A silent prayer from a little boy...

"Please make mommy and daddy stop fighting."
Moments later, they did—forever.

A heart's longing from an old sailor...

He looked toward the sky, "Dear God...maybe it's not
too late." The lines blurred and he thought he heard the
sound of children—calling him Papa.

A Divine connection for a wounded warrior...

Could anyone see past the scars and love a soldier, twice
burned—once in the flesh and once in the heart?

And all they ever wanted was a big, noisy, messy,
happy family. Was that too much to ask?

*God is near the broken hearted and puts the lonely in
families.*

The Voice

The Voice

Douglas Lee Spurling

Silver Spur Press

The Voice

Copyright © 2014 by Doug Spurling

Printed in the United States of America

2014—First Edition

DEDICATED TO...

HIM who sets the lonely in families, directs our paths
and delivers us from evil

Prayer Warriors—your valiant efforts avail much and
make dreams come true

Wounded Warriors—your scars are a badge of honor.

1

Sunshine, sailboats and seagulls were permanent residents of Tavernier Florida. Sometimes the sun took a day off, but not often—not today.

A few dozen sun-bleached sailboats rocked lazy along the pier. RJ eyed the boats and then stopped for a full minute in front of one that had a For Sale sign attached to the bow.

He made his way to the end of the pier, let out a slow whistle and shook his head. "What a mess, Sean."

Sean propped his forearm over the mop he'd been swinging and blew out a deep breath. He pulled a hanky out of his back pocket and wiped sweat off his face and neck. "I've got another swab bucket and mop."

RJ smiled, "Don't you just love this place?"

"I've got one word for this place. Salt. Salt water, salty air—" Sean wiped his face again—"and sweat."

"Exactly. If a man don't love that—he ain't worth his salt." RJ lifted a crooked grin.

Sean extended his hand and RJ shook it.

"I don't reckon I'll ever leave, but stuff like this makes me wonder, if I've gone plumb crazy." Sean glanced at the film of diesel fuel along the pier. "How long you in for?"

"I got a three day leave." RJ said. "Mac doesn't know I'm in. It's his birthday—sixteenth birthday."

Sean glanced toward the boat RJ had stopped in front of—the one with the For Sale sign. "So, did you stop here to pick out his birthday present?"

"Well, no, but now that you mention it...yes."

~

RJ snuck in the back door real quiet and when he found Mac sitting at the kitchen table putting a model sailboat together, he started singing, "Happy Birthday to you, happy birthday to you..."

Mac jumped up so fast the kitchen chair fell over. "Dad! I didn't know you were gonna be here. Awesome."

They hugged.

"About your birthday gift—"

"Gift? Dad, you taking off is a big deal—that's enough. You wanna go fishing? That'd be fun. Or we could go eat. How long are you in? What are you smiling about?"

"You are a big deal, Son. Sixteen already...how'd that happen so fast? Ask me about your birthday present—come on ask me."

Mac nodded, "Okay. Where is it?"

RJ poured a glass of water, "It's not here."

"Do we need to go pick it up somewhere?" Mac asked.

RJ sat down at the table. "Well...it's not exactly a pick-up-able gift."

Mac poured himself a glass of water too. "Huh?"

"Actually, it's an interesting story."

Mac sat down and smiled. "Oh—I see. It's one of your whopper tales. Let's hear it."

"Whopper tales? You mean one of my true stories?"

"Oh, right Dad, of course." Mac raised his eyebrows up and down. "Did you bring me that mermaid that follows you out to sea?"

RJ shook his head. "I asked, but she had a date."

Mac folded his arms. "Okay, then. I know. Being as it's my sixteenth birthday and all. You harnessed a dozen sharks, so I can go cruisin' around the bay. I'll bet none of my friends ever got a gift like that."

"You know, I may have exaggerated a little when I told you that story." RJ looked at the table. "It was only six sharks—not twelve."

"Oh, well if it's only six—forget it" Mac smiled.

"I really did get you a gift. And if I was a betting man, I'd bet none of your friends ever got a gift like this."

"Well, let's see it, Dad."

"You can't really see it" RJ said.

"What? It's invisible?"

"No. Well, maybe. It's something you do." RJ scratched his head.

"Do?"

"Yep. Do, and you're gonna love it. Matter of fact—you are probably the only young man I know who'd love this gift."

Mac stood up. "Well let's go do it or see it or whatever."

"It's at the marina." RJ stayed seated.

Mac stared blank for a second and then his eyes got real big. "A sailboat!"

RJ smiled at the ceiling and then at Mac. "Better—a whole fleet of them."

Mac narrowed his eyes. "Huh?"

"A job, you can start tomorrow—or this afternoon if you want."

"Seriously?" Mac looked at the table and then his eyes lit up. "At the marina? I got a job at the marina!"

RJ stood and nodded. "Yes sir."

Mac fast stepped toward the coat hooks by the back door. "I thought I wasn't old enough to work the docks."

RJ smiled.

Mac grabbed a hat that had an emblem of a sailboat and read, Captain. He smiled and tilted his head toward the door. "Today?"

RJ grabbed truck keys off a little oak table—the one Mac had made in shop class—and followed his son out the door.

By the time RJ had shifted the '64 Chevy into third gear Mac had already asked, "How'd you pull it off Dad? I thought I had to be eighteen to work there. ...Can't this thing go any faster?"

"I stopped by Mangrove Marina on my way home and lo and behold Sean was mopping up a big mess at the end of the pier."

"What happened?"

"Old Charlie Turner pulled his shrimper out before the fuel lines were removed. The main supply line from the on shore tank ruptured and spewed diesel fuel all over the place. It sprayed some of the finger piers, drifted sludge to several yachts, the ship to shore dinghy, the beach, it's a mess."

"Oh... I see. Yuck. Cool." Mac said.

"I reminded Sean that during a catastrophe the eighteen-year-old rule doesn't apply. I know it was meant for catastrophes like hurricanes and such, but...so?" RJ lifted one eyebrow and gave Mac a crooked smile.

"So? Did you ask him if I could have a job or..." Mac looked out the window toward the Gulf.

"Didn't have to ask, Sean's an old salt like me, he knew what I was thinking. He just said, "When can he start?" RJ looked at his son and smiled. "Happy birthday Mac."

And that was that. Mac had a job at the marina. A dirty, hard, dangerous job, cleaning the bottoms of yachts, and swabbing up a diesel spill. Only Mac would think that was the best birthday present a boy could ask for.

~

For five weeks Mac scrubbed every inch of the pier and the bottoms of several boats until not a trace of the diesel spill could be found.

Mac made one last trip up and down the pier to make sure he didn't miss anything. And then he put away all his tools and made his way into the marina store to tell Sean he was through.

"Whaddya talkin' about Mac? You're not through 'til I say you're through. I can't believe my ears. The son of such a fine sailor as RJ MacArthur quitting a job before it's through."

Mac cleared his throat. "Well sir, I can't find a lick of that spill anywhere...there's nothing left for me to do."

"Nothing left to do?" Sean narrowed his eyes and made a noise that sounded like a growl. "Don't ever let me hear you say those words again. Got it?"

"Okay but—"

"You'll always have something to do if you just do the next thing."

"The next thing...what next thing?"

"Don't matter. Just find one thing that needs doin' and that'll lead you to another. You won't ever get done and you won't ever get bored. Do you understand?"

Mac nodded.

"Okay then. What're you gonna do next?"

Mac shifted his feet and lifted his shoulders up and down. "I have no idea."

Sean pulled in a deep breath. "Okay, I'll help you get started. But the next thing is up to you. Understood?"

Mac said, "Yes sir."

Sean looked out the window and then at Mac. "You did such a fine job cleaning that first pier, now the other two look downright grungy—reckon you'll have to clean those too."

"Okay thank you sir." Mac headed toward the door.

Sean held up his hand. "One more thing. Did you notice how those cotton-pickin' diesel fumes started peeling the paint right off walls?"

Mac's eyes got wide. "Um...diesel fumes did that?"

"Darn right. What're you standing there for? You've got work to do. Let me know if you see anything else that needs doing. Of course, it's got to be related to the diesel spill." Sean gave Mac a nod and winked.

Mac opened the old wooden door and listened to the cowbell clang as it closed. He looked around and sure enough—the white paint was peeling off the wood siding on the marina store and the boat shed too. Mac doubted it had anything to do with diesel fumes, though.

But he got busy and stayed busy just doing the next thing. And just like Sean said, one thing led to another until Mac was handling all the dock work and boat maintenance for the marina.

He worked every day but Sunday and even then, he'd stop by the marina after church just to hang out and see if there was anything he could do...or perhaps catch a glimpse of that new girl he'd seen hanging around.

~

Something smelled. Sean laughed. "Someone's got a girlfriend."

Mac's face turned red as he walked toward the time clock to punch in. "What are you talking about?"

"Is that your dad's Old Spice I smell? And what happened to your clothes? No holes, no stains—they even look clean. Are you sure you can work like that?"

Mac grabbed his time card from out of a plastic envelope holder attached to the wall. "Why do we have a time clock? I'm the only employee."

Sean pushed a button on the cash register and a drawer popped open with a clang. He looked at Mac. "It came with the cash register, at an auction. Don't change the subject."

Mac slid his timecard into the clock until it clicked. "What subject?"

"You know what I'm talking about." Sean pointed a finger at Mac. "About 5'6", 110 pounds, big smile, green eyes. Don't tell me you haven't noticed her keeping an eye on you."

"Keeping an eye on me?" Mac shook his head. "You're just like my dad with your tall tales."

"She asked about you." Sean was dropping change into the cash register.

Mac was headed toward the door, but stopped and turned toward Sean. "She did?" He couldn't keep his lips from curling into a big toothy grin.

Sean nodded. "Yep, but don't worry, I told her you're already hopelessly in love."

Mac felt heat rush to his face. "I am not! ...You didn't."

Sean laughed as he slid the cash register drawer shut and then gave Mac a serious look. "But you are in love—" he tilted his head toward the docks—"with her...the salt."

Mac knew what he meant, and the old man was right. He loved the sea just like his dad, and his dad's dad. Anyone who wanted to be with Mac had to love the salt life or it would never work. Mac squinted at Sean and let out a deep sigh. "You didn't really say that, did you?"

"Sure I did Son, told her you were in love with the sea—just looking out for you."

Mac clenched his jaw and took a step toward the door.

Sean lifted both hands. "Wait, before you go off half-cocked. Don't you want to hear what she had to say?"

Mac let out a sigh and nodded.

Sean smiled. "She giggled and said, 'That's good, then daddy will like him, too.' That's just what she said Mac. Then she bought her Coke and went outside to sit on that bench, and gawk at you-know-who."

Mac grinned at the floor.

Sean leaned forward with both palms on the counter. "She's a good girl, Mac. I know her daddy. Sam—he's a good man. Navy. They go to my church."

"Well, I um, better get to work." Mac pointed toward the door.

"Get under, Our Thing, first. The Jaspers want to take her out this weekend."

Mac nodded, "Sure...what's her name?"

Sean gave Mac a look, "I just told you—Our Thing. It's the thirty-eight foot Hunter."

"No not—"

"Oh her…" Sean drew the words out long and smiled. "Her name is Maggie."

2

Mac went right to work swimming under Jasper's yacht, scraping barnacles off the hull. He started at the bow, which faced the shore.

The task was simple—but hard.

He'd dive under and scrape from side to side, starboard to port, then port to starboard. He'd scrape until he couldn't hold his breath any longer, and then he'd swim back to the surface and in one fluid motion fill his lungs, flip back and thrust under again. With each pass he'd work his way aft until he reached the transom.

On that day, each time he filled his lungs, he glanced toward shore.

He'd been at it for about three hours and was nearly finished when he saw her. He pretended not to notice how gracefully she floated off her bike and into the store. His heart skipped a beat when she sat on the bench, just outside the door and glanced his way—just like she'd done for three days in a row. This time he nodded, instead of looking away. She lifted a small wave.

Sean was telling the truth.

Mac filled his lungs with air and disappeared under the surface. He scraped barnacles until his lungs begged for air and he kicked back toward the sun. In a practiced motion he gulped and flipped, just like he'd done a thousand times without err. But this time, his timing was off. He had tried to gulp more air than usual to impress the gawking girl—watch how long I can stay under this time Maggie.

He was still sucking air when he thrust himself under the water. Seconds later he clawed to the surface, gasping and choking on salt water. He half swam and half splashed to the back of the yacht and managed to drag himself aboard the swim platform, which stuck straight out from the back of the boat and was only about three inches off the water. He spit, sputtered and coughed for a full minute.

Mac peaked around the edge of the boat and looked toward shore, to see if he could spot that long legged beauty. Her bike was leaning against the wood bench in front of the marina where she'd been sitting. She must be inside. He settled back and closed his eyes.

Maggie had walked to the end of the pier and saw Mac lying on the swim platform with his eyes closed. She ran the length of him with her eyes and smiled...then bit her bottom lip. Her eyes squeezed shut and she pressed the palm of her hand against her forehead and shook her head.

Mac opened his eyes to suntanned legs, faded cut-off jeans, a white tank top, sun-bleached light brown hair, green eyes and a smile brighter than the sun. He coughed twice to clear his throat—and his head.

Maggie let out a slight giggle. "Hi sailor...are you okay?"

"Well, I thought so. But maybe not...are you an angel?"

Maggie threw her head back and laughed. She put both hands over her face and shook her head.

He shook his head sending droplets of water all the way to Maggie's legs.

She shivered.

Mac sat up and wondered if she'd seen him splashing like a wounded duck.

Maggie smiled and looked toward the water. "It's obvious that you need swimming lessons...but other than that, you look good." She stretched out the word, good, a little too long.

Mac found it hard to breathe when he looked at her. "I, um, yeah, I might need swimming lessons—are you an instructor?"

Maggie blushed.

Mac stretched out his hand. "I'm Mac."

Maggie sat cross legged on the pier and reached out her hand to his, "Hi Mac—" their hands touched and Maggie lost her voice for a second—"I'm Maggie."

Mac held her hand and eyes. "Very nice to meet you Angel—I mean Maggie."

Maggie waved her hand. "Bet you say that to all the angels—I mean girls."

"Ha—" Mac laughed—"you think I need swimming lessons in there." He pointed at the water. "In relationships I swim like a rock."

For the next half hour they cracked open their hearts and talked about whatever silly thing came to their minds.

"So, Mac after you learn to swim, what do you want to be when you grow up?"

"That's easy. I'm going to work the docks until I graduate and then join the Navy. I'll save enough money to buy my own boat then I'm going to give sailing lessons and day cruises."

"Oh, I love that—it sounds perfect. What about other things like—" She hesitated and bit her bottom lip—"like family stuff."

Mac shrugged. "What do you mean?"

"You know." She looked out over the water. "Do you want to get married and have kids?"

Mac's smile reached his eyes "Well—it's kind of sudden, but okay."

Maggie's laugh echoed all the way to shore. "Seriously, do you want children?"

Mac let his smile fade. "I never knew my mother. She died giving me birth. My dad's been in the navy all my life. So, it's been him and me and a handful of nanny's. I spent a lot of time alone—maybe that has something to do with it. But, when I think of my future I want—" Mac looked at Maggie for the longest time and then pulled in a slow deep breath—"what I want more than anything else is to have a big, noisy, messy, happy family." He nodded his head once sealing his conviction.

Maggie nodded her head slowly a few times but never said a word. Their eyes were too busy talking.

Mac lifted a finger and smiled. "But first...our honey moon. We'll sail to the Bahamas and then around the coast for a month...at least."

Silence spoke through their eyes for an eternity of three seconds.

Mac whispered, "And you? marriage, children?"

Maggie blinked and her eyes got shiny. She whispered, "Yes, yes I do."

"That has got to be the prettiest words I've ever heard." Mac glanced away for a second. "I want to talk more but I, um, I'm almost done—" he pointed at Jasper's boat— "can I see you later?"

"Oh, right. Sorry, I'm keeping you from your work— drowning."

"Maybe when I'm done you can give me a swimming lesson or we can grab a Coke or I don't know...do the next thing."

Maggie tilter her head. "The next thing?"

"Yeah, the next thing—do that and you'll never get bored." Mac smiled.

"Sure. Okay. Nice meeting you Mr. big, noisy, messy, happy family guy."

"The pleasure was all mine, Miss swimming instructor."

Mac watched Maggie walk up the pier, when she glanced over her shoulder and saw him gawking, he rolled into the water.

She giggled.

Mac continued his work and Maggie waltzed into the store and bought a couple bottles of Coca-Cola.

She made her way back out to where Mac was working and kicked off her flip-flops and sat on the edge of the pier, her feet swirled circles in the water.

Mac exploded to the surface just as Maggie was taking a drink. She jerked and spit Coke across the side of the yacht and Mac's head and the front of her shirt and shorts.

After the laughter died, their eyes met. Maggie looked at her Coke-soiled shirt and shorts, smiled and slid into the water. She drifted the three feet to Mac at the back of the yacht. "Thought you might be thirsty."

Mac reached for the bottle of soda she was holding out to him, but instead gently pushed her hand to the side...and their lips met.

After several breathless seconds Mac whispered, "So, this is swimming lessons?"

Maggie bit her lip and made a nervous laugh. "Oh my, what you must think of me. I'm sorry. I never do this kind of—"

Mac placed a finger over her lips. "Maggie...teach me to swim."

~

They were married on the fourth of July, the year they graduated from high school. Two months later Maggie gave him the news.

"Mac do you remember the first day we met?"

Mac took a bite of the bologna sandwich Maggie had brought him for his lunch break and washed it down with a swig of Coke. He smiled and pointed toward the end of the pier. "Yep. Right out there. One look at you and I almost drowned."

Maggie leaned back on the wooden bench—their bench—the one they always sat on during Mac's lunch break at the marina. The bench they had scraped and painted together a few weeks after they'd met. "Do you remember what we talked about?"

"Of course—you asked me to marry you."

Maggie slapped Mac's chest. "What? I think you were confused—still are. But, what did you tell me about your dreams?"

"That's easy. I'm going to work the docks until I graduate and then join the Navy. I'll save enough money to buy my own boat then I'm going to give sailing lessons and day cruises."

Maggie smiled and leaned in close. "Right, good memory. But what else?"

"Um, then you asked me to marry you. You said something like, 'Mac you are such a hunk—do you want to get married and have kids?' "

She giggled. "Not exactly like that but close enough."

Mac swallowed the last of his sandwich and kissed his wife on the top of her head, her nose and then her lips. "I didn't exactly come through on the honey moon thing now did I...but I will. I promise. I'll work hard and we'll save and buy some old fixer-upper boats to sell and before you know it—"

Maggie pushed her finger tips against his lips. "Before you know it what you want more than anything else will come true, Mr. big, noisy, messy, happy family guy." She snuggled close and laid her hands over her stomach and smiled.

It must have taken a couple of breaths before it registered but then Mac's mouth and eyes popped as wide as a jellyfish. He jumped off the bench dropping his Coke in the process. He picked Maggie up in his arms and swung her around in two full circles shouting, "We're having a big messy baby!"

Maggie laughed so hard she couldn't catch her breath.

Suddenly Mac stopped and set her down like she was as fragile as a dozen eggs. "Oh Mags, oh no did I hurt you? I shouldn't have swung you around like that. I'm sorry. Wait here I'll go call the ambulance."

"Mac stop it I'm fine, I'm fine."

"But..." Mac touched her stomach. "Are you sure?"

"Yes, I'm sure silly—" she giggled—"we're gonna have a baby."

Mac let out a deep breath and dropped to the bench beside her. He held both of her hands in his. "Mags next to our wedding day this is the happiest day of my life." He dropped his head. "Saddest too."

"Sad? Why?" Maggie lifted Mac's chin to look in his eyes.

"I deploy in two months Maggie—I may not even be around for you." He wrapped his arms around her and clenched his jaw to hold back the quiver that had started in his chin. But it didn't help. His chin quivered and his eyes leaked a liquid joy and sadness all at once.

"It's alright Mac. God's got this. We'll be fine."

3

"Don't worry Mac, I'm fine, the baby's fine—" Maggie looked up from the bundle of joy she was cuddling—"your father and my daddy are worried enough for both of us."

Maggie looked at the two weary eyed men hovering near her hospital bed. She made a small smile and looked toward the door.

RJ looked at the door and then at Maggie. "You need the doctor?"

Maggie shook her head and pointed at the phone cradled on her shoulder.

"Oh, right." RJ looked at Maggie's dad. "Sam, let's get some more coffee."

Sam shuffled toward the door. "Yeah, we're too old to be listening to our kid's mushy conversation—might give me a heart attack or something."

"Dern right, I've had about all the excitement I can stand for awhile." RJ nodded at Maggie and slipped out the door.

Maggie shook her head and smiled into the phone. "You're going to have some big shoes to fill when you get back—my daddy and yours are spoiling us something awful..."

Maggie was hanging up the phone, when the nurse walked in, holding out her arms. "Let me see that precious child."

Maggie kissed her baby and let the nurse lift him from her arms.

"Hello Mr. Richard MacArthur Johnson, I'm Betsy, you remember me don't you? Of course you do, I helped bring you into this world. How's my handsome boy today?" She cradled the baby in one arm and pointed her finger at Maggie with the other. "As for you young lady—get some rest, and that's an order."

Maggie nodded and looked toward the window.

The nurse looked over her bifocals at Maggie and let out a slow breath. "Well...did you tell him?"

Maggie bit her bottom lip and shook her head. When she looked at the nurse her eyes started to water.

RJ and Maggie's dad walked in the room, each holding a cup of coffee.

The nurse turned to them and shook her head. "Now you two need to get out of here and let this poor girl rest. For crying out loud you both look awful. Go home and get some rest yourselves."

RJ looked at Maggie. "Did you tell him?"

Maggie wiped her eyes with the white bed sheet and let out a soft sob. "He wants a big, noisy, messy, happy family so bad—I couldn't." Maggie broke down and wept.

Sam went to his daughter and sat on the edge of the bed and held her in his arms. RJ stood on the other side of the bed and rested his hand on her shoulder. They all shed tears...including the nurse.

"I'll talk to Mac." RJ said. "Don't worry Maggie girl. You just rest and take care of that good looking grandson."

~

Mac tapped ashes off of a big fat cigar as he waited for his dad to answer the phone.

"Hello."

"Hi Grandpa!" Mac could hardly talk for the permanent smile plastered to his face. He leaned against the wall next to the pay phone and took a puff off the cigar—it made him let out a little cough. The cigar came out of a box that read, "It's a boy!" He'd given away all but one—which he saved lighting until this moment, when he called his dad.

"Hi Son—congratulations Dad."

Mac spun around in a full circle and stomped his boot on the ground. He let out a laugh when he got tangled up in the phone cord. "I can't believe it. I'm a dad. I just wish I was there."

"I wish you were too Son. But don't worry, Maggie's a strong girl and your son is as healthy as a horse. You just keep your eyes open and your head down and get back here safe."

"Don't worry Dad, I'll make it back. Me and Mags are gonna have a big, noisy, messy, house full of kids for you to spoil. This is just the beginning."

"Son, that reminds me, I need—"

"I just had a baby" Mac smiled real big at an elderly couple as they walked by. The couple picked up their pace. Mac yelled after them. "And I'm going to have more—a lot more!"

"Son, I need to talk to you about—"

"I know Dad, we're young and kids are expensive. But, I really think God has given us a vision for a big noisy messy happy family, and this is just the beginning." Mac tried to blow a smoke ring.

The phone was silent for a couple breaths. "Son, I have something to tell you."

Mac's smile faded a bit and he looked at the smoke floating away. "What? What's wrong, Dad? I thought you said—"

"I did. Everyone is okay. But...something happened." Mac listened as his dad explained what had happened during Maggie's delivery.

"A torn uterus? Is it serious?"

"Yes, the doctor said it can be very serious. Fortunately everything went well, and they're both fine. But..."

Mac dropped the cigar and crushed it with his foot. "But what Dad?"

Mac could hear his dad take a big breath. "Son... Maggie had to have a hysterectomy. She won't be able to have any more children."

Mac felt lightheaded. "Dad...I gotta go."He let the phone dangle from the receiver and slid to his heels with his back against the wall. With his head buried between his knees he felt his chin quiver and watched sorrow drip from his eyes to the floor.

RJ's voice could be heard over the line. "Mac, everything's going to be alright—God's got this."

"How!" Mac shouted at the dangling phone. "How does God got this?" He wiped a forearm across his eyes. "All I've ever wanted was a big, noisy, messy, happy..."

All of a sudden Mac scrambled to his feet. "Oh God no. It's all my fault." He hung up the phone.

~

Maggie woke to the sound of the phone ringing.

Mac's voice was hysterical. "Mags, Dad told me what happened. It's all my fault. I'm such an idiot. I'm so sorry Mags. Why didn't you tell me?"

"No honey it's not your fault." Maggie tried to sit up but was too sore.

Mac shook his head with a huff. "Yes it is. I knew it that day at Sean's. You remember—when I spun you. I'm sorry. What have I done?"

Maggie smiled but it was a sad sort of smile. "Mac, listen. You couldn't have done that—it'd be impossible that early in the pregnancy. Trust me on this. It's not your fault—not anybody's."

Mac looked up at the sky—toward heaven, toward God. "Nobody's?" The anger in his voice was obvious.

"That's right Mac, it was nobody's fault. You've got to believe God has a plan—"

"A plan? I do. Did. I know the plan and this ain't it! How could He let this happen? He put it in my heart—our heart—to have a big family. And now what? He just dangles it in front of us so He can rip it away?"

"Mac, if we let anger blind us because of what's been taken we won't see what's been given—who's been given. You're a daddy now...remember?"

Mac sighed. "I'm sorry Mags. I'm sorry. I thought I had it all figured out...and now, I feel like I'm about to drown."

"Well then, you're in luck—" Maggie whispered—"I'm your personal swimming instructor, and I won't let you drown."

"Mags, you know I've always tried to plan ahead, be prepared, but now we're off course and I don't know what we'll do—"

"We'll do the next thing Mac, and we'll keep doing the next thing—."

"Until we find shore." Mac's voice cracked. "I love you Mags."

Maggie pulled in a deep breath. "Lord, we thank You. We thank You for our son...our family."

Mac whispered, "Amen."

~

By the time Mac came home for Christmas Richey was already four months old. The four day leave passed in a blur and Mac didn't see him again until his first birthday. He was already learning to talk and Maggie had taught him to walk.

Mac wiped chocolate birthday cake off the highchair, the floor, the kitchen table and—of all places—the wall. He looked at the ceiling just to be sure.

Maggie giggled as she walked in the kitchen. "He's finally asleep."

Mac threw the chocolate covered rag in the sink. "Did our son eat any of his birthday cake or just paint the house with it?"He plopped down at the kitchen table. "Whoa, kids can sure make a mess. I don't know what we'd do with a house full of them...what was I thinking?"

"We need to talk about this." Maggie sat next to Mac at the kitchen table.

"There's nothing to talk about." Mac got up and poured a cup of coffee.

Maggie looked up at Mac, "We have other options...adoption."

"Mags, I have nothing against adoption. It's great— even better in some ways, because it's like rescuing someone."

Maggie lifted a shoulder up and down. "Well then?"

"It's just—" Mac sat back down—"it's just that I think I was wrong about the whole big family dream. If God wanted us to have a big family...things would've gone differently. Maybe it's His way of shutting a door."

"Or maybe not...Mac, maybe it was His way of opening one."

Mac leaned back and thought for a moment. "You mean, maybe what happened would cause us to want to adopt some child that needed adopting?"

Maggie placed her hand on Mac's. "Maybe."

Mac pulled in a deep breath. "I don't know. I just can't imagine God reaching down and causing you physical harm just so we'd adopt a child. He could just plant the idea in our heads, don't you think?"

Maggie nodded.

Mac took a sip of coffee. "Okay, we'll just do the next thing."

"Okay...what's that?"

"Dear God." Mac squeezed Maggie's hand. "If you want us to adopt a big noisy, messy house full of kids then put that desire in our hearts."

Mac opened his eyes.

Maggie still had hers closed. She squeezed his hand. "And Lord, help us to put the pieces where they fit even when we can't see the big picture."

They both looked at each other and said. "Amen."

Mac held her hands and stood. "There's another thing we can do."

She looked up at her husband and when she saw his crooked grin she knew. "We better hurry. Richey will wake up soon."

4

Mac turned off the ignition before the old blue pick-up rolled to a stop. He looked at the boy in the passenger seat. "Do you remember this place Richey?"

The boy read the sign on the two story brick building, "Florida Keys Community Hoss-t-i-pal."

"Yep—" Mac ruffled the boys hair—"Florida Keys Community Hospital."

"I don't 'member this place Dad."

"Yeah, probably not, it was a long time ago."

"Dad, I haven't been born long enough to 'member something from a long time ago."

"It was only a few years ago, you had to get a nail out of your foot, remember?" Mac opened the door.

Richey's eyes got real big as he looked at the building. "I don't need no more shots do I?"

"You do remember—nope, no shots today." Mac smiled. "Don't forget your boat."

"Yes sir." Richey pulled the door latch and pushed with his shoulder, the door opened with a creak.

As they walked to the door Mac asked, "How'd you learn to read so good anyway?"

"From you."

"That's not good. I'm not a real good speller."

"Yeah, I know. Mom helps me read your letters when you're out on the big boat. And then, she makes me look up in the dish-con-ary all the words you made wrong."

"Well shiver-me-timbers. I'm a pretty good teacher then, huh?"

"Yeah, you give me a lot of spelling words to look up."

~

Mac and Richey made their way to room 202 and slipped inside. RJ had his eyes closed and the only sound was the rhythmic beating of the heart monitor.

"Is he dead?" Richey whispered a bit too loud.

RJ must've heard because his mouth lifted into the slightest hint of a smile.

Richey set his model sailboat on the bedside cart next to a water pitcher and stepped closer for a better look. "Grampa? Don't be dead."

RJ growled and practically scared Richey to death.

The water pitcher clattered to the floor along with the model sailboat which broke into three pieces.

Richey's lip quivered a little as he picked up the sailboat—a gift for his Grampa.

RJ patted the bed beside him. "Sit down here little man."

Richey did as he was told.

RJ looked at the wooden pieces of the little sailboat and held out his hand. "You think if you sneak some glue in here we can fix it?"

Richey handed the broken boat to his Grampa. "I don't know. It'll never look the same. But we can try."

RJ smiled and blinked a few times. One lone tear showed up on his cheek. "We can try...that's what counts Junior."

Richey looked at the tear on his Grandpa's cheek and all of a sudden he had some of his own.

RJ cleared his throat. "Things are going to break. You can count on it. Some breaks will leave scars that never go away. But as long as a man is willing to try—those scars are badges of honor."

Richey rested his head on his Grampa's chest. "I can hear your heart beeping."

RJ let out a soft chuckle and then they both drifted off to sleep.

Mac sat in a chair next to the bed and watched his father and son sleep until a nurse came in and whispered, "I need to take his blood pressure."

Mac lifted Richey off his dad and onto the empty bed in the room.

When the nurse had left RJ gave Mac a weary smile. "You come in here because you need rest and as soon as you fall asleep they wake you up."

"Well, they're just doing their job. We want to make sure you're not going to have another heart attack." Mac stood beside his father, holding his hand.

"You and Maggie are doing a fine job with the boy." RJ rolled his head to the side to glance at Richey sleeping in the spare bed.

Mac nodded. "It's all Maggie, Dad. I've been deployed most of his life. It seems like yesterday I was handing out cigars. I can't believe he's already eight years old. But that's it—my tour is up and I'm out. It's time to spend some quality time at home."

"Mac you already have quality time—don't get it mixed up with quantity."

"But I've missed so much. I wasn't there when he learned to walk."

RJ lifted his hand. "Son, you taught him to ride a bike."

"That was because Mags made him wait until I was home. But, you were with him when he caught his first fish."

"That was fun." RJ smiled. "Mac, I'm proud of you Son, all I can say is, don't blink."

Mac said, "I'm afraid I already have. One blink and eight years have passed."

RJ looked his son straight in the eyes. "Don't forget what I told Junior."

"I won't Dad, I'll make sure he does his best—you know, make sure he tries." Mac nodded. "Good advice."

RJ puffed a quick breath. "Not him—you."

Mac wrinkled his brow. "What do you mean? I've never quit anything in my life. I've always worked hard—done my best. You know that. You taught me that."

RJ nodded. "Except for one thing. The one thing. It's never too late."

"Oh don't start that now Dad. We've wore that road out." Mac lowered his voice to a whisper. "I missed it. I thought God wanted us to have a big family—I was wrong. That's all." Mac glanced at Richey. "We're happy. No regrets."

"I know Son. But, I'm not convinced you were wrong. I think God gave you that dream for a big noisy messy house full of kids."

Mac shook his head. "Dad let's talk about something else."

"God knows the future before he gives a dream." RJ said. "So, if He gives a dream—I figure He has a way of making it come true—all we've got to do is keep dreaming."

Mac let out a slow breath and lifted a crooked smile. "That's quite a trick. Keep dreaming, but don't blink."

RJ lifted a big smile, looked at Mac and then out the window toward the Son. "Dream with your eyes wide open."

~

Mac didn't blink as rifles pierced the silence. He stood stone still as Taps floated into the cloudless blue sky. He saluted without so much as a tremble. At the presentation of the flag his voice never broke.

It never hit him until days later when he read in the obituary, "Survived by...one grandson, Richard MacArthur Johnson. RJ called him Junior."

Mac wept.

5

Mac and Richey carried supplies to the end of the faded wooden pier. Their newest project, a 38' Pearson, rested easy in their old familiar slip.

The paint was sun-bleached and flaking, the wood was faded and dry. But the hull was sound and the sails were good. Mac had said at least a hundred times, "Mags we'll keep flipping these boats until we can afford the one we want, and then we'll keep her—for our honeymoon. Really, we will, I promise."

Maggie would just laugh and say, "Please don't use 'flipping' and 'boat' in the same sentence. ...And Mac—" then she'd flutter her eyelashes—"I thought this was our honeymoon."

Mac looked her over real close and let out a whistle. "My oh my, she sure looks fine."

Maggie was on her hands and knees with her back to Mac and Richey. She slid sandpaper across the port bow trim a few more times. "She's a work in progress."

"A work in progress? She looks to be in ship-shape from here."

"Well thank you sailor." Maggie looked over her shoulder at Mac.

Richey flipped both hands in the air "Oh boy, here we go again. You're married for crying out loud. Aren't you two ever gonna stop flirting?"

Maggie stood up and held onto the mast while she stretched her back, and winked at Mac.

Mac said, "Son, flirting is important—especially when you're married."

"In a day or two we should be ready to start painting." Maggie said.

Mac stepped aboard and held out a hand for Richey. "Ahoy there matey come on aboard me ship."

Richey took a step and Mac carried him into the cockpit. "Let's pull all the old rigging and lines."

"Aye Aye Captain." Richey saluted. At ten years old he already knew more about stripping and rebuilding sailboats than most adult boat owners.

Maggie smiled at her son. "Well Richey, what number is this?"

"That's easy" Richey pulled the old weathered line out of the main sail rigging, and then stopped and looked at his mom. "Same as me—ten."

"Yep, our tenth boat." Maggie scanned the deck littered with old rags, some sandpaper, a couple of scrapers and an empty can of paint stripper.

"What should we name her?" Maggie looked at Mac.

Mac stuffed a screw driver in his back pocket and wiggled a cleat loose from the rear starboard corner. "Let's see now. This is our third boat since Dad passed, right?"

Maggie nodded.

Richey raised his hand as if he were in school. "The first one we named, Keep Dreamin'. That was my idea, remember?"

"And next one was, "Don't Blink" said Maggie.

Mac scratched his chin and looked out across the water. "This is a good boat—ugly but solid."

"The perfect fixer-upper," Maggie and Richey said it at the same time and then giggled.

"How about, RJ?"

~

The next day Mac painted, RJ, on the starboard side of the transom while Maggie and Richey sanded the deck trim.

"Richey, you sand around the hatch to the cabin." Maggie pointed to the spot she wanted him to work, safe in the center of the boat. "I'll finish the perimeter. When we're done, we'll get an ice cream cone. Deal?"

Richey scratched his head. "Sure. But—" he looked at the faded wood—"why can't we just stain it and skip the sanding part?"

Maggie smiled, "You know we've got to get to the good solid teak—that's where the real beauty hides. If we just skim over the top it might look good at first but the loose flakey stain and weathered soft wood will start to bubble and look worse than it does now."

"Alright, fine—I want a large hot fudge malt though."

"You got it."

Richey sanded for a few minutes and then watched a fishing boat chug by with seagulls swarming all around it. He spotted a couple of porpoises, too.

Maggie glanced toward the boat."They must be emptying their nets—throwing all the junk fish back into the water."

A swirl caught Richey's eye as a fin circled near the edge of the boat. He leaned over the edge to see if he could splash water like he'd seen in a movie. "Here Flipper," he said.

"No! Shark!" Maggie shouted.

The fin was three feet away—and followed by another.

Maggie scooped Richey up so quick his gum flew out of his mouth and the instant it hit the water—a shark flipped to the surface.

Richey saw the long row of teeth and wet his pants, right there on the spot.

It was rare to see sharks in the shallows, especially during the day.

They never forgot it.

~

A board on the front porch, under Mac's rocker, creaked to the rhythm of a frog's serenade.

Maggie backed out of the house holding two Mason jars full of ice tea. She hooked the screen door with her tennis shoe so it wouldn't slam and then handed Mac an ice tea and took a seat in the rocker next to his.

Maggie's chair didn't creak—it made a swoosh sound each time she'd rock.

For awhile, the chairs were the only ones to speak. Swoosh—swoosh—creak—swoosh—swoosh—creak...

"How's he doing?" Mac asked.

Maggie took a sip and stared out toward the west— toward the Gulf of Mexico. She pulled in a deep slow breath. "He's asleep. Acted like it was no big deal..." She shook her head and looked at the floor. "I should've been watching him—"

"It's not your fault Mags. You saved him from getting hurt—or worse." Mac looked at Maggie until her eyes met his. "I think it's time."

"Time?"

"This is our last flip. You and Richey don't need to work so hard anymore."

"Mac—"

"It's not because of what happened today. I knew it a few days ago. I just didn't want to listen—until today."

"Really?" Maggie's eyes got wide. "I had that same thought about a week ago. It was just a passing idea—I brushed it off."

Mac shook his head and stared toward the moon. "This'll sound weird, but—" he shrugged his shoulders—"I heard...something."

Maggie wrinkled her eyebrows and nose. "Something?"

"A Voice."

"Was it out loud?"

"I donno? I don't think so. I think it was inside my head."

"So, you're hearing things?"

"Maybe. But Mags...I think it was God."

Maggie pulled in a quick breath "God?"

The Voice said, "Well done. Sail on."

"Sail on?" Maggie took a drink of her ice tea. "God said, 'Sail on?' "

"The amazing part is the understanding that came with the words. All of a sudden I knew it was time to stop flipping and start sailing. Remember, we wanted to give sailing lessons and day cruises after the navy."

Maggie nodded. "But...life happened."

"True. It did, and does and will continue to happen—but I got off focus."

Maggie touched Mac's arm. "What do you mean? You love sailboats."

"Yeah, I suppose that's why I got confused. Somehow I flip-flopped making a life—for making a living." Mac rocked back. Creak. He lifted his ice tea. "But no more."

Maggie lifted her glass toward his and smiled. "Sail on."

After a few minutes of swoosh—swoosh—creak—swoosh—swoosh—creak Maggie stopped. "I pray Richey doesn't have nightmares...I pray I don't."

Creak...creak.

"About sharks?" Mac asked.

"Do you believe there's a devil?" Maggie looked scared. Swoosh—swoosh—swoosh.

"There's a God. And there's a devil. You know that Mags."

"I never felt him before...until today."

Creak—creak..."Sharks can scare the devil out of a person."

"No Mac. This wasn't normal." Swoosh—swoosh—swoosh. "It was evil—hatred." Her eyes glistened in the moonlight. "It wanted Richey." She let out a single sob and covered her mouth with both hands.

They both stood at once and she melted into Mac's embrace. The chairs creaked and swooshed to silence. Maggie's soft weeping muffled against Mac's chest until her breathing settled to normal.

And then it started, and the whole world stopped. Even the frog's and crickets stopped to listen. The waves hushed their slapping.

From the place where fear and pain are crushed to wine it sprang up. Like an old violin Maggie's voice sweet and pure echoed off the porch and drifted toward heaven.

"When peace like a river, attendeth my way,

When sorrows like sea billows roll;

Whatever my lot, Thou hast taught me to say,

It is well, it is well, with my soul."

And if a devil was anywhere near, Mac was sure it had to flee.

~

Sean paused for one breath before he stuck the key in the door—and that was all it took. Something caused him to turn and look just as sunlight chased shadows from the pier. He felt the wind wake up and make the boats dance in place like stallions in the starting gate. With his eyes he rode the waves out as far as he could see. He stuffed the keys back in his pocket and walked to the end of the pier, to where Mac and Maggie had their slip. He looked at the boat and read the name, RJ. He folded his arms across his chest and shook his head. "I miss you my old friend...sail on." He let his eyes sail one more time out into the Gulf and then forced his steps back to shore.

He plugged in the percolator and watched until the first bits of coffee bubbled. He shuffled to the corner and grabbed a faded blue cap that read NAVY. He pulled it over his thinning grey hair and reached for a broom standing in the corner.

Sean heard tires growl as they rolled into the gravel parking lot. "Good day for sailing." He said to the broom and swished it one more time across the floor. The sign read Mangrove Marina but all the old-timers called it, Sean's, since he'd managed the place for so long.

The door clanged open. "Hi Boss."

Sean let out a tired laugh and perched both hands on top of the broom handle. "Well, look what the tide blew in."

They shook hands.

"Sean, some folks do this thing called, retire." Mac said. "You ever heard of that?"

"I am retired—what're you talking about?"

Mac grabbed the broom out of his hand. "What's this?"

Sean reached for the broom but Mac pulled it out of reach. "That, is my oar. And this—" he swept his arm around the area—"this is my ocean."

"Sean, you need to expand your horizons. It's time to put some salt in that Navy blood of yours."

Sean took weary steps and sat on a stool near the counter. "Once upon a time...but not anymore."

Mac poured two cups of coffee and sat on the stool next to Sean. "How's Esther?"

"Some days are bad..." He took off his cap and rubbed his head, his forehead, his eyes. "Other days are awful. Doc says we're living on borrowed time." He let out a small laugh that was mostly sad. "His bills have us living on borrowed everything."

Mac pulled an envelope out of his back pocket and set it on the counter in front of Sean.

Sean lifted one eye brow. "What's this?"

"That my friend is your new home away from home."

Sean pushed the paper back at Mac without saying a word.

"The cure for all that ails a man can be found in saltwater—sweat, tears and the sea. And owning a boat gives plenty of opportunity for all three." Mac said. "Aren't you the one who taught me that?"

"Well I've had more than my fair share of sweat and tears." Sean took a sip of coffee.

Mac pushed the paper back toward Sean. "Now it's time for the sea."

Sean opened the envelope and pulled out the title to the sailboat, RJ. "Mac you can't just—"

"You gave me a job, taught me as much about the sea and sailing and life as my dad—it's an honor, Sir. Sail on."

Sean stared at the title and just shook his head. "Esther always loved the water."

6

Somewhere off the east coast of Florida the sailboat cut through four and five foot swells. *Maggie* was hand painted in blue across the stern.

Mac's eyes were closed and if not for the crooked grin one might've thought he was asleep. Richey was at the helm. "Captain for the day" Mac had told him.

"Must be some dream," Richey said.

Mac opened his eyes.

Richey looked at his dad and shook his head. "You've been sitting there sleeping with that goofy grin for at least an hour."

Mac laughed and adjusted his hat. "I wasn't sleeping. I was examining the boat...and your sailing skills."

"Yeah, right" Richey's crooked grin matched that of his father's.

Mac sat up a little straighter. "Close your eyes."

Richey looked out across the water and then at his dad. "Close my eyes? I'm driving."

Mac looked around at nothing but water as far as the eye could see. "I don't think you're going to hit anything—close your eyes."

Richey did as he was told.

"Now listen." Mac closed his eyes too.

"Okay...listen to what?" Richey said.

"The wind in the sails."

Richey closed his eyes and listened again. "They're not talking dad."

"Good. They're not supposed to. They're dance partners." Mac's crooked grin returned. "Slow dancing."

The thirty-five foot boat rose as it cut through a five foot swell. Richey squeezed the helm and opened his eyes. "I think the wind wants to fast dance."

Mac said, "The speed and the beat don't matter, as long as they keeping hugging each other close. No flapping. No clapping."

Richey laughed. "No doing the bump?"

"Right," Mac said. Now, close your eyes and listen to the water. Feel how she cuts the waves."

"Okay..."

"You want her to slice through the swells like a saw, not break through like a hammer."

They sailed along with their eyes closed. They listened to the melody of the wind hugging the sails, and they felt the waves cut smooth on either side of the bow.

Even though Mac bounced around these waters three or four times a week, running Maggie's Charter Service, he never tired of this—sailing with his son.

Time stood still as they slid across the saltwater dance floor—wearing matching crooked grins.

"When you're in deep salt," Mac said, "you've got to rely on all of your senses—not just sight."

Richey looked all the way around. "Yeah, speaking of that...I'm lost. Which way's home?"

Mac smiled. "Are you nervous?"

"Well, I'd feel a whole lot better, if the GPS was working."

Mac stood and watched a couple seagulls fly. "Do you know where you're at?"

Richey watched as the seagulls disappeared in the distance off to their port side. "No—if I did I wouldn't be lost."

"Narrow it down." Mac stared at the waves.

"Narrow it down?" Richey asked.

Mac nodded.

"Well I know we're in the Atlantic Ocean."

Mac shook his head. "You can do better than that."

"Okay we're in the Gulf Stream off the east coast of Florida...I hope."

"What else do you know?"

"Let's see. We need to go west. If we head east we'll hit the Bahamas...unless the Gulf Stream carried us too far north." Richey swallowed."In that case, we'd end up somewhere out in the middle of the Atlantic and possibly get swallowed in the Bermuda Triangle."

"Son," Mac said, "do you remember that radio tower near the house?"

"Sure. Me and Jake wanted to climb it. But, when we rode our bikes out there they had a big fence around it."

"Oh boy..." Mac grinned. "Me and a buddy climbed that tower when we were about your age. We hung an American flag from the top. About a week later they built the fence. It was a stupid thing to do. But, I learned something that day."

"What's that?"

"I didn't want to be in the air force. The height gave me the willies."

Richey frowned. "It's your fault we didn't get to climb the tower."

"I didn't build the fence." Mac smiled. "At least they still fly a flag up there."

"Anyway, why'd you ask me about the tower?" Richey looked around trying to spot it.

"Oh yeah, if you could see the tower, would you still be lost?"

"Well, no, of course not,"

"Why? You'd still be in the exact same spot you are right now. How would seeing the tower help you not be lost?"

"Well, I know where the tower's at. And from there I could figure out where I'm at."

"Exactly, so navigating the sea, or life, it comes down to paying attention to what's constant. Like, for instance, the sun always rises in the east and sets in the west. Knowing the placement of the stars is the way sailors navigated for centuries. The stars are a giant time piece and a map—you just have to know how to read them. Paying attention to the direction of the current and the wind and even the flight pattern of the birds—all can help to stay the course and not get lost. They're like road signs along the highway."

"Interesting...but that doesn't help today. It's cloudy. We're too far out to see land."

Mac took the helm from Richey. "Watch the waves." He turned into the wind and let the sails and the helm go free. After a minute, he tossed a buoy with a small rope over board and watched as they drifted apart. "See which direction we're floating? The Gulf Stream carries us north to north east."

"Cool. So..." Richey pointed with his right arm extended toward the way they were floating. "That's north."

Mac smiled and watched the sky. "Notice most of the birds are all headed the same direction. They're probably headed for land. They can fool you though because sometimes they're headed out to sea to go fishing."

"Okay, considering the current, I'd say the birds are headed west—toward shore." Richey ran tanned fingers through his blond hair and then pointed. "Follow those birds."

"Out on the ocean things can change fast—real fast. Your mind can play tricks on you, too. You've got to hold on to what's real. Look for something stable—that doesn't change. And hold on to it no matter how you feel."

Richey held the jib sheet and saluted. "Aye aye Cap'n. The radio tower is right over there...I think."

"You're a mighty fine sailor, Son." Mac smiled with his eyes. "Okay first mate—pull in the main, snug the jib, coming about."

Mac smiled as he watched Richey's strong arms pull in the sails. Not only do things change fast on the ocean—but in life, too. How'd Richey grow up so fast? Wasn't it yesterday he was still in diapers? And now look at him. We never saw our dream of a big family...but it's been good—as happy as we could've asked for. Probably won't be long before Richey finds a girl and is gone. The hum of the wind and the waves blurred together and Mac thought he heard the sound of a big, noisy, messy house full of children— calling him Papa. Mac rubbed the back of his neck as he looked toward heaven, and smiled.

Within fifteen minutes they could see the shore.

~

They lowered the sails and eased into their slip at Mangrove Marina. They still called it Sean's even though it'd been years since he ran the place.

Sean and his wife, Esther, practically lived on the boat Mac and Maggie had given them. They spent their time sailing up and down the west coast of Florida. The doctors said Esther wouldn't last a month out there—but, after five years or so, they told Sean to keep doing whatever it was he was doing. Sean just smiled and said, "Saltwater—it's good for what ails ya...and prayer, plenty of prayer." The empty slip told Mac they were still out there somewhere having the time of their lives. He smiled..."Someday."

Maggie walked out of the store and sat on the wooden bench by the door. She gave them a small wave like the one she gave Mac the first day they met...his heart still skipped a beat.

Mac and family had taken over managing the marina as well as operating their charter service. Richey followed in his dad's footsteps and was working the docs and cleaning yachts and was already signed up with the navy—he was scheduled to deploy at the end of the summer.

7

Mac propped his hands atop the broom handle and stared out the marina store window. "History echoes."

Richey stood on the end of the pier next to a girl with wavy red hair, a white tank top, cut off jeans and legs that seemed to run clean up to her smile. She was handing Richey something.

Maggie closed the ledger she'd been writing in and looked out the window toward where Mac was staring. "So that's why she bought two bottles of Coke."

"Mags, isn't that the exact same spot where you handed me a Coke...right before you asked me to marry you?"

Maggie went to Mac and looked out the window. "You've always been a little confused about that day."

"Maybe so—just glad you asked." Mac put one arm around his wife and held the broom with the other. Side by side they stood and spied on their son at the end of the pier.

Maggie shook her head and let out a fast breath. "I don't like her shorts."

"Why?" Mac asked.

"They're too short." Maggie walked back toward the cash register.

Mac shook his head and put his broom back to work. "I didn't notice."

"Like I said—confused."

~

Richey didn't have a problem with Jenny's short shorts...or her red hair, green eyes, long legs or any other part of her. As a matter of fact he thought he'd found his one and only true love. Their relationship took off in a whirlwind.

Jenny grabbed Richey's cap and plopped it on her head. It tilted to one side and covered her right eye. Although half her face was hidden behind the faded cap, even a blind man could see her beauty. She was happy and giddy. She was a lot like Maggie in her flirty sort-of way. Their playful zeal for life, their unconscious beauty; their act-first-think-later personalities made them appear similar in so many ways. Richey was smitten.

"I love you Jen...will you marry me?" The question popped out after Richey had only known Jenny for a little over two months. The words hung in the air and never got answered...not at first.

He knew he shouldn't rush such things. And as soon as the words spilled out of his mouth he remembered a conversation he'd had with his dad.

"You don't know a person 'til you've seasoned 'em." Mac had said.

"Seasoned 'em? Like salt and pepper?"

Mac had laughed at that. "Like all four seasons of the year. Then you'll know if they're worth their salt. Folks can put on a show for awhile—but usually not for a whole year."

Richey had nodded at the time and thought it made good sense...but surely it didn't apply to Jenny. She was pretty and funny and cute and outgoing and beautiful.

~

"Mac you've got to talk to Richey about that girl." Swoosh—swoosh—swoosh.

"You're going to wear a hole in the floor if you keep rocking like that." Mac started to tell Maggie that the girl had a name, and it was Jenny. He felt like he should say something about Richey being a responsible adult and able to make his own decisions. And he thought perhaps he ought to remind her that they met on the same pier in the same way as Richey and Jenny. But...he took one look at her set jaw and white knuckled grip on the armrest of her rocker and said, "You're right dear...what do you think I should say?"

Swoosh. Stop. "What? How am I supposed to know? He's your son. He's not thinking with his head that's for sure. He's thinking with...with."

Mac rocked a few times to buy some time. Creak—creak. "Mags this isn't like you. What's got you so riled up?"

Maggie's eyes got wide. "Do you know what he said to me? He told me to mind my own business. He's never told me that—not ever. He said he was in love. Love my foot! I told him if he was in love he wouldn't be so irritable."

"Come on Mags, you get...I mean, I get irritable sometimes—" he gave her his best crooked grin—"and I'm hopelessly in love with you."

"It's not the same thing Mac. You're irritable when it's not good sailing weather, not when we talk about our relationship. Richey's not in love. Love is irresistible—lust is irritable."

Mac sat back with his mouth hanging open. "Oh."

"The problem is—" Maggie pointed out into the night, toward wherever Richey might be with, that girl—"he thinks he's in love. And then, since he's had our example he won't quit. He'll do whatever it takes to make it work."

Mac wrinkled his forehead. "So, that's good right? They can make it work. It wasn't always smooth sailing for us."

Maggie pulled in a deep breath as she shook her head. "Mac, Richey plays for keeps. That girl plays for fun. Can't you tell? You're his father haven't you taught him anything about women?"

"I ah...well, sure I told him when the wind. No, I mean, I um showed him how to navigate rough—" Mac shook his head and looked at the stars, found the big dipper and then looked at Mags and rested his hand on hers. "I told him that things can change fast—real fast. Your mind can play tricks on you, too. You've got to hold on to what's real. Look for something stable—that doesn't change. And hold on to it no matter how you feel." Mac nodded once. "That's what I told him."

Maggie's jaw loosened a little and the hint of a smile pulled at the corner of her mouth.

"To be honest Mags...I don't know anything about women. I got lucky with you. Besides, he can find out everything he needs to know about a good women, just by watching you."

Maggie eased back and for the first time since they started the conversation she took a slow easy breath.

Mac said the two words that helped them weather every storm for over twenty years. "Let's pray."

~

The next morning Maggie sat alone at the kitchen table sipping coffee. Mac had left before first light to get their boat rigged for a sunrise cruise. She had made up her mind that she wouldn't pressure Richey again, and if he wanted to talk about his relationship it'd be up to him.

She was rinsing out her coffee cup when Richey walked in. "Mom, can we talk?"

"I'd like that." She poured him a cup of coffee and sat back down.

"Mom...she's the one." He lifted both hands in the air. "Don't you see, she's just like you."

Maggie rested her hands on both sides of her son's handsome face and drew a slow breath. "Remember the day you saw—thought you saw—Flipper?"

It was when he was around ten years old, and helping with one of their old fixer-uppers. He was supposed to be sanding around the cabin hatch, but he thought he saw a porpoise and reached over the side to see if he could get it to surface, like he'd seen on the movie Flipper. But, it turned out to be a close call, with two sharks.

Richey nodded and clenched his jaw.

Maggie rubbed her thumb across his cheek and held his chin in her hand. "Sometimes what we think we see on the surface isn't really what's underneath."

"So, underneath, you think Jenny's a shark?" Richey threw the words at his mother.

Maggie searched her son's eyes, looked into his heart. "All I'm saying is take your time. Sometimes what looks good on the surface can be dangerous underneath. If we hurry, it might look good at first, but in the end what's below the surface will bubble loose and we'll be worse off than before. It takes work to find good solid teak—and hearts."

"How can you say that? Jenny is just like you Mom."

~

Richey was irritated.

He hated that Jenny was everything he'd ever wanted on the outside...but inside she scared him, like a shark. The way she'd look at other guys and smile in a flirty sort-of way—the same way she smiled at Richey. The way she huffed whenever Richey mentioned something about God or church.

But she was just raised different that's all. As soon as they got married she'd come around and want to raise their kids in church, the same way Richey did. Under that beautiful smile was a heart of gold—not a shark, not a flakey piece of wood ready to bubble up and float away. Jenny, on the surface, was as playful as a porpoise and underneath it all, she was as solid and durable as teak.

Richey just knew it.

~

He was scheduled to deploy within the month, and he was ready—but he was scared. Not scared of combat or even death, but scared he might miss out on life. Like, what if he never got the chance to get married to raise a family...or to make love? Something he'd been thinking a lot about lately, since Jenny.

He'd already gone too far with her, not all the way— but farther than he felt comfortable. Jenny showed no hesitation and even encouraged him. So far in his life he'd kept himself from going over the edge with any of the girls he'd been with. He wanted to wait until he was married. He figured it was the right thing to do and the best way to show respect and honor to the girl he'd marry. But the fire he felt with Jenny—he wasn't sure he could quench. And knowing he'd deploy soon didn't help matters.

He carried his grandmother's ring in his pocket but he still wasn't sure. Maybe it wasn't fair. How could he ask a girl he'd only just met to commit to a life time with him, and then, up and leave her for God only knows how long? Maybe it'd be best to wait—to season her. Richey made up his mind to listen to the wisdom of his folks.

But, after a romantic dinner near the bay and a walk along the beach that wound up being more than just a walk. He found himself breathless at the sight and feel of Jenny's skin in the moonlight. He didn't recognize his own voice as he asked Jenny to be his wife. He felt guilty and giddy at the same time knowing that the girl next to him wore nothing but his grandmother's ring.

And so, three months after first laying eyes on Jennifer Maria Thomas, Richey made her his wife.

Mac cancelled all the charters scheduled for the week following the wedding, and after decorating the boat, they gave it to Richey and Jenny to use for a honeymoon cruise.

And then, once the whirlwind of, I do's, and, goodbyes, were said, reality set in. Richey was gone, and that girl Mac and Maggie barely knew had become their daughter in law.

The last thing Maggie said before drifting off to sleep that night was, "Mac, ready or not, we've got to get to know that girl."

~

The doorbell rang.

"Ready or not—here she comes." Mac dropped a handful of ice into a pitcher of sweet tea, and wiped his hands on his shirt as he headed toward the door.

Maggie placed a bowl of mashed potatoes on the table, blew a wisp of hair off her face and whispered. "Dear Jesus, help me."

Mac opened the door and there stood, that girl, Jenny, Richey's wife...Mac and Maggie's daughter in law. "Hi Jenny, come on in."

Jenny handed Mac a bottle of cheap wine and made a nervous chuckle. "Hi...wasn't sure what to bring."

Mac smiled and made a nervous chuckle too. "Nothing—you didn't need to bring anything. Just yourself—hope you're hungry."

Mac led her into the kitchen and asked if she wanted something to drink.

She looked at the bottle of wine and shrugged. "Sure."

Maggie removed an oven mitt, with a sailboat embroidered across the back and gave Jenny a hug. "You look nice. Have a seat."

Jenny sat down at the round kitchen table and then stood back up. "Can I help?"

Mac said, "Sure, here you go," and he handed her two tall glasses of sweet tea.

Maggie pointed at the table, "Just set mine right there Jenny, we're almost ready to eat."

Before sitting down Maggie grabbed a silver butter tray and a bowl full of hot biscuits.

Mac sat across from Jenny and next to Maggie. He took a sip of ice tea first and then stretched out his hands. Maggie put her hand in Mac's and folded her other hand around Jenny's in a motion so natural she must have done it a thousand times.

Jenny jerked her hand at first and then relaxed. She looked at Mac's open palm on the table and slowly placed her small hand in his.

As soon as she did, the corners of Maggie's mouth lifted and her eyes closed.

Mac's eyes closed too, and his mouth opened. "Dear Lord Jesus we thank you, not just for the food on the table but for the family around it—especially for our new family member, Jenny, our daughter. Thank you for expanding our family and Yours, for the revival of dreams and most of all for being with Richey and bringing him back home. Amen."

They feasted on fried chicken, mashed potatoes, green beans and biscuits.

Jenny talked about herself. Her job as a waitress, her dream of owning a beauty salon, how she planned to fix up the house she and Richey had rented.

Maggie smiled. "I love that cute little house, and it's so close you can walk—"

"We won't be there long, just until we can find something better."

Maggie dabbed a napkin across her lips. "Richey's always loved that place. When he showed it to us we both thought that front room would make the cutest little nursery."

Jenny hesitated, and then said, "That room will make a nice shop—where I cut hair and do perms and such."

Mac cleared his throat. "Well, if you need a hand—" he looked at Maggie and raised his left eyebrow, the way he always did when the wind blew their boat a little sideways— "I've got two. Pass me the tators they sure are good."

Maggie handed Mac the bowl of mashed potatoes and didn't smile. "Jenny, did you know this was Richey's favorite meal?"

Jenny wiped a napkin across her mouth. "Why do you say that?"

Maggie wrinkled her eyes and made a couple small shakes of her head. "Why? Well, because it is his favorite meal. Did he tell you something different?"

"You just said that to make me feel like I don't know anything about him. Well, I'll have you know...I know my own husband." Jenny dropped the napkin on her plate, leaving most of the food uneaten.

Mac watched Maggie's eyes get big and her neck stretched about an inch or two and then that vein on the side of her neck started pulsing—he knew she was about to say something she'd regret.

"I love your sundress where'd you get it?" Mac said it without thinking.

Maggie turned her head toward Mac in slow motion. Her mouth dropped open and then her lips moved but no sound came out.

Mac jumped up and grabbed the bottle of wine and started looking for a corkscrew. "Maybe it's time for some of this wine you brought...if I can figure out how to open it."

"It just pops off. It doesn't have a real cork." Jenny looked at Maggie. "And thank you Mac, I don't remember where I got this dress. I must have picked it up at a garage sale or something. "

Maggie let out a long sigh."Well, the colors are perfect; they compliment your eyes and hair."

Mac found the closest thing he could to wine glasses— three small jars that once upon a time held grape jelly. He poured them about half full.

"Here's to Richey and Jenny and a big noisy messy happy family."

Jenny raised her eyebrows and drained her wine.

8

The sun painted silvery streaks of orange and yellow from the eastern horizon all the way to a thirty-five foot Southern Cross named Maggie.

A month had gone by since the interesting dinner with Jenny, and Mac decided it was high time to fulfill a promise.

He had charted a course, like he'd done a hundred times before—but this time it was for the cruise of a lifetime. The long awaited honeymoon.

Mac and Maggie finished breakfast at the Pier Café and walked arm in arm like a couple of teenagers in love, Maggie was giddy.

The voyage from the Keys to the Bahamas was open ended. "We'll spend the day crossing the Gulf Stream—" Mac smiled—"and by sunset moor in Bahamas' Bay."

They stopped at a bench near the floating honeymoon suite. They sat close...as one. Mac's arm rested easy over his wife's shoulders, she rested against him. He kissed her hair. "I'm sorry Mags. Sorry it's taken so long."

Maggie made a comfortable sigh. "Mac, a lot of newlyweds spend their wedding night in the bay before going on a honeymoon cruise. She kissed his neck and whispered real close, "Our wedding night just took about twenty years." She giggled soft, pressed her palm over his heart and kissed his neck again in a way that took his breath.

A cool breeze drifted off the water. Maggie shivered.

Mac rubbed his hand up and down his wife's bare arm and watched the waves turn grey as distant clouds passed under the sun. He studied traces of a million smiles on Maggie's skin. "What if we never come back—never end the honeymoon?"

Maggie pressed closer to her husband but didn't say anything. The cloud passed and the warmth of the sun settled like a blanket.

Mac stretched his legs. "Almost time."

They watched the sun chase the remaining shadows from their boat. They planned to leave as soon as she was fully bathed in morning light.

Maggie leaned forward and looked at Mac, her eyes were shiny, her voice a whisper. "I'm sorry Mac."

He knew what she meant.

Since the first day they met they talked about family— a big noisy messy happy family. During this stage of life they figured they'd be learning how to spoil grandkids. And their honeymoon would be a precious memory stored in faded photographs.

Like a windmill in a hurricane the hands of time flew, and as wonderful and happy as they were, she still had one regret—only one child.

Mac folded his arm around her, "I don't know a lot Mags, but I know one thing for sure and certain—you have nothing to be sorry for." He kissed the side of her head, right where she'd spotted a grey hair. "Grandkids are better anyway. Spoil 'em and send 'em sailin' back home." He smiled and rested his head against his wife. "Richey will have a boat full that we can spoil—and that'll be just fine with me. Besides, we're sort-of busy catching up on an overdue honeymoon, remember?" This time he leaned forward and kissed her lips in a way that told her he had no regrets, and that he loved her more than the sea, and after all this time— she still took his breath away.

In a breathy voice Maggie whispered "My, oh my, Captain Mac...let's get this honeymoon started."

Mac's hands slid down Maggie's arms and held her hands as he stood. "Come with me, my dear."

As they walked arm in arm toward their slip Mac lifted his eyes to a few clouds. He studied the sky and the waves—calculating the wind speed and direction. He ran through a mental check list like any good captain.

The radar showed smooth sailing from sunup to sundown with only a small blip a hundred miles east of the Bahamas and it wouldn't cross their path until well after their estimated time of arrival at Bahamas Bay.

Another cloud and its shadow slid over the boat, and Mac felt a tinge of hesitation, because there are old sailors, and bold sailors, but no old, bold sailors. That's what he'd always been taught. That's how he'd sailed the world and always made it home safe to his Maggie girl. And that's how he'd sail today, with his bride on their honeymoon. They'd take their sweet time—and tonight they'd watch the sunset in Bahamas Bay.

Mac knew not waiting for calm seas and a gentle south wind was the most common cause for a bad trip across the Gulf Stream—but he couldn't ask for better weather. So why did he feel like he was dragging an anchor?

~

After they were in open water Maggie rested her hand on Mac's, "What's wrong...the boat?"

"I don't know—I don't think so."

Maggie searched Mac's eyes, his heart. "I'm concerned about Richey."

Mac took a deep breath and nodded. "We should pray."

They held hands. Mac didn't close his eyes, but rather raised them toward the sky. "Dear Lord, Richey's out there somewhere on this water. We don't know where he's at or how he's doing, but we know You do. And we know our prayers reach you, and You can reach him. So, Lord, we ask

You to protect our boy. If in the heat of battle wrap him in Your cool, calm embrace. Grant him Your peace and let Him know Your presence. Thank you."

Maggie had her head bowed and eyes closed. "And we pray for Richey's wife, Jenny." Maggie let out a sound more like a sob than a word. "We don't know what to do. Jenny's a sweet girl but..." She didn't know what to say, so she just let her heart bleed tears.

After Richey's deployment, Maggie had called Jenny several times. She wasn't home whenever they stopped by. Finally, the day before they left on their honeymoon, they saw her at the marina talking with another man—more like flirting with another man. They didn't want to believe it, so they'd convinced themselves it wasn't her. But down inside...

"Lord—" Maggie looked up—"You know how to reach Jenny." Maggie slid the back of her hand across both eyes and smiled. "And Richey sure would like a child."

Mac pulled Mags close and they sailed along like that for several minutes, just listening to the waves as they split off the bow and gurgled past the hull.

All of a sudden, a snow-white dove floated down and rested on the top of the mast. Mac and Maggie froze like statues.

Never, not once had Mac witnessed a dove landing on any of his vessels while underway at sea, seagulls sure, plenty of times, but a snow-white dove, never.

And the dove brought with it a blanket of peace that settled over the captain and his first mate. The Voice may have been out loud or maybe just an echo in their soul but both of them heard it as clear as the church bells on Sunday morning. *I am with you.*

It started out as a gentle hum and then Maggie let the song escape from her soul.

"When peace like a river, attendeth my way,

When sorrows like sea billows roll;

Whatever my lot, Thou hast taught me to say,

It is well, it is well, with my soul."

~

All Richey could think of was talking to Jenny and hitting the bunk. Come on girl answer the phone. Richey looked at his watch. He'd been on duty for sixteen hours straight when he was relieved for six hours of bunk time. But before he went to sleep he tried to reach Jenny, again. He'd told her exactly when he could call, but three times in a row he had to leave a message. He was exhausted and frustrated. Finally, thank God, she answered. "Hey baby, so glad you answered."

She sounded distracted. "Hey...what's up?"

The conversation was one sided with Richey doing most of the talking and it ended with Jenny saying, "I don't know about this whole sailor wife thing."

The words flew out of the phone line and kicked Richey in the gut. He felt like dying and knew there was no way he'd be able to sleep. So, when one of the guys scheduled for the recon got sick, Richey volunteered. Down inside a small part of him hoped he'd get hurt. Maybe that would make Jenny feel bad—wake her up.

The six member recon team loaded surveillance equipment in a large raft and explosives into a smaller raft that would lead. "Johnson since you're supposed to be in your bunk dreaming about your woman, you sit in back and hand out equipment to the ducks. Just don't fall asleep."

Richey clenched his jaw. His woman. "I'd like to take lead sir...it'll keep me awake." At the commander's nod he jumped into the front raft.

"Okay boys, sneak and peak. Jenkins and Johnson have the lead."

They tethered together with fifteen feet of rope between them. Jenkins started to slip over the side and then flipped back into the raft. "Good Lord man, that water is cold."

Richey was still hot from his conversation with Jenny and before he knew it he was in the water tugging both rafts toward shore. "Sissy," he said to Jenkins.

And then he saw something in the trees, near the shore, it looked like the shimmer of moonlight on metal...and then a flash.

~

The world stopped spinning. For the first time in over two decades Mac and Maggie had nothing on the schedule but floating with each other. They talked as long as they wanted about whatever...or nothing. They swam and snorkeled and built a fire on a deserted beach. Maggie sang and Mac listened. Mac sang and Maggie laughed. They fed each other by moonlight dancing off the water and fell asleep in each other's arms rocked to sleep by the waves. They learned to live again. Play again. They didn't think it was possible until it happened, but they fell in love again—deeper than they'd ever been. Days and nights ran together and for five weeks they never looked at a clock.

In the midst of all the joy, a solemn place remained. They could hear in their laughter, that last little breath that sounded sad. It was an awareness that storm clouds could gather out of the calmest of seas. Mac called it Wisdom's balancing act. It was at those times they'd say another prayer for Richey.

~

The sun was settling into the Gulf when they finally drifted into their slip at Mangrove Marina.

Maggie tugged on the back of Mac's shirt tail as he fastened the last loop around the last cleat to snug their boat to the pier in their old familiar slip. He yielded to her tug and walked backwards into her arms. She giggled and slipped down the companion way into the cabin.

"One more night Captain...please."

Mac followed her into their honeymoon suite. She thought for sure he'd seen the fear in her eyes. Maybe he did, but like her, he didn't want anything to interrupt this bliss. So they pretended not to notice the feeling that a storm was brewing.

The next morning before sunlight splashed across the bow Maggie's eyes peered into the dark. She felt Mac's chest rise and fall against her back, his breath warm against her skin and his arms, strong and gentle around her. She listened to the small waves pitter-patter against the hull and felt the ropes tug holding their vessel secure. All was well, but still she shivered. Her mind dropped through the bottom of the boat and she felt icy fingers of the deep reach for her.

She slipped out of Mac's arms and into the dark before the dawn. She prayed one more time, hoped and tried to believe one more time, that this time, her prayer would be answered...that it would be gone. She felt her breast, and a tear slipped from where it had been hiding. The lump was still there.

~

Mac furled the sails and secured the lines. The boat was a mess and Maggie knew he'd want to get it into ship shape before leaving.

She wiped down the cabin, folded clothes into a duffle bag and filled the cooler with food they didn't want to leave aboard. When she tried to carry the cooler above deck, another dizzy spell sat her back down.

Mac noticed and said, "I'm tired. Let's go home—I'll come back tomorrow."

Maggie knew Mac wasn't tired and she would have objected, but she just didn't have the strength. "Okay Captain, whatever you say." Maggie also knew that as soon as her foot touched the pier the world would start to spin again, she feared it might just spin out of control.

~

They walked in the door together. Mac unloaded the cooler and Maggie placed a finger on the blinking red light of the answering machine and then removed it. "Mac—" she waited until he looked at her. "We need to talk."

The tires squealed as he shifted gears toward the hospital. "Mags you should have told me...I knew something was wrong."

She lifted a small smile and placed a shaky hand on Mac's, atop the gear shifter. "It'll be alright...you can slow down."

When they got to the hospital Mac barged in carrying Maggie. "Where's Doc Lumis?"

"I'm sorry sir but Doctor Lumis isn't here today, Doctor Schultz is in. What's going on?"

Mac walked toward the emergency room door and shouted over his shoulder. "Call Doc Lumis, tell him Maggie needs him quick."

"Sir Doctor Lumis is in Miami. You can't go back—"

Mac disappeared through the door and went into the first room to his right—a room he'd been in more than once over the years. He set Maggie down on the bed and told her he'd be right back. He turned to go find a doctor—pull him into the room if he had to—and ran smack dab into a white smocked little man that Mac would've sworn was still wet behind the ears.

"Sir, my name is Doctor Schultz, what seems to be the problem?" Mac thought he saw a pimple and wondered if the kid had graduated from high school. He had a round face and round glasses and he didn't look old enough to shave. Maybe his dad's a doctor here.

Mac looked out the door, "Where's Doc Lumis?"

"I'm sorry sir, Doctor Lumis is unavailable. How can I help?"

Mac made a noise that sounded like a growl. "Where's a doctor."

"I'm Doctor Schultz and you are?" The boy stuck out his hand.

Mac looked at his hand and then at him and let out a small laugh that held no humor. "No son, we need a real doctor—now."

"Mac." Maggie's voice startled both of them.

Mac softened his tone. "Sorry, we haven't seen anyone but Doc Lumis in I don't know how long, probably longer than you've been alive—"

"Mac!"

"Anyway, my wife needs someone to look at her right away." Mac turned and looked at Maggie and pulled in a deep breath.

Maggie smiled at her husband, shook her head and then looked at the Doctor. "Thank you for seeing me Doctor Schultz, especially like this..." She mentioned finding a lump on her breast and feeling weak.

The doctor looked at Mac and cleared his throat. "Sir, would you mind waiting in the lobby?"

Mac considered throwing him out the window. Instead, he shook his head and pointed a finger in the kid's face. "Listen, this is my wife and if I want—"

Maggie put a hand on her husband's arm and nodded toward the door.

Mac let out a slow breath, kissed her on the cheek, nodded once and walked out.

When he got to the lobby he paced the floor like a caged animal—or a father waiting for his first born.

~

"When did you notice the lump?" The doctor looked up from his notes.

Maggie looked at the floor. "Five weeks ago."

"Five weeks? Why'd you wait so long to come in?"

She explained how she'd found the lump on her breast at the start of their honey moon and couldn't bring herself to tell Mac...to ruin their honeymoon.

Maggie was admitted into the hospital. Doctor Shultz ran preliminary tests and ordered a biopsy. On the third day the results came back.

9

The kitchen was still dark, except for the blinking red light on the answering machine.

Mac stared into cold black coffee. A steady stream of saltwater poured from each eye. Doc Lumis had confirmed the results but Mac still couldn't believe it. How could he? God had given him a big, noisy, messy, happy family dream. This must be a test. Like Job. But Job already had a big messy family.

"I can't do this. God I can't do this. Please. No. Not my Maggie. We just went on our honeymoon...it's too soon. Please no. She's so good Lord, Richey needs her. Richey's children need her. Mags grandchildren need her. Take me instead. Take me please, not Mags. She can do so much good for You here. Not me. I'm no good without her. Don't take her God, please don't take her. I'll do whatever you want. I won't ask you for another thing, please God, please."

He couldn't hold back the sobs, his shoulders quaked his hands shook the coffee spilt and his head fell to the table in a pool of tears and coffee.

When Mac opened his eyes the kitchen was light. Maggie sat across from him, watching, praying, smiling. He leaned back and wiped his face with both hands.

Maggie looked at the coffee tear mixture on the table and his shirt and face. "Good thing I taught you to swim, huh Mac."

Mac's eyes locked on Maggie's. He tried to speak but no words would come.

Maggie wiped off the table and then poured some fresh coffee for both of them but before she carried the cups back to the table she punched the blinking red button on the answering machine. "Maybe Richey called."

The machine beeped several times and then a voice stated the date and time of the first call. It was from four days prior—the same day they had gotten home but then taken Maggie to the hospital.

"This is Eddy Wills, Richey's friend. Captain Johnson sir, Mrs. Johnson, ma'am, I hate having to leave a message like this but, well, I don't know when, or if, I'll get another chance. I'm heading back out and figured you ought to hear from a friend—someone who was there. It was supposed to be a simple recon. You know, in and out. Richey was in the front raft—like always—always the brave one. It was so dark. And then, there was this flash from the trees and the next thing I knew, Richey's raft exploded. We blew the h—, um, we blew the heck out of the beach where the flash originated." He cleared his throat. "We searched all night and the next day. We only found pieces of the raft."

The message went silent for a few seconds and then, "A diver found Richey's dog tags...they were burned black."

Maggie collapsed onto the floor. Mac helped her to the seat next to the phone as the message continued.

"I suppose I could get in some kind of trouble for telling you all this. But, Captain Mac, Richey always told me that not knowing was the worst kind of pain. So, sir...ma'am—I'm really sorry, but thought you'd want to know."

Mac grabbed the phone and started to dial. "I need answers." Then he slammed the phone down. "Who can I call?"

Maggie's voice was small. "Mac, I need to rest."

Mac wiped his eyes and after a long embrace he carried his Maggie to their room. "I'll get your Bible and some water," he whispered. When he returned she was sound asleep so he sat in the chair next to the bed and watched her sleep. After an hour he crept back to the kitchen and tried to pray, tried to read his Bible, he even tried to reach Jenny...all he could do was weep.

The next morning at seven hundred hours the phone rang.

Maggie jumped from her sleep and then relaxed when she felt Mac's arm around her.

"A phone call is better than a door bell Mags." Mac answered the phone and was officially informed that Richey was missing in action. The caller gave fewer details than the voice message from the day before, but this call made it more real.

When Mac hung up Maggie had a blank stare and looked as if she'd aged twenty years over night.

~

Mac and Maggie were sitting down at the docks, where they met, where they made so many memories. By this time Maggie was too weak and Mac carried her to their favorite bench, the same bench where over twenty years prior he'd carved a heart and wrote Mac 'n Mags inside.

They watched the gulls float and dive and dance. They listened to the waves strum a melody against the pier and swish along the shore before rolling back out to sea for one more chance to do it again. Though words were few, they spoke much. Her smile, his touch.

A young couple walked hand in hand along the shore, Mac and Maggie smiled. But...as they got closer, Mac noticed something familiar. No—No it couldn't be. He touched Maggie's shoulder and stood. "I'll be back."

His stomach turned and a fire lit in his face. He quickened his pace until he was next to the couple locked in a passionate embrace.

Jenny pulled back with a giggle, and then she noticed Mac. "What are you doing here, Mr. Mac?" she slurred.

Mac grabbed her left hand and pulled the ring off her finger. He lifted it in his fist and glared at the scruffy looking blurry eyed punk she was clinging to. "Can't you see she's married?"

"Was married—you ol' geezer." He swayed a bit and pointed at Mac. "Her old man bought the farm, she told me so." He licked his lips and looked Jenny up and down. "I'm just helping her get over—"

It happened so fast Mac almost thought it came from somewhere else—except for the fact that his knuckles hurt. Blood was dripping from the punk's nose and mouth and he was out cold, flat on his back. Jenny started screaming things a sailor wouldn't repeat. She was going on about him having no right to stick his nose in her business that she was a grown woman and free to do what—

Mac tuned her out—he was thinking about how this would break Richey's heart—but when she stopped to take a breath, he simply said; "Just because you can, don't mean you should."

He turned to walk back to his precious Mags and didn't recognize his own voice when he barked over his shoulder telling Jenny he never wanted to see her again.

Mac's head was spinning so he had to concentrate to keep from walking off the pier and straight into the water. If it weren't for Maggie, he would. He'd walk right off the edge and sink to the bottom and not come up—ever.

This isn't happening. He pinched the bridge of his nose and blinked back tears. He didn't just witness his sleaze-bag daughter in law kissing some scum-bag punk. Surely he didn't just knock the punk out for mocking his son's death. No, this was all a dream. It had to be a dream— no, not a dream—a nightmare. His wife wasn't really eaten up with cancer. He'd wake up soon, and he'd be floating in his boat, with Mags curled up next to him. This was just a bad dream. Had to be.

That was the last time they went to the docks—the last time they went anywhere.

~

Maggie sat a little straighter in bed, smoothed the blanket across her lap, looked at Mac, her eyes clear, "I'm ready to win this fight."

Mac sat next to the bed and buried his head in her lap—his shoulders shook.

She placed a weary hand on his head and waited until he turned to face her. "I've got to sail out of cancer bay into heaven's harbor." She swallowed and lifted the corners of her mouth into a weak smile and allowed tears to trail down her sunken cheeks.

Mac stood and lifted her hands to his lips. She could feel him tremble. "I can't do it without you Mags...don't go."

She wanted to apologize, for the hundredth time for not giving Mac more children, for leaving him alone with no grandchildren to spoil, to teach how to swim and sail and fish. All the things they'd dreamed of. As good a life as they'd had, someone to share it with, some little ones to pass it on to would have made all the difference, but, she knew it was too late for that and saying sorry one more time wouldn't ease the pain or change a thing, so she simply whispered, "Thanks for the honeymoon, Captain. It was worth the wait."

Mac shook his head, and let out a single sob. His eyes squeezed shut.

"Mac," she waited until their eyes met. She squeezed his hands and shook them slightly. "You must let Captain Jesus take the helm." She looked up, "He's here to take me home." She looked at Mac, her eyes were strong. "Stay the course Mac." She pulled in a slow gentle breath, and the song in her soul drifted like a feather from her lips. "It is well...it is well...with my soul."

Her hands went limp, she settled back against her pillow, closed her eyes and, with a smile that radiated peace—the same peace they had felt the day the dove landed on their mast—she was gone.

But the words, *It is well...it is well...with my soul* echoed around the room like a chorus of angels.

Mac thought the words must have floated to heaven and back and across the water and around the world, because he shook with a holy presence so divine that he knew beyond the shadow of a doubt that Captain Jesus had indeed come to take his precious pearl Home.

~

Gold and orange waves massaged the island's white shore as a leather-skinned fisherman stood barefoot on the bow of his driftwood colored boat and cast a faded net toward the weed line.

Richey floated somewhere between life and death, with the ocean his tomb, and seaweed his grave clothes.

It's time. The words echoed from everywhere and it was understood to be a command that demanded a response.

Like slipping from a wetsuit he slipped from his skin and drifted to a place where he looked down as waves lapped across a burned and broken body wrapped in seaweed. He knew the body was his, but he also knew...it wasn't him.

He drifted higher until his body looked like a small meaningless dot.

He drifted even higher still and watched the ocean as it heaved great waves and pulled high tides, but at the same time it lapped gentle waves on a small island's white shores. He remembered how the saltwater licked his skin. He saw great beds of seaweed for hundreds of miles, but could still feel how it wrapped his flesh like gauze, soft and cold. At that moment he realized the ocean and everything in it, all of creation, worked to bring him life.

And then, he saw what triggered it all.

In another part of the ocean hundreds of miles away, he saw a little boat adrift. The vision drew clearer, and he could see the boat was a Southern Cross thirty-five foot cutter and two people were holding hands. He knew it was his mom and dad and they were praying...for him.

Prayer in the hands of love is the most powerful force on earth.

And then, in an instant, he was back in his body looking at the sky.

It was faint at first, but it carried a familiar sound. It echoed across the waves closer and clearer until he heard her sweet voice loud and strong. *It is well...it is well...with my soul.*

And then, he heard a fishing net slap against the water.

10

After Maggie's funeral, Mac sat on his front porch for a week, he didn't eat or sleep or change his clothes or take a shower—nothing. He just sat there. He was dead, except with each beat of his heart, water pumped from his eyes. He let the tears fall draining him of all emotion. As soon as he felt numb—like he could cry or feel no more—the tide would change and a new wave of pain would wash in.

Friends would stop by with meals, and encouragement. He pretended to listen, but their words were muted, garbled. He could see they were talking, but nothing could penetrate the fog of sorrow. He'd go through the motions of thanking them, but once they left, the food ended up out back in the dented metal trash can. How could he have an appetite for food when he had no appetite for life?

His heart beat on a bed of nails. His chest ached and he couldn't pull in a full breath. When he closed his eyes no sleep would come, only the feeling that he was sinking to the bottom of the ocean—so cold, so black, and so heavy.

His Mags, his best friend, his lover, his wife and Richey, his friend, a living breathing part of his own flesh and bone, his son—both of them, ripped from him. He wouldn't survive. It hurt too much to take another breath.

He'd watched plenty of sailors deal with death—so he knew just what to do. He sat on the front porch in his rocking chair with the biggest bottle of rum he could find and filled his coffee mug.

He stared into the liquid cure and slowly raised the cup to his lips and took a sip.

The bite made his jaw clench. He swirled the cup. "What am I doing?"

He lifted the cup and took a drink and then another.

He rocked back and warm fingers released the pressure on his heart.

He took a swig.

The knots in his shoulders loosened and his arms relaxed. For the first time in weeks, he was able to take a full breath.

He finished the cup and poured another.

He hadn't eaten in a week and the sensation was quick. A numbing flow through his veins told him he'd found relief.

Pain lunged from the shadows—"It's your fault she's dead—" and plunged his dagger.

Mac shook his head and wiggled a finger against his ear. "My fault?" He nodded and pulled a long slow drink from the cup—this time he enjoyed the taste. "Aye...it was my fault."

"You knew something was wrong. You should've come back early. You killed your own wife." Pain kicked Mac in the face.

"It's my fault. I killed my Mags." Mac's eyes got blurry. He put his cup down on the wood table that sat between Mac's rocker and Maggie's. The one where two Mason jars of ice tea would be sitting if...

A breeze blew across the porch and Maggie's rocker moved just a little. "She'd be sitting right there—but you were too selfish to notice she was sick and you killed her."

Mac stared at Maggie's rocker. "I'm sorry Mags."

"You may have gotten over the hurt but now you never will. Now that you know the truth—YOU KILLED HER." Pain pounded his brain.

Fear slithered out of the bottle. "Take another drink and the pain will go."

Pain hissed "It's never going to end."

"Unless you take another drink," fear whispered.

Mac stared at the bottle.

"Richey's dead too, because of you. MURDERER." The voices grew.

Mac wrinkled his brow and took a small drink. "Richey?" He took another drink of the liquid that seemed to help him think.

"All of your Navy talk pushed him to enlist. He did it for you."

Mac nodded. "I did."

"Richey should be at home making a big noisy messy house full of kids but, because of you—HE'S DEAD."

Mac finished the cup swallowed hard. "I'm such a stupid fool...I killed my own family."

Pain's jagged knife sliced the inside of his throat and ripped out his heart. "Everything you've lived for is over—your wife and your son are gone, forever—you might as well give up."

Fear whispered, "One more drink—it'll clear your head, help you relax, give you courage."

Mac could feel a fist beating where his heart used to be.

Pain gripped Mac's throat. "From now on your life is a black tunnel with no way of escape."

Mac couldn't breathe.

Fear growled, "There's only one way of escape."

Mac thought of the loaded revolver in the night stand next to the bed.

Pain's jagged knife rode every breath in and out of his throat making him despise every breath. "Just. Stop. Breathing."

Mac swallowed hard, and one word managed to struggle to the surface and escape through quivering lips... "God."

Fear not.

Mac dropped the bottle and rum and fear drained through the cracks and hid under the porch.

Mac had been in plenty of fights. He'd backed down from plenty too, but never when he was afraid. "Son, there's plenty of good reasons to back down from a fight—but never let fear be one of them." Mac could hear his dad's voice attached to the memory.

He'd always owned up to his mistakes and bore the pain without making excuses. It's the only way to be a man his dad had taught him. "Face fear—never, ever run from it. If you do, it'll track you down and never let you rest until you're overcome by it."

At that moment, Mac knew fear hid in the bottle—and he'd have no part in that. And taking his own life was the coward's way out.

Mac didn't think he could win this fight—he figured he'd eventually die from a broken heart. The pain was unbearable and he figured it'd kill him. But until then, one thing he wouldn't do, until his last breath he would not cower to fear. He'd honor Maggie and his son's memory by not bowing to fear and hiding in a bottle. Maggie deserved better than that—so did Richey.

He pictured Jenny with that poor excuse of a man at the docks—it disgusted him. He couldn't walk that same road. Masking pain was the coward's way. Mac couldn't—wouldn't do that.

~

Mac spent the following week cleaning out Richey's rented house since Jenny disappeared without a trace and Richey was still officially MIA. After that, he packed up a few things from his house, got in his boat and headed out to sea. He didn't check the weather. He didn't set a course. He just started sailing with no plan as to where he'd go or when he'd return—if he returned. He just had to leave. If he had any chance of winning this battle he'd have to fight it on his own ground—which in his case, was on the water.

He started out heading west—the opposite direction he'd sailed with his healthy beautiful wife celebrating their honeymoon. How could his smooth sailing life turn to stormy seas so quickly? That was another issue he hadn't even addressed yet. It was buried under an ocean of pain and sorrow—but eventually he'd have to deal with another sea monster lurking in the deepest parts of his heart. He was furious at God.

He ended up sailing around the Everglades and up the west coast of Florida. He lowered the sails near Sanibel Island and let the sea have her way. Sanibel's lighthouse stood in the harbor to the east. The sun leaked a path of orange and yellow and silver slow dancing on the tops of the waves as it melted into the western sea. The lazy waves rocked him closer to the harbor.

"Okay Mac how many days have you been gone?"

He couldn't remember when he started talking to himself. He said it was to break the monotony—but he wondered if it was because he was going mad. The only human voice he'd heard since he left was his own.

After an awkward attempt he pulled a new cell phone out of a new leather pouch on his hip so he could see the date and time. The phone was dead. Like it had been since the day after he set sail. "Piece of junk."

He pulled his arm back and prepared to launch the stupid cell phone into the water until he remembered. "Plug it in, you idiot." He always said he'd never own a cell phone, but after the message about Richey on their home answering machine, he changed his mind and bought one. He just couldn't figure out how to operate it half the time, and the other half he couldn't remember to plug it in.

He tried to count the days since he left, but it was a blur. "I don't know how many days—ten maybe."

He scanned the shore line, studied the waves and the wind.

"Alright then, when's the last time you had something to eat?"

He couldn't remember that either.

His appetite and his heart were lost and he had no idea where to go to find them. He looked at the helm. He knew how to steer a boat into harbor and out to sea—but he had no idea how he'd steer his life from here. He was lost in a sea of hurt. A gentle breeze drifted from the southwest, a sunset only God could paint, seventy degrees—perfect. But Mac didn't notice—didn't care. He was battling his own storm filled with typhoon waves of emotion and lightning strikes of pain.

"Stay the course, Mac and I'll see you again." Maggie's voice drifted across his memory like the wind. Another reason Mac questioned his sanity.

He made a single sob. "Mags...you were my course—" he looked at the sky—"you and Richey. Now I have none. No purpose—I'm lost."

As Mac drifted along, scenes from the past faded in and out like old movies starring his wife and son.

He remembered when time stood still as he and Richey slid across the saltwater dance floor—wearing matching crooked grins.

"When you're in deep salt," Mac had told Richey, "you've got to rely on all of your senses—not just sight."

Richey had looked all the way around. "Yeah, speaking of that...I'm lost. Which way's home?"

Mac taught his son that "on the ocean things can change fast—real fast. Your mind can play tricks on you, too. You've got to hold on to what's real. Look for something stable—that doesn't change. And hold on to it—no matter how you feel."

The cry of a gull pulled Mac from memory's movie theatre.

He rubbed a hand over his eyes and shook his head. "I wish it were that easy. I'm adrift and nothing is stable anymore."

I AM the anchor of your soul.

The Voice interrupted his thoughts like an Emergency Broadcast System Weather Alert. He didn't think he heard the words out loud, but they blared in his head as clear as a bell.

Mac made a small tired laugh. "I'm losing it."

Since the start of the trip Mac hadn't given God much thought. He ignored Him on purpose—just like God had ignored Mac and his family in their greatest time of need. But now he bristled, ready for a fight.

"God! Why'd you let it happen?" Mac growled the words and clenched his teeth.

The years Mac spent on the ocean made it all too clear that God existed. He'd watched the sun rise and set over the ocean too many times to ever doubt that God existed. He didn't think anyone really denied God's existence—down in the secret places of their heart even the atheist knew God was real. "God's as real as a sunrise—and everyone knows it." He'd say. "Some are deceived, but most are just mad at Him...or too self absorbed to admit the Truth." It was a hard line but he knew it was true.

When things didn't make sense, Mac would say, "God is under no obligation to fit into my logic. Obedience brings understanding."

Mac had already settled so many issues. The weakness of running to the bottle, the selfishness of turning to suicide, the stupidity of pretending God didn't exist and the childishness of blaming God all ran through his mind and emotions again. And, one by one, he'd thrown them overboard. But now, the last demon he had to wrestle climbed on board. The one he'd been ignoring.

He knew God didn't cause any of it. But what he couldn't figure out was, why, He allowed any of it. God could have stopped it all. Mac and Maggie had prayed she'd be healed and Richey would come home safe and sound. But no—God was silent. No miracles, no phone calls, no visits telling that Richey was coming home and the cancer was leaving—nothing to show that God had heard or was even listening.

Mac worked the muscles in his jaw and clenched his fist. "I would never let that happen to someone I loved if I could prevent it." He pointed his finger toward the sky and noticed he was trembling. His chin quivered, "You could have prevented this. All of it...and You didn't." Mac sunk to the cockpit sole and drew his knees to his chest. "Why would you do nothing? Why?" For several moments he sat in silence listening and heard only the waves lapping against the side of his boat.

He knew he shouldn't press so hard but he couldn't shake the thought. "If one of my sailors stood by and watched a comrade get killed when they could have easily prevented it—I'd have him court marshaled, dishonorably discharged and I'd forever brand him as a coward." He looked up, his eyes blurred with angry tears. "Now God, where does that leave us?"

No answer, just the gentle breeze, the lapping of the waves and the cry of the gull. "Yeah, ignore me some more—you're good at that."

Then, a nagging question hit him. Why'd you let Richey join the Navy? You of all people knew the danger.

Mac made a single laugh that held no humor, "That's not even the same thing God and you know it. Joining the Navy is not a death sentence. I didn't want him to get hurt, but I'd have taken a bullet for him if I could to protect him. I certainly wouldn't have stood by and watched without lifting a finger to help...like You."

Silence filled the atmosphere. Another scene drifted into Mac's mind. Richey stepped on a rusty nail when he was five. The nail was sticking out of the bottom of his shoe and Richey was hysterical. Maggie tried to pull it out, but Richey screamed bloody murder so they rushed him to the emergency room. The nail was removed, the area sterilized and Richey was sent to another room to wait for a tetanus shot.

Richey couldn't understand why, after already being poked in the foot, they would want to poke him again, with a needle, in the arm. "I'll be good—I won't step on no more nails. Promise...Please...Please...Please don't poke me no more."

He cried. Maggie cried. Even the nurse who cleaned the wound cried. Maggie held Richey on her lap and rubbed his back and when his breathing settled she whispered in his ear, "Do you trust me?"

Richey sniffed three times and tried to speak but could only make jerky little breaths. He squeezed his mom's shoulders and looked in her eyes through tears and lifted his head up and down.

A lonesome wave rolled under the boat.

Mac shook his head hard and the memory vanished. But as he did other questions appeared. Was it Maggie's fault he stepped on the nail? Did she make him? Why'd they hurt him again? The questions raced through Mac's mind faster than he could answer but he knew the answers immediately.

"NO! If Maggie had known, she'd have prevented it. And, sure the needle hurt—but it was for Richey's own good. It's not the same thing. How could cancer be good? How can whatever happened to Richey be good? Death is not good! Didn't you say, 'I've come to give life? Life not death!' "

Mac waved his hands in the air and looked toward the sky. His voice weak, about to break, "We don't know the future, we're just people—just stupid people...not God. Not eternal, not omniscient, omnipresent or omnipotent. I couldn't help Mags...or Richey. I'm just a man."

A single cry fell from his lips and he went to his knees, his hands clamped together and hung in front of him, his head tilted back facing the sky. Silence ruled for several moments. Mac listened to his racing, breaking heart. "I just don't understand."

One question rose to the top of a million others fighting for his attention. The Voice that asked the question was filled with compassion.

How can a man who doesn't understand, blame a God who does?

Line by line slapped his soul, like waves against the boat...

It's not My will that any should perish.

Life is a vapor.

The thief comes to kill steal and destroy.

There is none righteous, no not one.

My ways are not your ways.

Trust Me

Mac knew two things: the words rolling through his mind were from somewhere in the Bible, thanks to Maggie insisting he make Bible reading a daily routine; and he was exhausted.

He poured himself onto the starboard bench. Folded his hands behind his head and stared straight into the sky. He tried to see through the clouds through the blue, through the solar system and into heaven—where Maggie was.

Instead, all the scenes and questions rolled through his mind again—sailing with Richey, the Navy, the nail, the tetanus shot, Maggie. Mac watched the clouds, each one held a memory of Richey and Mags. But then, a vapor trail from a jet snaked into view. It floated like a water snake slithering across the sky.

That's when it hit him.

The venom that had bitten his wife and son happened not recently, but many years ago, back in a garden, where the world was right and good—God declared it very good and said, "I made this just for you, take the wheel."

Mac let out a deep breath and shook his head. "But we handed the wheel to the snake...and now this."

He pictured his wife and son.

Pain pierced its dagger one more time, but it was losing its sting.

Mac remembered Maggie's plea, as he lifted his eyes toward heaven and his hands in surrender. "Alright, Captain Jesus, take the wheel."

The dagger dissolved and a gentle peace flooded his soul.

The circumstances didn't change one bit—but Mac did. He knew that no matter what, somehow he was going to make it through this storm. Without making a conscious effort, Mac did what he'd always done—what he'd taught Richey to do when adrift and lost at sea—look for and hold onto, what's stable.

Although he knew there was an ocean full of things he didn't understand—he knew God was the anchor for his soul.

And that was enough.

11

Mac smiled at the clouds, "God...will you tell Maggie, I'll stay the course?" And then, with a voice as out of tune as an anchor chain and as loud as a cannon that could be heard all the way to heaven—all the way to his Mags—he belted out the song in his soul.

"When peace like a river, attendeth my way,

When sorrows like sea billows roll;

Whatever my lot, Thou hast taught me to say,

It is well, it is well, with my soul.

It is well, with my soul,

It is well, with my soul,

It is well, it is well, with my soul."

"Hey! ...Anybody aboard? Hello to sailboat—you're about to—"

Mac bolted upright and lunged to the bow just as he drifted into the starboard side of another sailboat about five feet longer and two feet higher than his.

How in the world—what are the odds?

"Ahoy mate, taking a bit of a nip are ya?" A tall bearded man that looked like a lumber jack looked down at Mac. He held a pipe in one hand and a bottle of rum in the other. "Nap! I mean nap—" he looked at the bottle—"I'm taking a nip, you're takin' a nap. You wanna nip?" He let out a laugh that could be heard on shore and held the bottle in Mac's general direction as he swayed like the mast of his 40' Catalina Sailboat.

"I'm sorry. I must have—" Mac shook his head and nodded toward the bench seat—"yeah...I uh...sorry." Mac looked at the bottle. "No thanks, I've had enough."

"Yah, I heard. Ya ain't exactly the best singer you know. But I heard ya coming before I saw ya—good thing too. I dropped them there rubber bumper gizmos just in time." The big man waved his bottle toward the bumpers. "Pretty smart sailin' huh?"

Mac looked at the bumpers and the boat—everything looked brand new, even the man's khaki shorts and Hawaiian shirt. Only the suspenders he wore over the Hawaiian shirt didn't look new—they looked, ridiculous. Other than the rum induced slur, Mac figured he sounded like a snow-bird from the mid-west. Wisconsin, Minnesota or Iowa—somewhere like that. Mac noticed the man's tanned face and whiter-than-snow legs. Yep, he's probably a farmer from the mid-west. Mac kept the boats apart and smiled up at the giant. "Yes, sir, that was some mighty fine seamanship. Thanks."

"There's another hitchin' post behind me if you wanna latch on to it."

Hitchin' post? Yep—a farmer. No doubt about it.

That's when Mac noticed what had happened. He wondered how he'd drifted into the Catalina so soon. Even though Mac had been preoccupied with his emotional roller coaster and wrestling with God—he still knew his location. It was like he had an internal navigational system. He subconsciously noticed the current and wind and calculated where his boat should drift. He had at least another thirty minutes before he drifted into the bay near the mooring balls.

So, why did he just run into a boat that was obviously tied off? Mac checked the channel both ways for boat traffic and wondered how this man had managed to miss the bright mooring balls anchored near the marina and had tied off on a channel marker. How can I tell him what he's done without making him feel like an idiot? "My name's Mac."

"Hi Mac! I'm Pete. You want me to help you get around, so you can hitch up on the other side?"

"Thanks, but I think I'll dock her for now." Mac pointed at the docks. "And then I'll tie off on one of the mooring balls closer to the docks." Mac went from pointing at the docks to pointing to the mooring balls—where Pete should have tied off in the first place.

Mac had maneuvered his boat away from the larger vessel and the natural current was now separating them. "Thanks again and I'm sorry about that."

The big man scratched his head and stared at the mooring balls. "Yah, you betcha—maybe I'll see ya later."

Mac noticed, Paul Bunyan was painted across the back of Pete's boat. Figures.

Later that evening, while Mac was picking up supplies on shore, he saw Pete. They exchanged friendly hellos. Pete smiled and pointed with his thumb toward the channel marker where he had tied his boat. "I wasn't parked in the right stall now was I?"

"Really?" Mac stepped to the side and looked around the big man toward the water. "Hmmm...you might be right." He noticed Pete had moved his boat out of the channel and had tied it to the pier, near Mac's.

Pete slapped Mac's shoulder and laughed like a big mid-west farmer would. His cheeks lit red and his meat and potato diet bounced his belly. "It was like hitching my mule to a road sign in the middle of the interstate and you know it."

Mac had to smile. But still, he was in no mood to carry on a conversation with anyone—unless it was Maggie or Richey.

Pete handed Mac a card. "If you're ever up in Duluth look me up. We've got an ocean up there too, you know." He laid both hands over his belly and laughed. "Only it's called Lake Superior." Pete's eyes were red and Mac could smell rum on his breath.

He nodded and put the card in his pocket and after small talk for more than a few minutes, Mac was back on his boat. That's where he felt safe. Even walking on land, after so many days at sea, made the earth feel unstable. He'd come a long way. But his heart was still shattered. It was too soon to walk around in a world that kept spinning like nothing had happened, like his world hadn't just fallen apart. No, he was better off—for now anyway out at sea. Just him, his boat, his God and memories of the life he once had.

After the sun had set, Mac listened to the quiet of the waves and occasionally caught a whiff of the sweet aroma drifting from Pete's pipe.

Pete had tied off to the mooring ball closest to Mac's.

Mac thought about how the big farmer had rambled on about how his wife recently passed away and how he sold the farm that had been in the family for over a century. How the kids wanted nothing to do with the farm and he didn't see any reason to mope around in a big old farm house full of his wife's memories. So he had done something crazy—sold the farm outside Duluth Minnesota and bought a boat in Florida. Only he didn't have a clue how to sail the thing. Mac hadn't really been interested but he nodded and offered just enough to be polite and make it through the conversation and back to his boat.

Maybe I'll talk to him tomorrow—and actually listen. Maybe I'll get a pipe.

Mac stayed moored there next to Pete for several days. He even gave Pete a couple of sailing lessons. They played chess from an outdoor patio overlooking the bay. They had talked about sailing and fishing and farming and the only thing they didn't talk about was what they wanted to talk about most of all—the big empty hole where their hearts used to be.

"Check." Pete smiled and sat back in his chair pulling his suspenders out from his chest with his thumbs.

Mac was staring at the sunset over the Gulf of Mexico and not paying much attention to the chess game they'd been in for over an hour. Mac looked at the board and noticed Pete had moved his bishop at a diagonal line across from Mac's king. Only he couldn't technically make that move because it exposed his king to Mac's queen. Mac didn't want to tell him, since Pete was finally getting the hang of the game. Mac moved and secretly rooted for Pete. Mac knew that, sometimes, losing was the best way to win.

Pete laughed more than any person he'd ever met. But after Mac started to listen, he could tell; it was a sad, hollow laugh. Mac knew Pete was masking the pain. The rum, the boat, the new clothes and new life style were an attempt to run away from the pain of a broken heart. "I miss my Mags, Pete. And my son. It hurts."

They'd told each other in bits and pieces about the past and their losses, but never delved into it more than a passing comment here and there. This was the first mention of the pain they were both feeling. Pete let out a nervous chuckle and a painful memory of his wife slapped his face red. "Yeah...well...I uh—" Pete slammed the rest of his rum and coke and chewed on a piece of ice—"I got you checked, again." This time he didn't smile.

Mac studied the board again, tired of secretly helping Pete stay in the game. He moved his queen. "Check...mate." The corners of his mouth pulled into a smile that didn't reach his eyes.

Pete looked at the board—dumbfounded. "How'd that happen?"

"You were blindsided—like me hitting your boat...like cancer hitting my wife. Like our lives. You never saw it coming."

"What are you getting at, Mac?"

"Nothing. I don't know. Everything. I've just been thinking. One day I had the best life a man could ever hope for and then..."

"Yeah" Pete nodded but never took his eyes off the board. "Just like that—it's over."

"You were happy out there tied up to the wrong buoy, in the wrong place, you didn't know it, but if you'd stayed there too long, chances are you might have been smashed into by a bigger vessel. But when you figured out there was a better place to be—you moved."

"Yeah, I moved only because you were taking a nap or giving yourself singing lessons or whatever, and ran into me first." Pete narrowed his eyes plopped his unlit pipe between his teeth and crossed his arms.

"That's just it. I wasn't taking a nap or...giving myself singing lessons. I was—believe it or not—talking to God. And I don't think running into you was an accident."

"You did it on purpose?"

"No Pete. I'm saying I think God wanted us to meet. Think about it. What are the odds?"

"I know, I know, but...God? I don't think so. He doesn't give a hoot about me or He'd have stopped my wife..." Pete shook his head. "Never mind, eat drink and be merry for tomorrow we die—that's my motto. I think that's even in the Bible somewhere. I worked hard. I was good— you know, did the right things—went to church, learned all about God since I was a kid. But what'd it get me?" Pete waved his empty glass at the waitress clearing a table. "Nothing, that's what." He set his glass on the wood table a little too hard. "A big fat nothing, no wife and a bunch of kids I never hear from."

"Pete, you want another sailing tip?"

"Sure" Pete nodded at the waitress who'd just brought him another glass of rum, and he took a sip.

Mac looked out at the water."That's the Gulf of Mexico it opens into the ocean and flows around the Florida Keys. The Ocean's average depth is 12,000 feet and plunges seven miles deep—deeper than Mount Everest is tall—in The Mariana Trench. It covers over seventy percent of the earth's surface, about 193 million square miles, 310 million cubic miles. Just south of here, the Gulf Stream flows east around the south end of Florida, past my home town and north up the east coast—a river in the ocean that travels north— sending millions of gallons of water an hour between Florida's east coast and the Bahamas. It can even change the weather.

"She's huge and wild and can't be tamed. Knowing about her won't help a hoot in a storm—you've got to know her intimately. And the only—"

Pete slapped the table like a side of beef and made a laugh that held no humor. "Intimately...you've spent too many hours alone out there, sailor."

Mac held up his hand telling Pete to let him finish. "And the only way to survive a storm at sea is, bow to the wind. Turn your back on her and she'll roll over your transom 'til your full to the gunnels. Try and cross her and she'll lift you up on a swell, and dump you on your side. But, face her head on, and you'll never have such a ride...but you'll survive." Mac looked at Pete. "My friend, we're smack in the middle of a storm. But, for this kind of storm, it's not the sea you've got to know—" Mac's eyes drifted out across the water and up into the sky—"it's the One who calms it."

Pete stared at his glass of rum and tilted it side to side. "That's what I'm doing. Instead of wallowing in the mud back on the farm, I'm taking the bull by the horns and starting fresh."

God please, give me wisdom. Mac let his eyes drift beyond the pier where the dinghies were tied, past their moored boats and out to where the channel marker bobbed alone—the hitchin' post where Pete first tied off. "My friend—" Mac looked Pete square in the eyes—"you might be tying your mule to the wrong post."

Pete lifted his broad shoulders up and down once and wiped a big palm over his shiny eyes. "My Liz talked about God like you. I always figured it was kind of strange when she said He was her friend. But, when she died, she was at peace...I could see that."

"She wants to see you again. And if God allows folks a window in heaven, maybe my Mags and your Liz are watching right now."

Pete grabbed his glass of rum and held it under the table. "You think they're watching?"

"I don't know if they are. But I know they're with God—and He is."

Pete looked up at the sky without saying a word.

Mac slid his chair back and stood. "Well, it's something to think about."

Pete stayed seated, still holding his drink under the table. "So...you're leaving tomorrow, huh?"

"Plan to set sail at first light." Mac looked out toward the water—it was calling him.

Pete shifted in his seat, started to pull the drink out from under the table and then stopped. "You really think The Big Guy's watching?"

Mac's eyes spoke the answer as he simply nodded.

Pete held out a trembling hand. "I'll give it some thought. If you're ever in Duluth, I'll spend the summers up there, and winters here." He looked toward his boat. "Maybe someday I'll even take her out of the harbor—thanks to your fine lessons."

Mac shook Pete's hand. "Maybe we'll bump into each other again sometime." Mac smiled. "So keep them there bumper gizmos handy. And, if I'm ever in Duluth, I'll look you up." But Mac knew he'd never leave Tavernier Florida, especially to go to some frozen tundra up north.

12

Mac was up before the sun preparing to head south. He'd listened to the weather report on his VHF and it was perfect sailing conditions. Mac had solar and wind generated power to keep the batteries charged and a diesel engine for motoring when the wind wouldn't cooperate.

He had finally remembered to charge his cell phone although he hadn't turned it on since the start of his trip. He unplugged it from the charger and flipped it open and pushed the red button to power it up. After a few seconds it vibrated to life—he always kept it on vibrate—he didn't like annoying ring tones, too much noise pollution.

After another second or two the phone vibrated again. He had a new voice message. Who'd be calling me? Probably the preacher. Mac pushed a button and waited, then dialed his access code and heard a ladies voice. "This is Florida Keys Community Hospital calling for Richard Johnson. We have found, um...Dr. Lumis would like to speak with you regarding..."

The phone went silent for a brief moment and then a man's voice came on the line. "Mac, this is Steve Lumis. Give me a call on my cell—" He left his number but Mac didn't get it because of what he said right before he left his number— "it's about Richey." Mac had to replay the message four times to get the number right.

Richey? What could Doc Lumis have to do with Richey—it's not even a Veterans Hospital. Maybe it's because he was born there. Maybe they sent records—Mac squeezed the bridge of his nose with his thumb and forefinger—death records. But why a civilian hospital? That doesn't make sense.

Mac dialed the number, sucked in a quick breath and held it.

"Dr. Lumis." He answered on the second ring.

"Doc this is Mac. What about my boy?" Mac didn't have time for niceties and small talk.

"Mac, where are you? You're not going to believe this, but Richey's here."

Mac couldn't breathe. He looked out across the water and tried to take a breath. Here? Did he say, here? Richey...there? Did he mean Richey? Mac swallowed. Or Richey's body?

"What, exactly, do you mean, Doc?"

"Richey is here Mac. He's alive. He was found down at the docks."

"Found! What do you mean found? Come on Doc talk—tell me everything."

"Yesterday Mangrove Marina called and said there was a young man sleeping on one of the benches. He'd been hanging around the marina for three days. Sean noticed him—"

"Sean?"

"Yeah, Sean and Esther are back on land for awhile. They're good—they asked about you."

"Anyway" Mac said.

"Sean saw Richey pacing the dock. He tried to talk to him, but before he could get close, he ran. He knew it was Richey, but Mac—he's hard to recognize—he's been burned and he doesn't remember anything. I have no idea how he got here. He was dehydrated and exhausted. I've admitted him."

"Richey's there—alive?" Mac's voice broke.

"Yes, he's going to be alright. He needs rest for starters and then maybe...hopefully, his memory will return. I'm praying for him. Where are you? How soon can you get here?"

Mac had already cast off and was hoisting the sails. "I'm on my way."

~

Mac kept the sails full and the motor running. Twenty-eight hours later he was standing in the Florida Keys Community Hospital looking at his sleeping son.

Anyone else would see a scarred burn victim. But Mac didn't see burns, he didn't notice scars—he saw his son. Mac had been to some of the most beautiful places on earth, and yet nothing compared to what he was looking at lying there in room 202 of the Florida Keys Community Hospital. Because love, doesn't see scars.

Mac's eyes blurred, his lip quivered, "I love you, Son."

Richey blinked, then smiled a crooked smile. "Dad—you look awful...where am I?"

Doctor Steve Lumis walked in. "Richey, good, you're awake." The doctor explained to Richey where he was, and how they had found him.

Richey had slept most of the three days since he'd been admitted and his memory had returned, all of it up to the day he'd gotten hurt.

Doctor Lumis pursed his lips and folded his arms. "Richey, what is the last thing you remember before waking up here? It might help waken the rest of your memory."

Richey inhaled a deep slow breath through his nose and closed his left eye.

Mac studied his son and for the first time noticed the burns; no eye brows, blotchy red skin, swollen lips, top half of his right ear was gone, and the right side of his face was a massive scar with his right eye swollen shut. Mac narrowed his lips and willed himself to remain calm.

"I remember we were on our way in to—" Richey shook his head slightly—"it doesn't matter. But we were on a simple recon. You know Dad—sneak and peak—set up surveillance, take pics and get out. We thought it was an uninhabited island, a drop spot for weapons and probably drugs—no one was supposed to be there. But—" Richey clenched his jaw—"something went wrong." A single tear escaped Richey's left eye.

Mac laid his hand on Richey's right arm and looked at Doctor Lumis. "Hey, Doc, maybe it's too soon. Son, you don't have to do this now."

"No, Dad, it's alright. Maybe it'll help. I need to know what happened...what happened to my team."

Mac nodded okay to his son.

"We were floating in on rafts. It was cold. Pitch dark. Jenkins was supposed to get in and swim us ashore but he complained about the water being too cold. 'Jenkins, you're a sissy' I told him and slipped into the water. It was deep—over my head. And so cold it took a few seconds before I could catch my breath. And then—" Richey stopped, his left eye grew big—"Incoming," he shouted. "I reached up to pull Jenkins out and..." Richey lifted his right hand as if reaching for Jenkins and then he froze with his hand suspended in front of him. His little finger and half of his ring finger were missing. The look on his face held no fear or shock. "It was too late. They didn't make it, did they?"

He shook his head. "Everything went red hot after that. My head was on fire, it felt like the water turned to lava. I swam as far as I could. I had to get out of the fire. Finally, it seemed like I swam forever. I ran into seaweed thick and cold."

Richey spoke the event as if announcing a play by play as he watched them roll through his memory. He relived the event in his mind. "The cold felt good—but I was burning up—my head was on fire. My right hand felt like it was being ground up in a propeller. I had to put out the fire in my head. I wrapped up in the weeds and stayed under water with only my mouth and nose sticking out. It sounded like bombs exploding one after another. And then everything went black."

Richey was quiet for a moment. His good eye got wide and darted around the room. "Where's Jenny?"

Panic grabbed Mac's throat and squeezed. He swallowed, hard. "Son, Jenny...she um—"

Suddenly Richey grabbed one bedrail with his left hand. "I've got to get back to my unit." Then, he grabbed the other bedrail with his wounded right hand and tried to pull. It was too much. He fell back, and a silent trail, leaked from his eye to the pillow.

Mac laid his hand on Richey's chest and felt his heart pounding hard. Mac's lips tightened, his chin quivered, "I love you Son."

Doc Lumis set his clip board down at the foot of Richey's bed, removed his glasses and wiped his fingers across wet eyes. "Mac, did you know Richey taught my son how to ride a bike? I was too busy back then. And now—" the doctor let out a single laugh that held no humor—"he's all grown up and I never see him." He slid his glasses back on, picked up the clip board and smiled. "We should let Richey rest—he's going to be alright."

"I need to alert the Navy. They may want to move him to one of their hospitals. And then—" Mac looked at Richey's wounds—"I don't know."

13

The clock ticked slowly these days.

Mac handed Richey a chocolate cupcake with a single candle poked into the center.

Richey stopped his rocking chair and watched as his dad lit the single candle. "What's this?"

Mac eased into the wooden rocker next to his son and for a moment they both sat on the front porch in silence and just stared at the candle. "One year ago today I raced into room 202 of the Keys Community Hospital and there you were...and now here you are."

"Thanks." Richey shook his head. "Wow, a year already?"

"You outshine the scars Richey." Mac's smile swelled all the way from his heart to his eyes.

"Outshine the scars?" Richey made a small laugh. "Yeah, right."

"I'm proud of you son." Mac looked at the flame. "Better blow out that candle—you wouldn't want to get burned."

Richey narrowed his one good eye and lifted a crooked grin. "That's sick." He blew out the candle ripped the cupcake in two and shoved half of it into his mouth.

Mac nodded. "Yeah, you're probably right—sorry."

Richey held the other half of the cupcake out to his dad and worked hard to swallow what he'd already shoved in his mouth.

"Thanks" Mac reached for the other half.

Just before he grabbed it, Richey pulled away and stuffed the rest of it in his mouth. "Too slow, old man." He garbled through a mouth full of cupcake.

"Now that's sick." Mac laughed and shook his head.

They both set their rocking chairs into motion.

Creak—creak—swoosh.

From the front porch they couldn't quite see the ocean, but they'd face in her general direction and imagine they were there. On quiet nights they could hear her calling; the gulls cry, the clanging of sailboat rigging, smell the salty air and if the wind was just right, sometimes they could even hear Maggie's sweet voice drifting all the way from heaven...*It is well with my soul.*

Richey had received the prestigious Medal of Honor. He didn't think he deserved it. But, Jenkins made Richey out to be some kind of hero. "Richey called out 'incoming' and jerked me from the boat," Jenkins said. "Then he pushed me deep into the water toward the back raft while the world lit up above us. At first I thought he was fooling around because I didn't want to get in the frigid water—but then, I realized, he saved my life."

They never found Richey and figured saving Jenkins had cost him his life. But, Richey was strong and the water was his home. He swam as far as he could, and then passed out in a cocoon of salt water and seaweed.

Three days later he was found by a fisherman and taken to an Island Convent where nuns cared for him for several weeks. His dog tags were missing and he was wearing nothing but charred rags, so identification was impossible. Richey kept saying, "Keys." Over and over he'd say it. "Keys please...I need the Keys." They couldn't figure out what he meant and figured he was still in shock.

About once a week, the fisherman who'd saved Richey checked in on him. On one of those visits he mentioned going to America, to the Keys, to transport a fishing vessel. Richey came to life. "The Keys, take me to the Keys."

After that Richey turned a corner and they allowed him to ride with the fisherman to America. The captain figured he could hand Richey over to the American authorities and let them handle it from there. Richey stood on the aft deck, as they pulled into port, and then he was gone.

The fisherman reported what had happened, but Richey was never found, until he showed up at the marina.

After Richey was released from the hospital he settled in at his dad's place and without missing a beat they got busy. At first they did it just to keep from thinking about the way their lives had turned out.

Richey visited the VA hospital, VFW, and nursing homes. He was thrilled listening to his heroes tell their stories. They were thrilled to have someone to tell them to. He was a member of the Military Order of the Purple Heart and organized a program for the tax deductible donation of boats. One hundred percent of the proceeds went directly to wounded veterans; many of whom received little or no compensation from other sources. He also set up distribution locations at local shops and marinas for the Purple Heart Viola; the organizations official flower, assembled by disabled and needy veterans.

He told anyone who'd listen about how he floated between life and death in a saltwater grave and then drifted to a place where he was looking down at his broken burned body and how he saw his mom and dad praying for him and he'd always say, "Prayer in the hands of love is the most powerful force on earth." His beautiful blue eye would swim when told a part to the story that he didn't remember until several months after it happened. "And one more time, I floated up toward Him—the One at the helm—closer and closer until I was absorbed right into Him and I saw through

His eyes at the helm of the universe. The earth floated like a bobber in an eternal ocean. But, like myself, as small and insignificant as the earth appeared—in the vastness of the universe—it was incredibly valuable, like a priceless pearl in the midst of the sea."

After that, life became precious, but the details weren't important. Richey tried to view everything through those eternal eyes at the helm. "What matters for eternity? That's what's important." It helped him see with an eternal passion, beyond the scars. He said he could see better with one eye than he ever did with two.

"I see eternity in my right and what's left—with my left."

It helped him forgive Jenny for her wayward heart. Secretly he hoped, someday she'd return. He never stopped praying for her. And even though he didn't want to, he couldn't help it—he'd never stopped loving her. On good days, he believed she could look beyond the scars and see his heart.

But he tried not to dwell on that too much, because if he did, it led to what hurt the most: he'd never realize the dream of having a family. He'd never teach his kids how to walk and ride a bike and fish and swim and sail and love life with eternity in view…or carry on his father's name by giving him a boatload of grandchildren. Because, who'd want to be with a beat up, one-eyed sailor, with half a hand, half an ear and a burned up face? That dream would take a miracle.

Richey found the only way to keep from dwelling on his shattered dreams was to stay busy trying to help other people's dreams come true. He tried to remember that in the big picture—through the eyes of the Master Helmsman—all of God's children are family.

Mac spent most of his time on the boat. Richey usually stayed behind and looked after the house. Time eased along like a slow wave, and little by little, their hearts mended.

They'd developed a motto that seemed to get them through the hardest times; the times when Richey couldn't stand to look at himself in the mirror and the times Mac thought he'd die for missing his Mags. They'd take a deep breath and, do the next thing. When they didn't think they could go on one more minute they'd, do the next thing, whether they felt like it or not.

"Well, I'll go mow the lawn...Well, I'm going to go visit the VA...Let's go fishing...The truck needs the oil changed...

They just did the next thing, until little by little they could finally talk about their past, without the conversation falling like a silent painful tear.

They'd even learned to smile through the pain, toward the memories. Like the time they were painting one of their fixer-upper boats and the paint pail slid off the bow and landed on Maggie's head. Or, when she baked peanut butter cookies—Mac and Richey's favorite—she'd always shape some to look like sailboats. Or, how out of the clear blue, no matter where she was at, she'd start singing right out loud. And how—even though it had happened a long time ago—she cried like a baby when the preacher told the story about Horatio Spafford. The writer of her favorite hymn had lost his four year old son due to illness and then his business due to fire. Then he sent his wife and four daughters across the Atlantic and the ship sank after colliding with another sea vessel. All four daughters died. His wife Anna survived and sent him a telegram, "Saved alone..." Horatio traveled the same waters to meet his grieving wife and as he passed over the spot where his daughters had died he penned the words to the famous hymn, It Is Well With My Soul. Some days Maggie would play that hymn over and over all day.

Mac and Richey kept doing the next thing, breathing in, breathing out, surviving second by second, day by day, week by week and month by month, until it turned into a year and that year turned into two and then five and then seven.

~

Just when everything had settled into a comfortable routine, Richey started itching for change. The worst season was approaching—summer. The heat never bothered him until after his injuries and now he couldn't stand the hot Florida sun. It hurt his eye and his skin burned whenever he was exposed too long. And worst of all—the dreams. Strange dreams, more like nightmares, kept him awake. He'd always see the same thing; a terrible car accident, and then a little blond haired boy crying himself to sleep.

In his dream, Richey would reach out to comfort the child, but then, pull back—not wanting to frighten him. Even when awake, Richey couldn't forget the big blue eyes and the silent tears. The next thing that would happen always caused Richey to sit straight up in bed. The boy would lift his left hand and place it on the scarred right side of Richey's face and as tears dripped off a quivering chin, he'd say one word—the one word Richey was sure he'd never hear in real life…"Dad."

At first, Richey didn't say anything. He figured it'd pass. But it didn't. Now he was worried. What could it mean? "Was I in a car accident when I was a kid?" Richey had asked Mac one evening after supper as they sat on the front porch.

"No, never a car accident—but I do recall the time you rammed one of our fixer-uppers into the pier and cracked the starboard bow." Mac let out a soft chuckle. "Why?"

Richey explained the reoccurring dreams.

Mac rocked his chair and then stopped mid rock. "Maybe the car accident represents the Titanic, and the crying little boy is you, grieving. But now you're ready to wake up and move on to bigger and better things."

They had started calling the time when Maggie died, Richey was injured and Jenny disappeared, the Titanic. That was the time when everything in life appeared to be smooth sailing. Mac and Maggie were finally taking their long awaited honeymoon and Richey was pursuing his career in the Navy and dreaming of a big happy family with his new bride. But, hidden just below the surface, the icy fingers of death and pain slammed into the hull of their lives, and all their dreams sank.

Richey lifted his head in one slow nod. "I thought it might have been something I'd forgotten—you know, like a car wreck or something from when I was a kid. But, maybe you're right. It's strange now that I think about it. That face...it was familiar."

"Reckon we oughta pray about it" Mac said.

Ever since Mac had that heated discussion with God—the one by Sanibel Island where he smacked into Paul Bunyan—he turned to prayer as his primary source for problem solving. All the time he had spent talking to Maggie was now transferred toward heaven. He didn't pray to Maggie, of course, but he found a peace through prayer that nothing else would give. And it didn't hurt knowing that Mags was up there somewhere, too. Maybe God even let her listen. Probably not, but maybe, Mac didn't know. He whispered a simple prayer for wisdom and then set his chair back into motion. "You'll figure it out Son." He smiled. "Maybe God's preparing you for something. Don't worry. I have faith in God...and you."

The dreams continued.

The next week the temperature climbed to over a hundred and Richey found himself hating the place he'd always loved. He was scrubbing the deck of their boat. If they didn't scrub and clean on a regular basis, the moist salty air mildewed and corroded in a hurry. Usually, Richey loved the work, the smell, the sound of the gulls, the splashing waves, but the heat...the heat was more than he could take.

"I've got to get out of here." He threw the scrub brush into the five gallon bucket and walked up the dock toward the marina. He used to dive in the water to get refreshed, but now, that didn't even sound good.

Later that evening after eating the steaks Mac had grilled, they sat in their usual spot on the front porch, the sun was beginning to set and the breeze cooled enough to make it tolerable. Mac reached into his shirt pocket and pulled out a card. "What do you think about Minnesota?"

Richey shook his head. "What're you talking about?"

"I met this man—during the Titanic. He lived in Minnesota. Duluth, Minnesota. He said they had an ocean up there, a fresh water ocean—Lake Superior."

Richey looked curious. "And...?"

"He also said it was a good deal cooler in the summer and a whole lot colder in the winter. I thought maybe we could go for a visit and check it out."

"You mean check it out to visit, or to live? Dad, you love this place—it's a part of you." Richey smiled and made a soft chuckle. "If you moved...the whole place would fall in the ocean."

Mac looked at Richey, "You're a part of me, Son. This place is just dirt." He sat back and looked off into the distance. "You know...it might just be God's way."

"What do you mean, God's way?"

"Well, just think about us sitting here in these rocking chairs. We're content to sit for quite some time but then, we get uncomfortable and switch positions or get up and move somewhere else. When we get uncomfortable where we're at in life—it may be God's way of getting us to get up and move. Make a change."

"Hmmm...but leaving Tavernier?"

"I've traveled the world by water. These eyes have seen the most beautiful places. But out of all those sights, there was only one that I could never tire of—no matter how many times I laid my eyes on it."

Richey cocked his head. "Duluth?"

Mac's eyes smiled first. And then the corners of his mouth lifted. "You and your mom...my family. In all my years, I've never seen a more beautiful sight. And of all the places I've been—there's never been a place I'd rather be than with my family. Family—the greatest place on earth. Besides, don't you think it's kind of hot down here?"

"Minnesota?" A queasy feeling soaked Richey's stomach. "Isn't that where, Jenny—" Richey drew a deep breath—"moved?"

They'd gone over this before. At times Richey had wanted to find Jenny. But all he had to do was run his hand across his face and feel the scars or glance in the mirror, and he knew it was hopeless. No woman would want a man who looked like him—especially Jenny. She was too beautiful...too wild.

Compassion took up residence on Mac's face. He leaned toward his son and placed a hand on his knee. "That was a long time ago, son."

Richey swallowed hard. "What if she decides to come back...and we're gone?"

"Come back?" Mac pulled in a slow breath. "Like I said, it was a long time ago. She thought you were..." He didn't need to finish, they both knew what he meant. She thought he was dead. They all did.

~

Not that it would have mattered to Jenny if Richey were dead or alive. It took depth of character like Maggie's for military wives to wait for their husbands during long deployments at sea. Something Richey knew Jenny didn't have.

If only he'd have waited, maybe he'd have met someone else. Maybe he'd have met someone with the inward beauty like his mom. If only he hadn't jumped the gun and gotten married so quick, maybe he wouldn't have been so anxious to volunteer for that recon mission.

But it was too late. Now he had to suffer the consequences for rejecting advice, for being in a hurry. Not only did he have to pay—but his dad did, too. Now they had no one to continue the family name. No children to love, no family to come home to. With him their family lineage would end—all because he was in a hurry to make life happen.

Richey made a long slow sigh as he released the breath he'd been holding and nodded at the card in Mac's hand. "Did you know fresh water isn't nearly as hard on boats as salt water?"

Mac let out a single laugh. "So, I've heard."

And Mac and Richey...did the next thing.

14

"Ricky's a sweet boy." She drew a heart on the file folder labeled, Richard MacArthur Johnson. "He's a bit of a mystery though." She colored in the heart with a blue ink pen and looked over her glasses at the Paulsens. "Are you sure about this?"

The young couple sat on folding chairs on the other side of the social worker's desk. Martin squeezed his wife's hand. Rebecca smiled. They both nodded.

Marilyn Harper pressed hard on the pen and drew a dark jagged line across the heart.

"He hasn't said a word in over two years. Not a single word since he was around five years old...since the accident that killed his mom—" she narrowed her lips and inhaled sharp through her nose—"and dad." She spit the last word out like it tasted awful.

Marilyn folded her arms and looked at the broken, scribbled heart. "Doctors say it was from the shock. He didn't sustain any serious head trauma from the accident, and other than a broken nose he was fine...physically, anyway."

Someone sniffed, and when Marilyn looked up, Martin and Rebecca Paulsen were wiping their eyes. Martin grabbed a couple tissues from the box on the edge of Marilyn's desk and gave one to his wife.

Marilyn flipped through Ricky's file one more time and then shook her head.

"What's wrong?" Martin asked.

"Oh, probably nothing—it just feels like I'm missing something. Too many cases, not enough time." She closed the file.

"Alright, all background checks have been approved, the home inspections passed at every level. If you're absolutely sure, we'll proceed on a foster care basis. It may be harder than you think. He's been through a lot." She handed them her card.

"Let's meet again in about ninety days. At that time we'll discuss adoption, if you're still interested. Contact me sooner if it gets to be too much...if you change your mind."

"We will" Rebecca said. "But we won't change our mind. We've prayed about this for a long time—especially our daughter, Sally."

Martin stood. "We're sure."

Marilyn tapped her pen on top of the folder, "Oh, and one more thing; it may be nothing, but he wears a necklace, and rubs the pendant when he gets scared or nervous—it's a little sailboat. I don't know why, but it seems real important to him...maybe that'll help."

~

Mac and Richey brought their Florida life style with them, everything but the salt water—and Richey loved it.

Maggie's Charter Service was up and running without a hitch. Richey was happy to find so much volunteer work available with veterans. And he especially fell in love with winter. He was able to walk out in public and not feel the eyes of pity, or horror. Of course, it was because he was bundled up from head to toe—but it felt good just the same. He felt at home in this new haven of snow. The summers were warm but not nearly as hot as Florida, and the upkeep on the boat in fresh water was much simpler and not required as often.

It was a good thing they showed up when they did, too. Pete didn't let on over the phone, but he was in trouble. He'd sold his big boat—the one Mac drifted into at Sanibel Island—and he used the money to buy an old run down bar called, The Tavern. Fisherman, iron workers and dock hands were the main customers. In the winter it was pretty slow. Pete got a loan to refurbish the place during the winter, but drank most of it and fell behind on the payments. The building was on the brink of foreclosure and Pete wasn't sober long enough to care.

Mac tried to talk him into selling, The Tavern, but Pete wouldn't hear of it. So, for months Mac and Richey did the next thing. They helped Pete renovate—and make the payments.

Richey tended bar a couple nights a week so Mac could take Pete sailing. Mac insisted Pete go along because, he needed a first mate to help with the rigging. The truth was what he'd told Richey; "Sailing's good for the soul—and Pete's soul is sick."

Richey wasn't thrilled with the idea because he didn't have the foggiest idea about bartending and being around a lot of people made him nervous. He was still scar-conscious around new people, even though Mac always told him he outshined the scars. But, since it was to help a friend, he pulled his Navy cap down tight, wrapped a bandana around his neck and in the dim lights he looked almost like everyone else—at least nobody seemed to notice.

And even though it wasn't his choice of environments, he started to enjoy the company. The Tavern was like coming home for them. Like families sit around a dinner table and discuss the day—they'd sit at the bar and do the same. They just wanted to be a part of a family.

~

Ricky's new mommy and daddy—Martin and Rebecca Paulsen—didn't yell at each other, hit each other, call him bad names or anything like that.

At night they tucked him in with hugs and kisses and Ricky would feel his tummy giggle—that was something new—he liked it. And when his new sister, Sally, called him brother, he felt his heart smile—that was new, too.

At night Ricky dreamed of sailboats. He'd sail the ocean blue, where warm sun danced off shiny waves.

But sometimes he'd feel a chill. He'd see the ocean turn black. The waves would toss the little boat across dark water, and the name splashed in mean red letters across the back would wake him crying and in a cold sweat. ALONE.

Then the thoughts would come.

"You killed your parents you wicked child," the voice would hiss inside his head, and then he would relive, one more time, that horrible event...

His dad was driving drunk and yelling at his mom—like usual.

From the middle of the back seat Ricky leaned forward and placed a trembling little hand on the man's shoulder.

"Stop...please stop."

Ricky didn't see the elbow that slammed him back into his seat.

"Sit back and shut up you little brat!"

Ricky went silent—at least on the outside. But inside he screamed. God, make them stop fighting...please.

His tears continued to fall—big, silent tears. Blood ran from his nose, across his lips and dripped off a quivering chin, but Ricky never made a sound. Not when the deer shot out in front of the car. Not when they swerved, but still hit the deer. Not when the car rolled three times and came to rest upside down, at an angle, leaning against a large oak tree, with a hand painted sign nailed about eight feet up which read: YES, Jesus loves me —Ricky never made a sound.

The paramedics figured Ricky broke his nose during the crash. Ricky never told them otherwise—but he knew.

No next of kin could be found and he wouldn't speak a word. He was a ward of the state.

He bounced from foster home to foster home. Never in one place more than a few months. The only thing that didn't change was what Ricky took with him: a necklace with a silver pendant in the shape of a sailboat and a quivering lip followed by big silent tears.

~

Mac and Richey had never considered themselves to be counselors. Matters of the heart were always Maggie's territory. But after surviving the time they called the Titanic, they found themselves saying "I'm no counselor, but...I understand where you're coming from."

Richey found a compassion he never knew he had for patrons at the bar. Although he didn't agree with the method of using liquid medicine to heal their pain—he understood why they did. He marveled at how words flowing from his lips carried wisdom beyond his own, as if a Voice told him what to say—all he had to do was listen.

Mac could easily understand what Pete was going through. And somewhere in the midst of sailing, he found words filled with comfort and healing to help Pete sail through this storm called life.

Pete confided in Mac that his financial trouble went further than just with the bar. He had fallen behind on his taxes, and the penalties and interest were skyrocketing out of control. Pete had to sell the bar.

By this time Richey had gotten interested.

"Can a Christian own a saloon?" Richey asked his dad.

"Reckon, we oughta pray about it," was Mac's predictable reply. But, he didn't just say it—he actually did.

After praying, they realized the answer was quite simple. God will not be put in a religious box—Christian or otherwise and even if it sounded weird...God wanted Mac and his son to buy, The Tavern.

Pete stayed on as bar-keep but he didn't touch a drop. He quit smoking his pipe, too. He gave it to Mac. "Comes with The Tavern," he'd told Mac. He started calling Mac, Boss. Mac told him not to but he did it anyway. Pete even got to where he could beat Mac at chess every now and then— fair and square.

After all the dips and curves, life was turning out okay. Not like they'd planned. Not like they wanted. But they figured they were going to make it.

They'd rather have Maggie still alive. They wished they had someone to carry on their family name. Richey would rather have not been twice burned—once in his skin and once in his heart. They'd rather have a big noisy messy happy house full of kids and grandkids rather than a bunch of tough old mariners, iron workers and washed up, worn out misfits. But they'd make the most it—no matter which way the wind would blow. And either way, they'd have a family—because that's what mattered most of all.

~

"Mom, how long has Ricky lived with us?" Sally folded a pair of Ricky's white tube socks and stacked them with the others on the kitchen table.

"Well let's see"—Rebecca pulled a t-shirt out of the laundry basket—"I think it's been about three or four months now...seems like a week." She folded the shirt and set it on the table.

Sally watched her mother fold a couple t-shirts and then grabbed one out of the basket. "I don't think he likes it here."

Rebecca's forehead wrinkled a little. "Why do you say that?"

Sally tossed the shirt back into the basket after her second attempt at folding it. "Because I hear him crying at night—that's why. I sure wish he'd talk."

"I think he likes it here—especially when I make peanut butter cookies." Rebecca folded another shirt in slow motion and smiled at her daughter. "Maybe Ricky is having some bad dreams...he's been through a lot."

Sally stared at the white kitchen table top and nodded. "Yeah, bad dreams...that's probably it."

Rebecca pulled in a deep breath and nodded. Her smile was gone.

"I gotta pray for him Mom. If God will make the bad dreams go away, maybe he'll start to talk—wouldn't that be awesome, huh Mom?"

Sally prayed.

Every night, for what seemed like forever, she'd stop by Ricky's room before going to bed. She'd whisper a prayer and say, "Good night Ricky, I'm sooo glad you're here. I prayed for a long time for a little brother—I love you."

Sally leaned against the wall just outside Ricky's room. A quiet sigh escaped her lips as she shook her head and shuffled toward her room.

"Sis...me too."

Sally squealed, ran, jumped and landed right in the middle of Ricky's bed. She cupped his face in her hands. "You talked Ricky, you talked!" She giggled and hugged him close. "Sis...you called me Sis!" She gulped a big breath. "What'd ya mean, 'me too?' Huh, Ricky, what'd ya mean? Say some more! Oooh, you're so cute."

She squeezed his cheeks between her palms, making him look like a blue-eyed guppy.

Ricky stared with those big blue eyes, "Ebry'ting."

~

The day of the accident, in many ways Ricky died. Emotionally, he was still five years old. And now, when he spoke for the first time in about three years, he sounded more like a five year old.

But, he knew what he meant. Everything Sally had been saying and praying night after night.

He was glad to be there, too. A place where he was loved—not just baby-sat for a pay check. He had prayed too, not out loud, but in his head. He prayed to belong to a family—like one he'd seen on TV. And, as much as he knew about love, he loved Sally—and his new mom and new dad.

Ricky smiled and his chin quivered a little.

Sally rubbed her thumbs under his eyes, wiping away fresh tears.

When she did that—wiped away his tears—Ricky felt loved, more loved than he ever imagined possible.

Then, Sally kissed his forehead, and he closed his eyes and drifted off to sleep with the hint of a smile pulling at the corners of his mouth.

That night he wouldn't dream of being alone, but surrounded by family and friends and he'd be the captain in charge of sailing the biggest ship in the sea.

Sally ran downstairs and pulled both parents back up to Ricky's room. For the longest time they just watched him sleep.

Sally said, "Should I wake him up, so you can hear him talk?"

Martin reached out his hand. "Let's pray."

Sally stood between her parents with her head bowed and eyes squeezed shut. Two blond little braids wove like a crown from her forehead back to a large pony tail that draped over one shoulder—a princess in her white cotton gown. She was the reason they were here—in this room with that little boy.

~

Beck wondered about the timing—they all did.

It had been around three years since Ricky's accident...and since Sally started kneeling by her bed every night and praying for a little brother. Sally said it was the same night as Ricky's accident, that she had started praying.

Maybe she was right. Perhaps, there was a Master plan at work.

Martin and Beck had prayed too, but they couldn't make it happen. They tried everything. Timing, diet, stress reduction, fertility pills, exercise, Martin started wearing boxers...they tried everything. They were tired of trying.

But then one day at school Sally met a new friend. Her name was Sara, and she was a foster child.

"Mom, I know how you can get me a brother!" Sally had burst through the back door after school.

Beck looked up from the cookie dough she was pressing with a fork. Oh my...they're teaching birds and bees already?

"Mom, it's better than having your own baby."

What? "And why is that?"

Sally counted on her fingers. "Well, for one, you don't have to get fat." She put her hands out holding an invisible pregnant belly and waddled over to pat her mom's flat stomach.

"And for two—" she held up two fingers—"you can pick the one you want." Sally crossed her arms and looked around the room real serious like, then her face lit up and she pointed, as if she'd just found the perfect child sitting there waiting for her.

"And for three, you can choose if you want a boy or girl. That's nice 'cuz we want a boy." Sally made a small giggle then.

"And for five, or I mean four or...anyway, you can pick the age you want."

Beck slid the cookie sheet into the oven and sat down.

"And for seven, you can send them back if you don't like them." Sally planted both hands on her hips and stared at her mom as if to say—well, let's go get one.

"Oh...I see. Honey, you can't just go to the store and pick out a child like a loaf of bread." Beck smiled.

Sally wasn't listening. "Oh! And the most bestest thing of all—them little kids need a mommy and daddy really, really, really, really bad. My friend, Sara, at school, said she used to cry herself to sleep every single night in some place she called a, group home. But now, she falls to sleep with a smile on her face."

~

So, here they stood, in the reality of a little girl's prayers, watching a little boy sleep. A little boy that a year ago they didn't even know existed. They could never send Ricky back—no, not ever.

They held hands and Martin whispered. "Dear Lord, thanks for letting Ricky come into our lives. This is a special night, he's found his voice. And Lord—" Martin's eyes found Rebecca.

Her green eyes smiled, knowing what he was about to say, because it was only the day before when Martin had asked, "Beck, how would you feel about Ricky living with us—permanent I mean—you know, adopting him for real?"

Rebecca's eyes had glistened. "I've been praying you'd ask."

"I'm scared though." Martin had said. "We don't know how to care for a child that...that won't talk." Martin stared into his coffee cup. "If only he'd talk."

Now, Martin sucked in a deep breath, smiled at his wife and continued his prayer. "Lord, if you'll allow it, we'd like for Ricky to find more than just his voice here. We'd like for him to find his home."

Sally kept her eyes closed but she lifted her heels until she was way up high on her tippy-toes.

"We'd like Ricky to become a member of our family...for good."

Sally squealed and bounced up and down with little jumps off her toes.

Ricky rolled onto his side, but didn't wake.

After a stifled giggle from all three, Martin continued. "Lord, thanks again for helping Ricky find his voice, and for helping us, find Ricky. Amen."

Ricky talked more and more, especially to Sally—sometimes she missed the quiet days.

15

"A whole two dollars and fifty cents...every single week?" Ricky's blue eyes couldn't get any bigger.

"Yes Son, as long as you keep up with your chores, can you remember what they are?"

Ricky felt that happy feeling in his tummy when Mr. Paulsen called him Son.

But, how come his other dad never called him Son? How come he never said, I love you? Mr. Paulsen says it all the time. Ricky's other dad didn't even act like a real dad—didn't look like one either, with those mean, black eyes.

Mommy lived with him though...so he must have been his real dad, right? But then, how come he hated him so bad?

Maybe I was bad.

He didn't wanna think about that no more 'cuz it made his eyes feel sad, that's why. Besides, Mr. Paulsen feels more like a real dad than anybody ever could anyway. I'll pretend he's been my real dad, forever and ever.

Now, he wants to give me real money. He's got to be the bestest dad in the whole wide world. I gotta remember to tell God thanks, before I go to sleep tonight.

Ricky smiled, "Yes sir, Mr. Paulsen. I remember. Take out the trash, make the bed and keep the toys picked up in the room I sleep in."

"You got it Son." Mr. Paulsen knelt down to Ricky's level and looked him in the eye, "You can call me Dad now you know, that is—if you want. And it's your bed, your toys and your room, so you can say, 'make my bed and keep my toys picked up in my room.' "

Wow—that was another new thing. Ricky couldn't get used to the fact that he had a real bed and toys and a room he could actually call his own. It felt strange. It felt great. And was kind of scary, too—because, the Paulsens might get tired of me and send me back to the Brown County Shelter for Boys, that's why.

Ricky looked at the floor and bit his bottom lip. "Um, Ok." He looked up and the corners of his mouth made a shy smile. "Mr. Paulsen sir, I mean, Mr. uh, Dad sir, does 'llowance mean I can actually um, you know...buy something new, my very own self?"

Martin nodded.

"With real money, and real new, like from a real store, not like a supply room with old dirty toys?"

Martin's eyes got a little shiny and he blinked a few times. "Whatever you want, Son, from a real live store." He ruffled Ricky's hair. "Two-fifty won't buy much though, so if it cost more than that you'll have to save it until you have enough."

"How much 'llowances makes enough to buy a sailboat? Not a real sailboat a'course but a model, like the one you got me, long time ago, when you and Mrs. Pauls— Mom, I mean, and Sally brought me home?"

Martin smiled, "Well those models range from ten to twenty dollars."

Ricky's eyes got real big. "Oh...will it take 'til I'm big like you to save enough 'llowance?"

Martin said, "Not that long, only about a month or so. That's about four allowances." Then he counted on his fingers, "one, two, three, four."

Ricky did his chores and saved each allowance until he had enough to buy a model sailboat—the wood kind.

The room where he worked was simple with one window looking out over the yard. The twin size bed had a blue and white quilt patterned with sailboats of all shapes and sizes. The wood chest of drawers and desk used to be pink, but before Ricky moved in, the Paulsen's found the set for twenty-five dollars at a garage sale, brought it home and painted it blue—Ricky's favorite color.

He'd spend hours putting those little boats together. He'd glue every piece and paint every tiny detail. And as soon as the paint had dried, he'd give it away.

Most of the time, he gave them to family members or friends, like his Sunday school teacher, or baby-sitter, even the mail man.

He even gave one to a perfect stranger.

~

Captain Richard MacArthur Johnson attended more and more funerals every year. "Hey Pete, how come all my friends are getting so old...and dying?"

Pete smiled, but it didn't reach his eyes, "Living causes that, Mac."

"I'll head out in the morning and try to make it back tomorrow night—try not to die on me."

"I won't die—you just don't go killing yourself trying to get back here either. Me and Richey got it covered. If you get to visiting and it gets late, just spend the night—you ain't that much help around here anyway Boss."

Mac waved his hand like swatting a fly. "Visiting's for folks who've got nothing to do. I'll pay my respects and head back. Simple as that."

Mac wouldn't have known about the funeral at all, except a few months earlier, Scott and his wife, Beth, had chartered a three hour sunset cruise on Mac's sailboat—Maggie.

Usually Mac would take four people at a time—even though, his boat could handle six, Mac figured four was more comfortable for the folks.

Pete had told Mac, "You can make more money if you book six—all the other charters around here book six."

But Mac said, "The right way to do a thing ain't measured by dollars and cents." And then he followed with one of his favorite lines, "Just 'cuz you can, don't mean you should."

Scott and his wife had bought all four seats, so they could be the only passengers on the cruise. Scott was wresting through the final stages of lung cancer and getting back out on open water was on his bucket list.

When Mac found out Scott was his old Navy comrade and why they were taking the cruise, he gave them a full refund and wouldn't even accept a tip, even though they offered—several times.

Mac had simply told them, "Thanks for the honor of letting me escort you across our fresh water sea...the only thing I ask, is that you keep me posted." The couple held each other and nodded, too choked up to speak.

Beth had kept Mac posted via e-mail—the news was sad:

Dear Mac,

Yesterday at sunset, Scott sailed to the other side. Thank you for making our last outing so special—and thank you for your prayer that day. Something happened to us after that—helped us get our heart back where we knew it should be.

Mac, I know it's a long drive and you may be too busy, but I wanted to at least offer the invitation.

She left the date, time and place of the funeral.

If Mac had thought about it, he'd have agreed—he was busy. He had back to back charters scheduled everyday for three weeks and it'd cost him business to make the trip.

But, Mac didn't think twice. "Doin' right don't take thinkin,' it takes doin'."

Mac was up way before dawn steering his 1964 Chevy pickup out of Duluth Minnesota. During the five hour trip south he stopped once for fuel, coffee and a breakfast burrito and made it to Mankato with plenty of time to get cleaned up at a truck stop and attend Scott Meyer's funeral—another funeral.

If all went well, he'd make it back to Duluth before dark.

After the funeral, Mac paid his respects and told Beth "If you ever need an ear—or a shoulder—I've got two." Then, he meandered his way through a maze of her family and friends and made his way out to his old pickup.

It was two-thirty in the afternoon and Mac figured he could make it back to Duluth before dark. But, all of a sudden, before he made it out of Mankato, he got tired—so tired he couldn't keep his eyes open.

I better get a room and leave at first light.

After checking in at the Comfort Inn he collapsed on the bed, even though it was only around three o'clock in the afternoon.

An hour later, around four o'clock, he was wide awake—and hungry. He looked out his window and saw a Culver's hamburger joint and a Jiffy Lube.

It's close to supper time—a burger sounds good. Mac yawned and stretched his arms over his head and glanced at his old blue truck sitting in the parking lot. ...I should've changed the oil before I left home—I'll do that too.

~

Ricky was sitting in the Jiffy Lube waiting area with his dad. The TV mounted near the ceiling was tuned to a news channel and couldn't hold Ricky's attention. A magazine rack had nothing of interest for him, either. He fidgeted in his seat until he saw a grey haired man sitting on the tailgate of an old blue Chevy pickup.

For three full minutes Ricky stared through the window at the old man and then cupped his hands over his mouth and whispered something into his dad's ear. His dad smiled and nodded.

Ricky got up, walked outside and up to the old man. He handed him his newest creation and for an eternity that lasted only two seconds, their eyes locked. Ricky always felt a happy feeling when he gave one of his boats away. But, this time was different, something he'd never felt before, maybe 'cuz he's a stranger, Ricky thought.

Old, sea weary blue eyes danced at the freckle-faced, blue eyed vision. The old man showed the slightest quiver in his whiskered chin, and the little man felt his blue eyes pool and almost spill.

The little boat was blue on the bottom and white on the deck. Ricky's skillful little hands had painted a small blue cross on the top of the main sail. He had said it was his mostest special boat yet, and so he put a cross on top of the sail, because crosses are special, that's why.

The old man watched the boy walk away and then use all of his muscles to wrestle open the big glass door and slip inside.

Ricky sat next to his dad and looked out at the old man still holding the little wooden boat in one hand, and wiping his eyes with a white hanky in the other. Ricky put his hand on his chest, why is my heart beeping so fast?

~

Mac had the weathered eyes and whiskers of an old sailor, but his feet swung like a child's under the tailgate. His eyes turned to blue pools and added the only thing a little sailboat needed—saltwater.

One soft chuckle escaped as he turned his head toward the sky and whispered, "Well, shiver me timbers...I thought I was here for an oil change."

The next day Mac was up at first light to make the two hundred fifty mile trek north, but his thoughts never left a blue eyed boy at a Jiffy Lube parking lot in Mankato Minnesota.

The boy stirred an old familiar ache.

The emptiness gnawed at the hole in his heart. The place he'd always reserved for a big, noisy, messy, happy family.

But now, when he thought of his home, the only sound was the ticking of the oak ship wheel clock.

Despair settled like fog, in the cab of Mac's truck.

For about the hundredth time since he left Mankato, Mac eyed the little blue and white sailboat on the seat next to him.

What are the odds?

He cranked down the window and looked toward the sky. "Dear God...maybe it's not too late."

Mac stared at the white lines sailing by and listened to the wind, and in the midst of it all, the lines blurred and he thought he heard the sound of children—calling him, Papa.

Hope filled the cab, leaving despair spinning in a dust-devil on the side of the road.

Mac smiled and cranked up the window—sealing hope inside.

16

The only sailboat Ricky kept was the one given to him by the Paulsens the day they brought him home. It sat next to his bed on that little blue wooden table. He'd pick it up every night before drifting off to sleep and imagine it was real, and he was the captain sailing the ocean blue.

He'd spend every afternoon he could up in his room putting little model sailboats together.

"Steady as she goes." He smiled at the sound of his new found voice. He tied the sail to the mast with as steady a hand as any sailor that ever sailed the ocean blue.

"Take your time you'll get there faster" he whispered as he glued the tiniest rudder to the transom. The hours flew like minutes—but he never got in a hurry.

Except, when he got a whiff of what was drifting up the stairs. Then, he had just one speed.

He pressed the cap back on the glue. Jumped up. Yelled "I love peanut butter cookies" and sailed down the steps, bounced off the landing wall.

And then it happened.

He heard it as he slid across the wood floor in the foyer. The words he loved to hear but rarely did before moving to the Paulsens.

I love you.

He couldn't tell if The Voice was out loud, or in his head.

He was already running across the living room carpet and almost to the kitchen when he spun around and headed back to the foyer.

Like a hunter at the edge of the woods, he stood. Under the archway that divided the living room from the foyer, his boots were half on carpet and half on wood.

He looked across the foyer, to the open staircase and his eyes climbed the oak spindled railing—nothing.

He scanned the right wall of the foyer. The solid oak entry door was closed and locked. The old fashioned metal milk can stood undisturbed holding umbrellas, a wooden cane, and his baseball bat—a Louisville Slugger—the one he'd gotten when his dad took him to a Minnesota Twins game.

Ricky was at that age where the line between imagination and reality clouded. Yet, he knew he wasn't imagining things. He would never imagine those words—*I love you*—they were too precious.

Who said that? He scanned the left wall of the foyer. The closet door was open a little. Aha—Sis must be hiding in there.

He sneaked as quiet as pointy-toed-cowboy boots could tip-toe across a hardwood floor. He stopped in front of the closet, and rested his hand on the knob.

He sucked in a deep breath, and all at once, with all he had, he swung open the door and let out his best lion's roar—RAAHR.

Nothing.

Nobody in the closet. Nothing, but coats and boots and mittens—and a note crumpled up on the floor. Oops, that's a note from teacher, I'm 'posed to give to Mom. It was something about the field trip and a bag lunch. It must have fallen out of his backpack. Oh well.

He pushed the door shut.

What's going on around here? Ricky scrunched his freckled nose and rubbed the top of his blond, crew-cut. He folded his arms over a red and black checkered flannel shirt and tapped his cowboy boot—a little man, deep in thought. I know I heard something. Hmmm. I better get some cookies and come back and 'vestigate.

I love you.

Ricky jumped. Heat rushed to his face. His cheeks and the tips of his ears turned red and his chin quivered a little.

He inhaled deep and held his breath.

His wide eyes drifted from the closet to the picture. Without as much as a breath, he inched with slow, small, sliding steps, he paused between each one.

Hanging in the foyer, opposite the entry door, was a picture framed in silver. A small light illuminated from the top. Actually, it was three pictures in one, a 3-D picture that changed depending on the angle it was viewed from.

Ricky stopped about four feet to the right of the picture. The first thing he saw was the face of Jesus.

Whoa, His eyes are looking right at me. Did He say it? Pictures don't talk, do they?

He sidestepped, slow, eyes glued to the eyes glued, to him. As Ricky moved front and center the picture transformed from the face of Jesus, to Jesus on the cross.

Ricky's head tilted and jaw dropped, his eyes got even bigger. Holy Moses, I've run by here a hundred trillion times and never seen that before.

The Man's head was bleeding from what looked like pointy sticks. That must be the crowny thorn thing teacher talked about in Sunday school—that must've hurt bad. He looked at the blood that ran down His hands and feet and side.

But, what Ricky noticed most, were His eyes. How come He's still looking right at me?

When he felt his chin start to quiver he knew what was going to happen, but he didn't know why.

First, his lips narrowed and the corners dropped, making a shaky upside down smile. And then, three jerky inhales, and a whimper caused his eyes to leak—every time, just like that.

Ricky's sister always knew the dam was about to break whenever she saw that quiver. Kids at school knew, too. And they were cruel. "Cry baby's quiver, here comes the river," Ricky hated it. But, he couldn't help it.

His eyes dropped to his pointy boots, as a tear hit the floor. His chin quivered—and then came the river.

Ricky didn't know much about the Man in the picture. No one ever taught him. Before moving in with the Paulsens, he'd rarely been to church.

Ricky slid the sole of his boot across the liquid soul dripping to the floor. He moved two steps to his left, toward the living room, wiped his eyes with the tail of his shirt and sniffed.

When he looked again, the Man in the picture wasn't on the cross at all, but floating in white puffy clouds. He's still looking at me. A white robe—like a sheet—wrapped around Him. He had scars like holes in His hands and feet, but He wasn't bleeding. His hands and arms were open wide, as if to say, *I love you.*

Like dominoes falling in reverse, like a flailing flopping sail finally catching wind, every good word Ricky ever heard about the Man in the picture, stood up and came to life.

Ricky's eyes blossomed. "I get it" he said right out loud as understanding rolled through his mind.

He walked to the right side of the picture, where he could see the face of Jesus. "Jesus sees me."

He stepped to the center where he could see Jesus on the cross. "And then...a'fore the mean ol' devil can beat me up, He says, *No—beat Me up instead.*"

He sidestepped left to where he could see Jesus in the clouds. "Then...His Daddy—God—makes Him all better...and He wins...we win."

Ricky fingered the sailboat pendant.

"And we sail away to heaven, and live happily ever after...like a big happy family."

Then Ricky saw it. Right there, at the bottom edge of the picture frame, with raised silver letters:

YES, Jesus loves me

He remembered the song they sang in Sunday school—there was something else familiar about those words...but what was it?

The quiver quickened, and the river flowed and a little boy's knees hit a wet wood floor. Little hands rose toward the man in the clouds. And a quiet little voice slipped through quivering lips, "I love you, too."

Ricky wasn't sure why he knelt, or why he said what he did—but it felt right...like he was sailing away to live happily ever after. That's all it took—three little words.

I love you. The words Ricky never heard when he bounced from foster home to foster home. And then, before the accident, he rarely heard them—and when he did it was only from his birth mother, Jenny. Sometimes she'd tuck him in at night. She smelled funny and her words were slurred, but Ricky remembered what she'd said. "I love you. Someday we'll sail away...and live happily ever after."

The last time she'd told him that was the night before the accident. "Here you go little man." She knelt next to Ricky's bed. Her outstretched hand swayed.

"What is it?" The house was quiet...finally. But Ricky's head still echoed with the sound of angry voices; someone being hit—again; shattering glass, and the slamming screen door that pounded to a blaring silence—all too often, his bedtime story.

"Something I got from your d—" She never finished that word, but when she opened her hand a silver necklace with a sailboat pendant dropped into Ricky's trembling fingers. "It'll help you remember." She had touched her cut and swollen lips with the tips of her fingers and then pressed them to Ricky's cheek. "I love you. Someday we'll sail away...and live happily ever after."

And that's all he wanted. To know he was part of a family—and to be loved. Was that too much to ask?

His mom meant well, Ricky knew it too, but she never did what she said. They never sailed away, and they never lived happily ever after.

After a short time living with the Paulsens Ricky learned love was more than just words. It was action.

And now, as he knelt there on that hard wood floor listening to three little words echo in his soul, he knew something more. He didn't understand it, couldn't explain it. But one thing he knew for sure—everything he needed was wrapped up in that Voice.

"It's more-better than the yummiest peanut butter cookies in the whole wide world, forever, that's what."

Ricky wiped his eyes with his sleeve. And that's when he noticed Sally, kneeling next to him. He put his arm around her shoulders and they rested their heads together.

So, this is how love feels. Ricky didn't understand what he was feeling, but he felt it just the same. No fear. No embarrassment for hugging his sister—even though she's a yucky girl, and she laughed when he slipped on the ice.

Neither spoke for several moments. The world stopped turning, time stood still. Ricky felt love—real love. He actually belonged to a family.

Ricky whispered, "Did you hear it, too?"

Sally tilted her head away from Ricky, so she could see his face. "Hear what?"

"I love you." Ricky whispered.

Sally brushed a strand of blond hair from her face and tucked it behind her ear. Last week she turned ten—two years older than her brother—so she wasn't a little kid any more. She looked into her brother's eyes, "I love you too." She smiled and then giggled..."Hear what?"

Ricky shook his head. "No, not that, I meant—" and just then his stomach growled—"hear that." He jumped up and ran into the kitchen. "Peanabuddacooookies!" His voice faded along with his pain filled memories of the past.

~

Sally stayed on her knees and stared at the picture. She felt sorry for Ricky, but she couldn't help but laugh yesterday on the way home from school, when he had slipped on the ice and landed right smack dab on his butt.

When Ricky had gotten up from the frozen sidewalk his little lip had already started to quiver. He rubbed his bottom with both hands—must've hurt, but not nearly as much as his embarrassed broken little heart when he looked across the street and saw Suzy Smyth.

Ricky had taken two careful steps and kicked his sister right in the shin. Suzy didn't see that, because she had turned her head and was walking fast toward her house, which was kitty-corner across the street.

Ricky and Sally had walked the rest of the way home in silence. He pretended his rump didn't hurt, and she pretended her shin didn't. But it stung like the dickens—thanks to those stupid pointy-toed boots.

That night Sally had prayed:

"Dear God, hi this is Sally. My little brother Ricky, he can be a real pain, especially when he's wearing those stupid pointy toed cowboy boots. But, I love him anyway. Only, I don't think he believes it. I don't think he believes anyone loves him. I know when he kicked me he was embarrassed because Suzy saw him fall. He likes her—not just like, but like-like. So...I'm sorry I laughed. The kids at school laugh at him all the time. And it makes him real sad. So God, I have an idea that might make him not be so sad."

At this part of her prayer she had smiled up at her bedroom ceiling and giggled a little.

"God, will You tell Ricky You love him? I'm sure if he hears it from You, he'll believe it. And that will make him happy instead of sad. ...Oh, one more thing. If it's not too much trouble, can You make his feet grow out of those stupid pointy toed boots? There, that's all for now. Thanks God. Love You, Amen."

Sally had drifted off to sleep after saying that prayer and didn't even think about it again until just now, after she saw Ricky kneeling in front of the picture of Jesus.

She dropped her eyes from the picture to the floor—the floor still wet with Ricky's tears.

"God, You answered my prayer, didn't You? You told him, right? You know...that You love him. That's why he hugged me and didn't act all weird about it, right?"

She squeezed her eyes shut and tilted her head toward heaven and opened the ears of her heart.

I Am a Father to the fatherless, and near the broken-hearted.

Her eyes popped open. Not sure if she heard The Voice out loud or in her head, or in her heart, never-the-less, with childlike faith, the kind that moves mountains, she believed. And that was enough.

"Thanks God—that's sooo cool. Now, Ricky won't be sad anymore."

17

The eyes of HIM who sits on The Throne roam to and fro throughout the whole earth delivering strength to those whose hearts are pure and faithful

In The Throne Room he stood. The opposite of everything around him: darkness in the presence of Light; the putrid in the midst of Purity; the divisive in the face of the Divine. lucifer slithered and crouched and searched for a shadow, but finding none, he simply stood, and watched the eyes of HIM who sits upon The Throne.

The Eyes stopped roaming to and fro, and lucifer followed the gaze all the way from heaven to Saint Peter, not the man...but a small town in southern Minnesota. They looked into the heart of a child.

lucifer shuttered at the sight of the kneeling child and two angels by his side. One was none other than the Archangel Gabriel.

lucifer slipped from The Throne Room to a horde of demons waiting just outside The Gate and dispatched his vilest demon to steal the Seed-Of-Faith from the heart of the kneeling child.

Like a hissing black cat lucifer's voice polluted the atmosphere as he reentered The Throne Room. "Wait! i know that boy...he belongs to me." he pointed a crooked accusing finger toward the earth. "The generational curse is in force—the sins of the father passed to the son—he is mine, as his father, and his father's father. They're all mine."

An orchestra of all that is good and holy and right rose in perfect harmony with voices singing "Holy, Holy, Holy is the Lord God Almighty who was and is and is to come, be glory and honor and praise."

HIS Voice rolled like thunder amidst thousands upon thousands of crashing ocean waves.

The atmosphere shook.

The accuser dropped like wax in the face of the sun.

A Holy hand stretched from an unapproachable light and pointed. *"LOOK."*

A holographic scene rose of a woman in her late twenties. Her eyes sparkled and tears slid down her cheeks. She dropped to her knees, bowed her head and folded her hands.

lucifer jerked his head away and closed his eyes. But the scene didn't vanish. he shook his head but the scene remained. Like lightning it burned inside his brain and he couldn't erase the vision of what he hated the most, the thing he feared almost as much as The Voice.

The very sight of someone in prayer affected the accuser; his voice was raspy, weak, barely a whisper. "She has nothing to do with this."

"She prays for her daughter." The Voice vibrated with a quality that said—*I am well pleased with this child.*

The scene before them changed to the woman tucking her daughter in for the night.

lucifer cursed as confusion saturated his mind. "How can some random woman p-p-praying for her daughter have anything to do with...she doesn't even know who he—"

"She prays for her daughter's future...and the man she'll marry." The Voice once again shook the atmosphere.

The brightest flash exploded in lucifer's head. he knew no weapon formed against a parent's prayer for a child would prosper—especially prayers for their future mate.

Those prayers knew no bounds. They were generational blessings that crossed bloodlines and broke the generational curse. They were invisible seeds that wove divine unities and multiplied forces of heaven stronger than any force against the hordes of hell.

It birthed God's favorite word—and lucifer's worst nightmare—*relationship*.

~

Blind with rage lucifer clenched his entire being and screeched "NO! NO! NO!"

The words echoed from The Throne Room, through the solar system and down through the atmosphere all the way to the front foyer of a little house in a little town in southern Minnesota where a young boy knelt on a tear splattered floor.

The Archangel Gabriel heard the echo of evil that screeched from The Throne Room. He was sent to witness the awakening and stood watchful just to the left of Ricky.

Another angel—Ricky's Guardian Angel—David, stood by Ricky's right side.

Ricky knelt on a wood floor wet with tears, his hands raised toward a picture of Christ. His sister, Sally knelt beside him.

Pacing back and forth behind them was dribgnos—the demon assigned to Ricky. dribgnos covered his ears as the echo pounded his head like a migraine, NO! NO! NO! he stopped six feet from the weeping child, pointed a trembling, crooked finger, and tried to imitate the sound that echoed like a roaring lion in his head. But when it came out it sounded more like a scared cat. "no. no. no."

The child, Ricky, heard nothing but The Voice whispering, *I love you.*

The voices of angels and demons are at a frequency the human ear cannot hear—like radio waves. They echo all around but can only be tuned in through the spirit.

Ricky didn't know it, but the moment he spun around and headed away from his craving for cookies, and toward The Voice—he tuned in to The Spirit...and started a war.

dribgnos growled, "He's mine."

Ricky whispered toward the picture, "I love you too."

dribgnos dropped low, his voice like a siren. "Nooo...lucifer will have my head."

Gabriel looked at the demon dribgnos, and could still remember the creature's former self, before the rebellion, before the fall, before he was cast from heaven, and before his wretched decision to turn—turned him inside out.

"Praying, Songbird?" Gabriel asked.

"Don't call me that." dribgnos covered his head to hide his quivering chin.

"Cat got your tongue...Songbird?" David's voice flowed like a pure mountain stream.

"It's not over...i'll get the kid." dribgnos whimpered, and then looked at Gabriel. "Why?"

"And why not? It's a simple message, from HIM." When Gabriel mentioned HIM, he looked toward heaven.

dribgnos looked toward hell, and cowered like a whipped pup. "But w-wwhy... you?" dribgnos stammered. he knew the rules. he knew Gabriel was sent directly from The Throne Room. And only God could give the command to vanquish him into eternal damnation. That order could be given at any time, and Gabriel could carry it out. All demons know their final damnation will come sooner or later— sooner, is what they fear.

Gabriel's heavenward gaze slowly drifted back to earth, back to dribgnos. "I was sent from The Throne Room to echo His words, the words He tells everyone—*I love you.* It's nothing new. And you should know...the Lord is always near the broken hearted."

Gabriel looked at Ricky and smiled. "He has a special assignment."

The demon jerked to attention. "Special assignment?" he'd heard Gabriel say those same words about other humans—one of them was Billy Graham. Then, he stared at Gabriel with an intense hatred. "Leave us alone." The words sounded like gravel.

Both angels took a step toward the demon.

dribgnos stood his ground, and narrowed his eyes to yellow slits. "Just like the good-ole-days, at the orphanage, right David?" he sliced a hideous talon across his own throat. "i'll have the kid slit it, before you'll use him."

For hundreds of years dribgnos had been assigned to orphanages. His miserable existence had been spent terrorizing children. Orphanages run by the ruthless and cruel were largely dribgnos's doing.

David could still remember the last time he faced dribgnos. It was in the early 1800's at an orphanage in Philadelphia. Eight year old Timothy succumbed to the wiles of dribgnos. And for five long years David and dribgnos battled over this lad's soul. Finally, at thirteen years old, Timothy took his own life with a knife to the throat.

David stared right through the evil before him. "You forget one thing dribgnos—I escorted Timothy to The Father. And that's where's he's at right now. His last breath on this earth was his first in eternity, where you can't touch him, ever." David smiled. "Just think about that...right now, at this very moment, Timothy is filled with a pressed-down-shaken-together-and-running-over, kind of joy, as he sings praises to his KING.

"You know what? Timothy never even thinks about you—he doesn't even remember those days. But, you remember don't you? Once upon a time, before the fall, you stood up there—" David looked toward heaven—"maybe where Timothy is standing right now. You sang praise too, right? You felt joy once too, right? But now look at you." David shook his head at the pathetic creature.

dribgnos pointed at the sky, "Th-that was wrong and you know it. Timothy committed suicide, so he should be damned. That's against God's own law—thou shalt not kill—God broke His own law. He's unjust. That's why lucifer had to stand up to Him. he saw through your God's hypocrisy."

David didn't want to have this conversation. He knew it was pointless but he answered anyway. "dribgnos, you are blind and don't know the Love of God, nor can you know it. Do you remember September 11, when people jumped from the towers to escape the pain of burning to death?"

dribgnos nodded.

"I suppose you think all of those people should be cast into hell, too—for the same reason, right?"

dribgnos nodded, again.

"Well, I don't expect you to understand this, but, sometimes people's lives are like a burning building, and they jump out, to escape the pain.

"Only God knows the condition of a heart, and the trauma it's in. God is good. He's not looking for ways to cast people into hell—like you are.

"As a matter of fact, He sends no person to hell. It was created for you, and your master. Anyone else...goes there by choice. The Father holds the cup of salvation for all to drink, and be cured of the sickness of sin—but He forces no one.

"His desire is for all to be saved—and you know it. But, your choice to follow lucifer's rebellion has seared you beyond any rational feeling or hope of repair."

"SHUT UP—" dribgnos trembled with hate—"You talk too much." he pointed a crooked finger at Ricky. "This kid is mine and you know it. i'll steal The Word. He'll stammer and stutter and drive himself crazy. i'll confuse his mind, and no words will come. Special assignment...HA!"

A putrid stench filled the unseen realm as laughter drooled from the demon.

"So...you'll try and make him turn out, just-like-you?" David spit the words at the demon.

dribgnos ignored David's words. "Hey angel boy you like quotes from the The Bible right? Here's one, "The Voice of one crying...blah blah blah." dribgnos swirled his hand in the air. "Oh...and how about, Cry baby's quiver—here comes the river." dribgnos danced. "That one's dribgnos 3:16."

Gabriel and David took another step toward the demon wanting to step on the wretched parasite, and squish him like the bug he was.

David wished angels could spit on demons.

Gabriel stopped, but David kept walking toward the rodent and towered over the back pedaling demon.

He waited for the go ahead to behead, the putrid being, and send him forever to the pit where he belonged...but no such word was given.

~

"Sing for me Songbird. Remember? We used to sing HIS praise?" David challenged the demon.

"Stop" whimpered the smoldering dribgnos. Mad that his name was reversed from Songbird to dribgnos, a cursed reminder of his former being—and voice.

Once upon a time he sang like, well, like his namesake—a songbird. Now his voice sounded like a gravel-pitched hoarse whisper.

"How would you like us to change your name? How would you like...um, let's see, how about—hoarse whisperer?"

dribgnos lifted his eyes and dared to look into David's. he would like his name changed—not to that, but—to something other than what it was. he hated the constant reminder of the reversal in his destiny. Every time his name was spoken, he had a flash back. One moment he was singing, the next he was stinging. he used to sing to The LORD, and what joy filled every fiber of his being.

Songbird's place was right beside lucifer. But—little by little—lucifer inched away. Songbird liked the way his voice and lucifer's would blend when they sang praises to The KING. he liked the sound so much, when lucifer started inching away, Songbird inched with him.

Songbird had thought for a moment, while they sang, that his voice sounded even better, than his singing partner. he thought he detected a bit of gravel in the otherwise silken voice of lucifer.

When lucifer announced he was moving to a higher location of heaven, Songbird chose to follow, thinking perhaps, he would be promoted to the new worship leader.

Even when, The KING, reached out to Songbird and asked him to stay, he knew he should, but he didn't. Three times he was asked to turn around, he wouldn't. But his name did. Everything turned inside out the moment he chose to turn his back on The One True GOD, Creator of the universe.

Songbird became dribgnos.

Oh, how The LORD longs to share The Truth. Even the English language reflects the reversal. devil in reverse is lived—a constant reminder of how the devil's choice to leave the very presence of Life turned him inside out.

When memories of The KING would flash, dribgnos would hang his head and cover his eyes unable to bear the thoughts of how far he'd fallen. But now, he wouldn't go back, even if he could, he was too bitter, too cold, too angry, too heartless...too dead.

The same way his preying, would leave Ricky once he got through with him. dribgnos pulled his mind back to the task at hand. Focus on the kid, Songbird—arghh—dribgnos. Keep your mind on destroying the kid. Deceive the kid and keep yourself out of the abyss...and the snarling jaws of lucifer and his tormentors.

Slow and calm Gabriel spoke. "Try as you may, dribgnos, The Voice has spoken—it will come to pass."

With his eyes closed dribgnos spoke, barely above a whisper, "Gabriel, you forget one thing...CHOICE." But it was too late. When he opened his eyes, Gabriel was gone.

dribgnos sized up David.

Angel stared at demon.

The ever present fear, of being vanquished from earth, and cast into a fiery eternal damnation, paralyzed dribgnos.

Eternity wears no watch. An eternity passed. But, only one second clicked off earth's clock and Ricky's eternal destiny changed forever.

Ricky and his sister had been kneeling in the foyer when Ricky suddenly jumped up and headed toward the kitchen. dribgnos started to follow, but David stood between the child and the demon.

And that's where he planned to stay.

18

FOUR YEARS LATER.

Ricky knew he shouldn't wet the bed at his age. He tried everything to quit. He wouldn't drink anything after supper. He always went to the bathroom—real hard—before he went to bed.

But, those dreams deceived him. They seemed so real. He would wake up, get up and walk to the bathroom, just like he was supposed to. But, most every morning—when he found the wet sheets—he'd realize he had only been dreaming.

The shame, the humiliation, and the helplessness he'd feel caused the lip to quiver and the dam to break. And, that's how Ricky started most of his days.

Ricky's greatest fear came upon him that day when family friends stopped by for a visit. They stayed for supper, and by the time they were ready to leave, a good old fashioned Minnesota blizzard had set in. The roads were simply too dangerous—company was going to stay.

"We're havin' a sleep-over!" Five year old Matthew's eyes lit up as he looked at Ricky. "Oh goody, I can sleep with you. Won't that be fun?" When he saw the fear on Ricky's face he said, "Don't worry—I'm a big boy—I don't wet the bed no more." He stuck out his chest and smiled at his mother. "Right, Mommy?"

Ricky felt sick. He went straight to his room, plopped down on his twin bed and hugged his pillow. He could smell the fresh clean sheets. Clean, because he had just washed them that morning...and the morning before that.

He had learned to do his own laundry. It had become an unpleasant morning chore. Sometimes he'd wake up long before everyone else and sneak down to the basement and wash his wetted sheets and clothes, and then he'd sneak back upstairs and make his bed and put on clean pajamas. He'd lay in bed and watch the night turn to day, pretending he was waking up after a good night's sleep—dry.

He longed to sleep through the night, and wake up dry...especially tonight. His lip quivered and the river flowed.

The words from the kids at school echoed in his head. Cry baby's quiver, here comes the river. Ricky rolled on his back, hugged his pillow over his face, and wept.

What am I gonna do? ...I'll just stay awake all night. I won't let myself go to sleep. God, don't let me fall asleep. This kid is younger than me and doesn't wet the bed. What will the kids at school say? Laughter like a thousand voices pulsed in Ricky's head. Cry baby's quiver, here comes two rivers...and one's yellow.

God help me. Ricky groaned.

A soft knock at the door jolted Ricky. Using his pillow he wiped away the tears and jumped up. He pretended to be looking out the window.

The door slowly opened.

"What's up Bud?" His Dad whispered and wiped a stray tear from the young man's cheek.

Ricky held his breath and looked at the door expecting, the kid, to walk in.

"He's still downstairs." His Dad whispered.

Ricky's lip started its quiver and so he looked out the window to hide the welling water works.

His Dad knelt on one knee and looked out the window, too. "A little nervous?" He said it like it was no big deal. Not like it was the end of the world—which it was.

Ricky sucked in a breath, "Yeah."

His Dad looked him straight in the eyes, "If you don't want to...just ask God." Then, he waited.

Ricky, shifted his weight back and forth, wiped his nose with his sleeve and whispered out the window toward the wind. "Dear God—" his voice broke and bottom lip took off on a beat of its own. He spun around into his father's arms. "Please God make me not wet the bed—ever."

After several long moments and Ricky's breathing had settled to a normal pace, his dad stood and spoke the words as a matter-of-fact, "Okay, now you won't—ever." He patted Ricky's head, turned and walked out the door.

Ricky tilted his head and stared at the space where his Dad had just stood. How does he know? How can he be so sure? He'd never known him to lie. So maybe...

That night the little visitor, Matthew, talked to Ricky about everything under the sun. Ricky wasn't listening. He was thinking about his little prayer and what his dad had said.

If you don't want to...just ask God.

Ricky took prayer real serious. He didn't blabber on and on about nothing—like Matthew.

He remembered praying in the back seat of the car when he was small, praying for his parents to stop fighting, not his new parents, but his old parents, with the mean dad. And wham! As soon as he prayed, a car wreck stopped them from fighting—forever.

Another time he prayed for a new home and pretty soon the nice Paulsen family came along and adopted him. Prayer was a pretty big deal.

So what about this prayer?

He replayed his dad's words. Okay, now you won't...ever. Ricky thought about that for a long time. He thought about how people, normal people, would sleep all night and wake up without wet pajamas. He thought about other people who would sleep, and then wake up and have to go to the bathroom, but they didn't go in their bed. He thought about how much he'd like to be one of those people… and the next thing he knew, Matthew shaking him.

"Ricky, Ricky, Ricky!"

Ricky bolted upright afraid that—"What!"

"Come on sleepy head, your mom made pancakes!"

"Go…go. I'll be down in a minute. Don't eat 'em all." Ricky sat up and leaned against the headboard. He was still trying to figure out if he was awake or dreaming. And then it registered…he was dry.

He was awake and he was dry. He kept double checking—just to be sure he was dry.

A sleepy giddy grin crossed his lips and he thought about prayer. He wondered how it worked. How could God hear him…and someone else a mega-jillion miles away on the other side of the world—all at the same time?

Maybe it's like a cell phone. Prayer is calling God's cell phone number. No, that wouldn't work…'cuz what if a bunch of folks called at the same time? God doesn't have busy signals or answering machines.

Ricky's Sunday school teacher had said God is everywhere. Maybe…God's like air. Air is all over the place—God is all over the place. You can't see air—you can't see God. Yeah, that's it. And somebody…maybe the preacher, or Ricky's mom or dad or maybe even Sally acting like a teacher, one of them said God will live inside a person, if He's invited. Well, that's like air, too, because air goes inside a person when they take a breath. Ricky took a deep breath and smiled. Yep. God is all over the place like air. That's why He can hear everybody when they pray.

Air is good, it pushes sailboats.

But, what about underwater, where there's no air? Maybe, that's why God made it so people can't talk underwater.

Ricky's stomach growled at the smell of pancakes. Maybe prayers are like smells.

I don't know how He does it, just glad He does.

He hopped out of bed and followed the sweet pancake aroma down the steps...in dry pajamas.

As he passed through the foyer he glanced toward the picture of Jesus and whispered, "Thanks." And deep inside his heart he knew, beyond the shadow of a doubt—God heard him.

And from that day, Ricky didn't wet the bed—ever.

~

Winter was slowly losing its icy grip and spring break was only a week away. Ricky's youth group would be heading north to their annual youth rally. And Ricky, confident the bed-wetting prayer was going to stick, asked if he could go. Five days and four nights, away from home all the way up to Duluth. It would be the first time he'd been away, for even one night, since he moved in with the Paulsens.

"Oh Ricky...are you sure you want to?"

"Yes! Mom, I don't w—" embarrassment slapped his face red and he looked at the floor—"I can handle it...now."

"Well, what do you think?" Ricky's mother dropped into a chair at the kitchen table and looked at the newspaper her husband was hiding behind, pretending to read, but she knew he was listening.

The paper leveled and his father looked Ricky right in the eye, "Well, there comes a time in every man's life when he needs to find his voice. If Ricky says he's ready, well, then by golly, I believe it."

That was that. He was going.

The next day at school, Ricky remembered his Dad's words. There comes a time in every man's—Ricky's chest stuck out a little farther. Dad called me...a man. Ricky grew a little taller.

Steve Shostrum was a bully, and Ricky was his target. It had gone on for so long Ricky couldn't remember a day when Steve hadn't picked on him, in one way or another. Ricky never said a word. He tried once or twice, but his bottom lip would start to quiver and his eyes would well with tears.

The hard part was—Ricky liked the bully. Somehow when he looked at Steve, he didn't see his freckled face and creepy scar under his left eye. He didn't notice the wild fiery red hair, he just saw a boy who had a mean dad. He felt sorry for him. He knew what it was like.

But, just the same, the kids would laugh when Steve would trip Ricky, or knock his books to the floor. And as soon as Ricky's lip started to quiver and his face got red, the kids would laugh. "Cry babies quiver, here comes the river."

The tears would fall. Even if he could find his voice, it wouldn't be heard over the laughter of a thousand tongues.

Ricky would just walk away...and pray. He never had trouble finding the right words when it came to talking to God. It was people he had trouble with.

Ricky was replaying his dad's words from the day before—there comes a time in every man's life when he needs to find his voice—and then, he was watching his books slide down the polished terrazzo floor. He knew what happened. He knew better than to carry his books at his side. Usually, he didn't. He'd hold them cradled tight to his chest. But today, he didn't walk in fear—he walked like a man.

Steve had slapped Ricky's books and sent them sailing across the floor. Ricky hurried to pick them up, knowing it would only be a matter of seconds before some kid kicked them—sending them sailing down the hall like a hockey puck. He also knew from experience that about the time he would bend over to pick up his first book, Steve would be right behind to push him over. But this time, Ricky's mind stayed clear, an idea flashed.

Ricky turned his head just enough to see Steve slithering up from behind, and just as Ricky started to bend over, acting as if he were to pick up his book, he dropped to his hands and knees.

Steve pushed, like usual, but this time his hands met air, and his knees met Ricky's side, and head over heels he fell, straight over Ricky's back.

The hall went silent.

Another flash, and Ricky thought of a prayer. Since he was already on his knees—he folded his hands, and bowed his head, he found his voice, but he regretted the words as soon as they came out of his mouth, "Father forgive him, for he doesn't know he's so stupid."

The hall filled with the laughter of a thousand tongues, but this time they weren't laughing at Ricky.

He looked at Steve scrambling to his feet, his face as red as his hair, and Ricky felt sorry for him. He wished he could trade places. He wished the kids were laughing at him instead of poor Steve. That's just the way it was with Ricky.

He looked at the floor and whispered under the roar of the laugher, "Father forgive me—that was stupid."

Ricky started to get up, but with one knee still on the floor he stopped. He noticed his shoe was almost untied. He'd grown out of his cowboy boots and wore soft soled sneakers. He had an idea.

He looked at Steve and smiled. Ricky grabbed his book off the floor and at the same time pulled his shoe string. And then he stepped on it—on purpose—and tripped himself.

The laughter aimed at Steve swiveled to Ricky. But he didn't hear any of it. He was too busy thinking—you the man, Ricky, you the man.

The history teacher, Mr. Hansen, walked out of his classroom and tried to settle the crowd.

Steve had bumped his elbow on the hard floor and was rubbing it, his face was still red and he had a deer-in-the-headlights look on his face. Ricky was tying his shoe...and smiling.

The only part of the story Mr. Hansen heard was that Ricky flipped Steve over his back. And that was enough. For the first time in his life, Ricky was sent to the Principal's Office—the smile never left his face.

~

Only David and dribgnos heard the explosion. The prison door to a cell called fear was blown off its hinges, as Ricky stumbled through, by tripping over his own shoe string.

19

Normally, Ricky would be afraid to sleep anywhere but in the privacy of his own room. But he hadn't had the scary nightmare in a long time and he hadn't wet the bed in months.

Just last week his dad—not his mean dad, but his real dad, Martin Paulsen, the one who adopted him, the one who prayed with him, the one who would never get drunk and beat him, that dad—had called him a man. And then, the very next day Ricky found the courage to stand up to the school bully—things were looking up.

His lips curled into a smile. He was seated by himself, near the back of the church bus, on the driver's side. He bounced along staring out the window. Maybe I'm not a loser. Maybe the wreck wasn't my fault. Maybe, just maybe...I'm not cursed.

A fracture appeared in the chain around Ricky's soul. He couldn't see it, but the hurts and scars of the past forged a shackle that weighed heavy on his heart.

He'd always blamed himself for his parent's death. The words he prayed in silence the day of the accident were branded in his memory. God, make them stop fighting—please. They did. Forever.

Almost immediately after he had prayed, he saw the deer lope from the left shoulder. All his dad had to do was slow down. But instead he swerved onto the right shoulder and hit the gas. The car fishtailed as soon as the tires hit the gravel shoulder and the right front corner hit the deer and sent it spinning along the side of the car.

Ricky could still see the whites of the poor things eyes—wide and bulging with fear—as its head splattered against the passenger window. They had haunted his dreams for years. Both parents died, the deer died—why not me?

He never thought it possible that a deer just happened to run out in front of the car, and his dad's drunkenness slowed his reaction time, blurred his judgment and caused the wreck.

He never thought God might have saved him from a life of abuse through the hands of a violent man. He never considered another option other than thinking he was responsible for causing his parents' death—until now.

The fracture became a crack—the chain slipped.

New thoughts rushed through Ricky's mind like the scenery outside the window.

Maybe God doesn't kill everyone that dies. Maybe people have a say-so in the matter. Bad choices get bad results. Drink, drive, die. Maybe, just maybe, it wasn't my fault. Maybe God didn't kill them—maybe drinking and driving did.

Ricky leaned his head against the window glass. The cold window made him shiver. All the things he'd heard at youth group and read in his Bible started to come together like the pieces of one of his model sailboats. Words formed in his mind almost as if they were being whispered in his ear.

I set before you life and death, blessing and cursing—choose life.

Ricky could see ahead, the road curved slightly to the left, and then split, one lane veered off to the right and the other continued to the left. Which way will we go? One road goes to Curseville and the other—maybe the narrow one—goes to Blessingville.

God has a plan, I can choose to follow, or veer off and go my own way.

If Gus swerves this bus into the ditch or takes the wrong turn and we get lost or get into a wreck because of it—that wouldn't be God's fault, or the road builders fault, or the bus's fault—it would be a result of bad choices.

Ricky whispered, "I choose Life."

They caught up to a long train chugging along on the other side of the left ditch. They eased by the caboose and Ricky started counting the rail-cars. They passed each one like a slow motion race. Fifty-nine, sixty, sixty-one, sixty—what?

Jesus forgives...do you? was spray painted on the side of one of the faded red box-cars.

Do I forgive? Sure I do. I forgive everybody—even the bully Steve. Ricky felt pretty good about himself...until a flash of his mean dad yelling in his face blasted to the forefront of his memory. He doesn't count...he doesn't deserve to be forgiven.

Forgive or you won't be forgiven

I can't forgive him.

Ricky pictured Jesus on the cross saying, *Father forgive them for they know not what they do.*

He rubbed a hand over his eyes, looked toward the sky and nodded. Okay, if Jesus could forgive them, maybe I can—he let out a slow breath—I forgive him, too.

There was a sound that could only be heard in the realm of the spirit—it was the sound of chains clattering beneath Ricky's feet.

Ricky felt a smile swell all the way from his heart to his eyes.

When he heard the giggle, he shifted his eyes back inside the bus. He knew that voice, and it made his face turn a little red.

Ricky's mom might have thought he was too young, to start liking girls. But, Suzy Smyth was no girl—she was an angel.

She proved it on the first day of seventh grade when each student had to stand in front of the English class and introduce themselves. Ricky had tried but when he opened his mouth to speak nothing came out but a squeak. The whole class burst into laughter—everyone but Suzy. She just looked at Ricky with a sad sort of smile—a sad, beautiful, angelic smile—with a dimple on her right cheek.

Suzy knelt on the bus seat directly in front of Ricky, her forearms rested on the back of her seat. "Whatcha smilin' about Ricky?"

Suzy's sing-song voice made his stomach kind-of bubbly, and her dimpled smile made his head a little fuzzy. He felt heat in his face, which told him he was turning red, and knowing that, made him even redder. He looked out the window.

He really wanted to talk, but what should he say? He couldn't tell her he thought she was an angel. He didn't have the nerve to say she was the only person that kept him from running out of class and dying, that first day of school. He certainly didn't know how to tell her he liked her—and not just like, but like-like. And he wouldn't even begin to know how to put into words the rolling thoughts about God. What did she ask me anyway? What am I thinking about...no, that's not it. Oh boy. He looked at the angel in front of him and cleared his throat—twice.

"I don't know."

Her eyes dropped, darted out the window and then back at him. She smiled a shy kind of smile, looked at her hand, and tossed a folded note into his lap before spinning around and sinking deep into her seat.

All Ricky could see was the top of her blond pony tail, tied with a pink thing. Ricky's sister had one just like it, he'd heard her call it a crunchy or scrunchy or something like that. Ricky watched her hair. A fountain of glittering gold bounced with the rhythm of the bus.

He covered the note with his hand and looked around to see if anyone was watching. Thomas Laury—the preacher's kid, a senior, an amazing drummer and a not-so-amazing hockey player—sat in the seat across the aisle from Ricky. He was either asleep or listening to whatever was stuck in his ears.

Everyone else was asleep or playing with their phones. The note was folded in a triangle, the way he'd fold a piece of paper to play table football during study hall. His name was written in fancy blue letters with a red heart for the dot above the *i*. After scanning for spies one more time, he fixed his eyes on the bobbing blond pony tail in the seat in front of him and unfolded the note.

Dear Richard,

I'm not sure if Richard is your real name but I suppose since they call you Ricky that you probably have a name like Richard for your real name. I use it because this is a serious letter and mom always uses my whole real name when she's real serious. "Susan Roxanne Smyth, clean your room right now. I'm serious." Like that. That's why I'm using your real name (or at least I think/hope it's your real name.) If it's not—um, well—just pretend it is for now, for seriousness, okay?

Anyway, I have to tell you—I noticed you looking at me, a lot. Well, I want you to know Richard, I won't put up with this kind of behavior. If you like me, then you will have to do more than just look at me. And I don't just mean—like—I mean like-like. Like, more than just friend like.

So, if you like me you have to tell me. And Richard, I know you are kind of shy, so I was trying to figure out how to make it easy for you to tell me you like me—that is, if you do. My mom said girls like to talk—boys like to eat. So, I figured out a secret message that only you and I would know. I hope you don't think it's stupid, but here it is.

Me and mom made some peanut butter cookies, and I brought some with me. If you like me, all you have to do is tell me, "I like peanut butter cookies." And then, I will know you like me, and want to be more than just friends...and I might even share.

And then she drew a smiley face and signed her name.

Ricky's cheeks hurt from smiling. After looking to make sure no one was peeking, he read it again, and right out loud without thinking he said, "I do. They're my favorite."

Laury opened his eyes, looked around, shook his head and closed his eyes again.

Ricky folded the note and stuck it in his pocket real quick like. He took a long deep breath—the first one in several moments.

~

Suzy barely breathed. She was listening for five simple words from the boy sitting behind her. She'd be fourteen soon, in six months, so she was a year older than Ricky. She knew she liked him, and thought he liked her. She made it easy enough for him to tell her, and even tempted him with homemade cookies.

It had been ten minutes since Suzy tossed Ricky the note—but it felt like an hour.

Ricky hadn't said the secret message. All she heard him say was, "I do. They're my favorite." Was he talking about her cookies...or was he talking to Laury about some stupid hockey game? He probably doesn't even like me. She stuffed her hand in the bag of cookies and grabbed two. I just made a fool of myself. She chomped a cookie.

"Boys are stupid."

Suzy heard her mom say that after she'd opened her Valentine's gift—two tickets to a Minnesota Wild hockey game.

Suzy's dad, Chet, was the local high school hockey coach. He wanted to go pro when in college. But, a knee injury ended that dream and he settled for coach. Going to a professional hockey game must have been the most romantic thing he could think of.

Suzy took another bite. Boys are stupid.

~

Ricky cleared his throat, again, and leaned forward to say those secret words...and chickened out. Again.

But then something happened. He smelled peanut butter cookies. His stomach growled.

He checked the secret message again, leaned forward and whispered into the golden cascade, "I like peanut butter cookies...they're my favorite."

She heard the words just as she bit into her second cookie and gasped, which sucked cookie crumbs into her throat and made her cough so hard she couldn't breathe for a few seconds.

Ricky wasn't' sure if she was laughing at him—he didn't think so but...

Finally, Suzy let out a long breathy sigh and inhaled long and deep. She turned and her eyes were watering, but she wore a smile. She lifted a plastic bag of peanut butter cookies. "Want one?" She lowered the bag a bit and raised one eyebrow. "But, be careful"—she coughed—"they've got a kick."

"Well, I um...I'll take my chances" Ricky said.

The corners of her mouth lifted in a way that made Ricky feel like he was being hugged. "So, you like, peanut butter cookies?" She drew out the word, like, long and slow. And then she lifted her eyebrows and spoke through a smile that was bigger than before. "And they're your favorite." She drew out the word, favorite, long and slow too.

She tilted her head and held the bag next to a smile that took Ricky's breath.

He didn't know what to say, she's flirting. This was new territory. His throat was tight, he could barely speak, let alone eat—but he figured he'd give it a try. He reached toward the bag.

"Take them, these things are dangerous." She pushed the plastic bag full of homemade cookies into his hand. Their hands touched—and the world stopped.

Ricky's stomach did a back flip. He swallowed hard. Time stood still. The hum of the bus and the chatter from the other kids fell away; all went silent—except for the beat of Ricky's heart. He was never more alive.

Their eyes locked as Ricky sat back, in slow motion. He rested his hands—and the cookies—in his lap.

A light pink appeared in her cheeks, just above an adorable dimple. A few cookie crumbs lay on her bottom lip, and the corners of her mouth lifted. She knelt facing the back of her seat—toward Ricky.

He reached into the bag without taking his eyes off her. He lifted a cookie toward his mouth, and then he had a romantic thought—one from a movie—he slowly raised the cookie to her mouth.

Her lips parted—but then she jerked her head back, coughed and laughed. "Are you trying to kill me or what?"

He looked at the cookie, frowned, "are these poison?" and shoved the whole thing into his mouth before she could answer. Through a mouthful of cookie he moaned, "Oh, I just love peanut butter cookies, they really are my favorite." He swallowed and grabbed another and shoved it whole into his mouth.

Suzy's eyes got huge, her smile grew wide and her hand rested over her heart. "You love peanut butter cookies." She drew out the word love in a long dreamy sort of way that made Ricky's head spin.

They were an item.

Laury watched the whole thing, shaking his head with his mouth hanging open. "Kids" he said, and then shouted "Gimme one of those."

20

Earlier that morning, before the sun had chased the shadows from the church parking lot, a handful of grey haired men and women, two moms toting babies, one man in a business suit and another wearing oil stained jeans, had walked the perimeter of the bus. They spoke one at a time, but not to each other. They spoke to God.

They asked for His hand of protection on the bus and everyone in it. They asked for angels to surround the bus and not allow any demonic influence to enter or interfere with His good and perfect will. The gathering lasted for about fifteen minutes, at the most, but the results stayed with the bus and every passenger in it.

And for that reason, dribgnos drifted just outside Ricky's window, watching but unable to enter the bus hindered by a force-field of prayer and thwarted by a host of heaven's guardian angels.

~

Ricky's face turned pale and his jaw dropped. A split second later the driver hit the brakes—hard.

Suzy—still turned around in her seat, sitting on her knees and facing Ricky—fell.

The world shifted into slow motion. Ricky leaned forward and just before the back of Suzy's head smashed against the metal seat in front of her, Ricky latched onto her hands and held—with a strength beyond his own.

Eyes couldn't see the angelic arms of David, wrapped around Ricky and Suzy holding them in place and keeping them safe.

From sixty-to-nothing in zero seconds flat, the bus came to a crawl. The tires didn't slip and the bus didn't swerve, but, of course, the passengers were propelled forward.

Bibles, notebooks, cell phones and backpacks spewed all over the floor. An apple bounced from somewhere in the back and splattered against the front of the bus—as did a can of Coke which sprayed a slow fountain all over the bus driver.

Fortunately, miraculously, no one was hurt.

"Hey! Everybody Okay?" Gus shouted as he eased the bus onto the shoulder. "Stay in your seat until we're stopped."

As soon as the brake was set, it was musical chairs. Kids rummaged in and out of seats gathering up belongings scattered everywhere.

Charlie grabbed his spewing Coke and held a finger over the puncture. He looked at Gus, who was wiping soda off his face with a hanky...and then, without thinking he opened the can and sprayed Gus all over again. Charlie covered the opening with his mouth until soda came out his nose and made his eyes water. When the spewing stopped Charlie choked out, "Oops, my bad...sorry Gus."

He downed the rest of the Coke, crushed the can and tossed it in the basket behind Gus's seat. Lifting his shoulders a couple times he gave Gus a crooked grin. "It was my last can." He burped real loud and walked back to his seat. That was Charlie.

After the kids had settled down, one-by-one they stared out the windows on the right side of the bus. All eyes were on the deer; one doe and two fawns. They had loped from the left shoulder and crossed directly in front of the bus. Now they grazed in the ditch, unaware of the chaos they had just caused.

All eyes were on the deer—except Ricky's. He stared trance-like out the right front window. He made his way to the front of the bus, not watching where he was walking, but feeling with his hands on the seats. He tripped on a backpack sticking out from under one of the seats, and caught himself on the seat back. But he never once took his eyes off whatever they were glued to.

When he got to the front of the bus he said, "Open the door."

Gus shook his head. "Ricky, we're almost there. Can you wait?"

"Open the door!" This time Ricky screamed the words and the whole bus fell silent.

Gus slowly pulled the lever opening the door.

Before the door was open all the way Ricky scrambled out and half ran half staggered toward his target.

"Stay seated!" Gus yelled as he followed after Ricky. Everyone obeyed—except Suzy. She followed Gus but kept her distance.

Ricky stopped in front of a large oak. About eight feet up, nailed to the tree, a faded sign hanging crooked, read: YES, Jesus loves me.

Ricky's chin quivered, the dam broke. A flood of buried memories woke and drove him to his knees. He could see it all.

~

"Ricky! Ricky!" His mother's voice was garbled, like she was choking on something. He couldn't see her. He was stuck, upside down. Blood dripped from his nose and ran into his eyes—everything was blurry.

"Mom, what happened? Are you ok?" That was Ricky, always taking care of mom.

"I'm fine." She lied. "Are you ok? Does it hurt?"

"I'm ok Mom. I think I'm stuck in the belt seat." He always mixed that up and called the seatbelt a belt seat.

"Hey, little man. Can you tell me somethi..." She was fading.

"Sure Mom." He said through quivering lips. She didn't sound right and it scared him.

"What's the song you...you know...in Sund... Sch..." Her words were slurred and short.

"Mom, how come you're talking like that?" Ricky had heard his mom's words slurred often from drinking too much—but this was different. "Where are you? I can't see you. Come here Mom."

He jerked on the belt seat with both hands as hard as he could. He jerked and jerked and jerked and wiggled and tried to get free with all of his might, his mom needed him but he was stuck in the belt seat.

Finally he stopped and through bloody, quivering lips he sang. "Jesus loves me, this I know, for the bible, tells me so. Little ones, to Him belong, they are weak, but He is strong..."

His mother, Jenny, smiled a sad broken bloody smile. She lay on her back just outside the twisted vehicle. If she turned her head she could barely see Ricky through her swollen eyes. "You think He loves...even me?"

Ricky sniffed, "a-course, Mom—He loves you more'n ever."

A dark reality stood before her—bad choices and a lifetime of regret. "Sorry...I'm so sorry."

"No. No Mom, you don't have to be sorry. It's not your fault. The deer and Dad—"

"Ricky, your dad's not here."

Jenny looked at the man she'd lived with for the last half decade, the man splayed out on the ground in a pool of blood. Why'd she always fall for his type? The long neck bottle was still in his hand.

There was a time when the canvas of her life was a colorful painting filled with hope and beauty and then...her lust for fun stepped in and splashed it black. All black, with one small dot of white—Ricky.

"Mom...is he dead?"

She let out a slow breath that drained her lungs. "He's sailing."

Ricky wasn't listening because he was pulling on the belt seat again, trying to get free to help his mom.

Then, he remembered a prayer from Sunday school. His mom didn't go to church, but she let the church van pick him up sometimes—when she could get out of bed in time.

"Mom, say this. Dear Jesus, sorry for my sins—that's bad stuff you do that don't make God happy—please forgive me, amen. And mean it. You gotta mean it or it don't work. That's what, Miss Carroll, my Sunday school teacher said. But if you mean it, then you can know you're gonna go to heaven when you die."

Then, he got real scared. "But...you're not gonna die, right mom?"

She lay there silent for several moments. Tears and blood mingled in the dirt. "Okay, Jesus." With each raspy word blood spilled from her mouth. "I don't have a right to ask favors—" she grabbed a ragged breath—"please take care of my little man."

Sirens wailed in the distance.

Tears and blood and sorrow drained from her. Regret laced icy fingers around her throat. With the last bit of breath in her soul she wheezed, "God, I don't deserve it...but, will You forgive me?"

She could only hope it was true.

Her face rolled toward the sky. For a moment her eyes cleared and the black canvas faded to a brilliant light shining through the trees.

Ricky heard her read the words out loud, YES, Jesus loves me.

The corners of her mouth lifted.

And she was gone.

"Mom!" Ricky yanked and groaned and strained and cried and banged on the belt seat until his little arms fell limp dangling over his head. His whole world got fuzzy. "Mom, wait, we never sailed to happily ever..."

The next thing Ricky knew was waking up in the hospital. He couldn't remember anything past the scared bloody eyes of the deer slamming into the window.

He lost a lot of blood—and all of his desire to speak.

~

As Ricky knelt there filling in the blank spots of his memory. He remembered his mother's last words as he read the sign, YES, Jesus loves me

A black hole in his heart filled white. He felt the corners of his mouth lift.

And then Gus's hand on his shoulder, "What's going on man?"

Ricky eased to his feet never taking his eyes off the sign. "This is where it happened, Gus. My mom and—" the word dad got stuck in his throat and he made a small cough—"died right there, under that sign." He lifted his hand slow and pointed toward the old faded sign and held his hand in the air as if he could touch it.

Gus knew Ricky was adopted, but not much more. "Oh, wow."

"Mom went to heaven, I know that now. But him—" Ricky looked at the ground—"I don't know...doubt it. But you know something Gus?"

Gus shrugged.

"I don't hate him." Ricky looked at Gus. "I don't know how...but I forgave him. Not saying what he did was right—but I'm free of those chains. I've given it to God." Ricky's hands shot in the air like a man just freed from prison.

Gus let out a small laugh. "Hey, I'm uh...just the bus driver...but I'd say you met God today."

"Just the bus driver? Are you kidding? There's no just about that. God digs the small stuff Gus. You may not even know it, but you could be right smack dab in the middle of a special assignment from God—" Ricky pointed at the bus— "just driving that bus, right there."

Gus smiled at this bold side to Ricky, "Preach it man."

Suzy started to walk up from behind. Gus held up his hand at first, and then waved her over. She knelt next to Ricky. The ditch grass was warm on top from the sun, but cold and damp near the ground where the snow hadn't melted.

Suzy read the sign and as quiet as a breeze, she started to sing. "Yes Jesus loves me, yes Jesus loves me, yes Jesus loves me, the Bible tells me so..."

One-by-one the kids filed out of the bus.

Right there, on the side of the road, in a snow sloppy ditch, a bunch of teens, joined hearts and hands.

They dropped to their knees, in front of an old faded sign, under a large oak tree.

It didn't matter if the ground was cold and wet, because they met God, and sang with the angels, and came to know for sure and certain that...Yes, Jesus loves me.

21

Gus was shaking his head and talking to himself. "It had to be a miracle." He was thirty-three years old, born in the church and never missed a service. But in all those years, he had never felt the presence of a loving God like he did that day.

"It had to be a miracle."

He never should have been able to stop the bus in time. With all the weight, and the brakes aren't the best. The road's slick from sand and salt. He glanced toward the tree line where the deer vanished after Ricky jumped from the bus—they ought to be venison by now. He looked in the overhead mirror.

Suzy was sitting next to Ricky.

Before shifting the bus into first gear, he shifted his gaze into the sky "It had to be a miracle. Thanks."

~

The rest of the bus ride to Duluth was quiet. Ricky thought about what had just happened. Did he really remember? Or was his mind playing tricks on him. And what was it that his mom had said?

"Your dad's not here...he's sailing."

Ricky closed his eyes. What was mom trying to say? An angry voice echoed from somewhere in his past.

"Shut-up you big baby—you sure ain't no kid of mine!"

Ricky popped his eyes open and shook his head to shake the memory.

He looked at Suzy seated next to him. Suzy smiled a shy smile and slid her hand closest to him down to her side—he did the same—and they held hands. All the painful memories dissolved and Ricky floated on a cloud. The hollow pang in his heart—a constant companion for as long as he could remember—was gone. He felt like he could fly beside, rather than ride in, the bus. But, sitting next to Suzy was better, and his heart was soaring just the same.

~

dribgnos had hoped, when he scared the deer, that it would cause a wreck and wipe out a bus load of church kids. But, instead his plan backfired and he caused the bus to stop right where Ricky would see the sign...and remember.

The angel, David protected the area around Ricky and Suzy. Other guardian angels had helped slow the bus, that was on a collision course to slaughter a family of deer—or worse.

What the demon meant for harm, God used for good.

dribgnos knew he was off. his timing was off, his tempting was off. he couldn't even scare a few deer onto the road at the right time. his last ditch effort to show lucifer some recent progress before his meeting, had failed.

Why couldn't lucifer summons me a few months ago? Just a little while ago i was set. The kid was scared of his shadow, he wet the bed, and wouldn't open his mouth for fear of being laughed at, but now...

dribgnos shook his head. Ricky didn't just grow out of it. The worst possible thing happened—he prayed out of it. The bed wetting and the nightmares too.

To top it off, the strangle-hold dribgnos had on the boy's confidence was cut loose when that ditzy googly-eyed blond showed up. And not just any blond—the one lucifer warned him about.

"Make sure you keep that kid away from the girl they call Suzy. Her mother prays. She'll ruin everything." lucifer had spit the word, prays, out like it was a hot coal on his tongue.

dribgnos was a master at manipulating children, but this whole, peanut butter cookie I like you thing was like trying to stab a fly with a pitch fork.

They're just kids. lucifer won't look at this as a setback. i haven't failed. i have time...lots of time.

Besides, what lucifer doesn't know won't hurt him. he wants me to think he knows everything—but i know better. he's not all knowing like, The Creator. he can't be everywhere at once like, The Creator, either. So, he doesn't need to know.

i'll tell him about the nightmares, the bedwetting, the fear of speaking—he doesn't need to know any of the rest. After all, it's too soon to tell if any of it will stick anyway.

Better not stir the caldron.

And for sure i won't mention the sign where the accident took place, the one that jogged Ricky's memory about his mother, the one that planted the original seed, the one that just kicked Ricky's faith into overdrive, the one that says **YES, Jesus loves me**.

No, i won't definitely won't tell lucifer about that... no matter what.

~

dribgnos found lucifer in his usual perch located in the highest point of earth's eastern atmosphere. It was the closest he was allowed to get to The Throne Room without an invitation.

"What's happened to you?" lucifer hissed.

"What do you m—"

"Silence! you used to control entire orphanages and now you can't keep one quivering-lipped child under control?"

lucifer narrowed his eyes to slits. "Are you planning a rebellion?" he was obsessed with the fear that someone would take his authority. And refused to recognize, Someone already had.

"i should cast you into the pit myself."

lucifer didn't have authority to cast anything into the pit, or the lake of fire or any part of hell created by The God of Heaven, but he liked to act as if he did.

lucifer did, however, control an army of demons called tormentors. he could sentence someone to be tortured by them. And using that fear is how he controlled the hoards of hell, and many people living on earth as well.

lucifer glared at dribgnos. "Maybe the tormentors will stir you into submission."

"nomylordlucifer." dribgnos slurred the words together through quivering lips. his head bowed low.

"Silence! i can't believe only a third of the angels had enough sense to follow me out of heaven—and you had to be one of them."

lucifer paced, growled and clawed the air. he cursed the demon in charge of Ricky, cursed the angel David and cursed the God of Heaven.

Then he stopped and pointed a charred leather-like finger straight at dribgnos and seethed. "Go to the boy. Say nothing. Do nothing. Only repeat the words of the angel David, or anything you hear HIM say to the boy." He pointed up and hissed as he said the word HIM. "And nothing else. You got it—NOTHING." When lucifer said the word nothing, his hand snapped into a fist—a shaking, angry, fist.

dribgnos whispered what he thought he just heard. Couldn't believe it, but dared not question it. Slowly, he lifted his head with questioning eyes.

"Only, repeat what you hear the angel David, or The God of Heaven say. Repeat it to the boy. Do you understand?" Again, when he made mention of The God of

Heaven, he pointed up and hissed, only this time, he spit and spewed a putrid odor of hatred and fear.

dribgnos started to nod yes, that he understood, but then shook his head hard and closed his eyes. No, he didn't understand—not at all.

"Of course you don't—you're an idiot!"

lucifer hated with a perfect hatred and wanted to kill this demon—but knew he couldn't. If he could, he'd kill them all—every living thing. he hated everything, everyone and especially the God of Creation. And the best way he knew to hurt HIM was to take the thing HE wanted most—a relationship with HIS Creation.

dribgnos kept his head bowed and wouldn't look lucifer in the eye.

"Repeat after me, dribgnos."

"Yes my lord."

"i will only speak the words i hear the angel and his God speak."

dribgnos feared this was a trap, but he repeated the words slow, with his head and eyes low.

lucifer's voice softened, he was transforming into his angel of light façade. he liked to perceive himself as a wise ruler willing to deposit profound truths into his devoted followers. "my dear songbird, you have lost your voice with the child because he has heard The Voice.

"Now, you must regain your position. His followers call this—the sin of familiarity. But nothing could be further from the truth, it's not a sin. i'm not asking you to tempt him to do evil, just repeat the very words as i've instructed you. And his eyes will be opened to another familiar voice, another point of view."

lucifer's smile vanished and his voice went to gravel again. "Even you should be able to do that, right?"

"my lord lucifer. I understand." he didn't understand—he didn't have a clue, but fear kept him from saying so.

lucifer eyed the demon, knowing he still didn't understand. he pointed at dribgnos and whispered, "Loooook." he drew the word out, slow, long, as if casting a spell.

Instantly, dribgnos envisioned a stadium packed with people. A preacher's voice echoed "God loves you...God loves you...God loves you..." dribgnos could hear lucifer repeating the exact same words along with the preacher, but little by little they sounded different. "God, loves...you?"

With an emphasis here and a pause there, it sounded like a question. God, loves...you? Others, maybe—you? Doubtful.

lucifer snapped his fingers.

dribgnos blinked.

"Same words, different meaning, yes? Echo the angel and his Lord until the subject second guesses whose voice he hears, and its meaning. That's all you must do to create doubt in these creatures. Create doubt and faith will waver, and you will have regained your foothold."

lucifer folded his arms, nodded his head signaling the meeting was over.

dribgnos finally nodded with understanding in his eyes.

"Go!"

With that one word lucifer was gone. And dribgnos was plummeting back toward Ricky.

22

When the bus pulled into the parking lot at the Duluth Hyatt, Youth Pastors Rory and Deb Williams were waiting. They had driven up earlier to make preparations.

Gus eased the bus to a stop. "Okay, everybody stay in your seats." He pulled the door lever and the youth pastors climbed on board.

"Hey, our prayers have been answered—everyone had a safe trip." Rory said it loud to get everyone's attention.

"You have no idea—" Gus smiled at Rory and Deb— "tell ya later."

Rory continued. "We've prearranged your room assignments. Don't get nervous if you're not rooming with your best friend—we did that on purpose. It'll give you a chance to get to know someone outside your comfort zone— expand your horizons—it'll be fun."

Scattered moans could be heard around the bus. A thousand butterflies took to flight in Ricky's stomach.

Rory lifted his open hand, "And then, of course we had to place the rooms in strategic locations. We've scattered the Junior high kids closest to the chaperone's rooms—you know, so they don't miss out on any of the fun, in case a pillow fight or gross fest breaks out—we don't want any of the adults to get too bored and not come back next year, right?

"We've placed the boys on one floor and the girls on another—we don't want to have to have a teen mom retreat here next year, either." Small laughter fluttered, mostly from the junior high kids.

He nodded to Deb and she handed a stack of papers to the front row and told them to take one and pass it back.

"We're handing out a schedule of events and a list of names and numbers so you can contact—"

"The cheerleaders from East Bethel," Laury ducked behind the seat. Laughter rolled.

Deb held some of the papers over her head. "I used to be one of those cheer-leaders—thanks for the reminder Laury. Bethel's team captain, Shelly Moore called and asked if you were going to attend. I told her you were and she said, 'Well then, I guess we won't.'"

She shrugged her shoulders and grinned.

A piece of paper flew across the bus and hit Laury on the back of the head, "What'd you do Laury?" An array of voices spoke at once. "I changed my mind—Can I go home now—Call her back Deb, tell her Laury won't be here—"

Rory, held both hands up, "Alright, quiet down. This list is the names, room numbers and contact information for all of our chaperones. You'll also find your name and room number. Keep this with you at all times. Remember, you can call or contact, any of us, at anytime, no matter what—we're here for you."

Deb walked back to Laury and ruffled his hair. "You know I'm kidding. Actually, the Bethel girls are going to be here...and you, sad to say, may be one of the reasons. Shelly asked about you."

"Seriously?" Laury lifted his eyebrows twice, pursed his lips and patted out a quick drum solo, using his hands, the seat in front of him and the top of Max Thompson's head.

Ricky shook his head, "Kids."

Laury looked at Ricky, pointed both index fingers at him, nodded and laughed—a respectful laugh, one that said: That was a good one kid.

Yep, Ricky was on top of the world.

After Rory prayed they filed off the bus and found their respective rooms.

As it turned out Ricky and Laury were roommates.

"So kid, you and Suzy huh?" Laury stretched out on the bed nearest the door and flipped through the TV channels."

Ricky fingered Suzy's letter in his pocket. All he wanted to do was read it again and again and again. He couldn't believe this was his life. He had a girl, his dad called him a man, he stood up to the bully, he didn't wet the...never mind that.

"How old are you anyway? Aren't you too young to be looking at girls? You probably still wet the bed, huh?"

Ricky could feel his face turning red but figured the best comeback was to tell the truth. "Yeah, well, I haven't for a few months now, but this is my first trip away from home so, if I do, or if I get scared, can I jump in bed with you?"

Laury's face went blank for a second and then he blasted Ricky with his pillow. "You're funny for a kid—I like that. No wonder Suzy-Q thinks you're a cutie-pie."

The impact of the pillow knocked Ricky back a few steps and he poised to throw the pillow back, but Laury had his hand up and his eyes focused on the television. "Close your eyes kid."

A behind the scenes report of the making of the Sports Illustrated Swimsuit edition had Laury dazed. Ricky tossed the pillow back onto Laury's bed and sat back against the head board of his own bed and opened the letter. As tempting as the pictures on the television screen, his heart was drawn to the words penned on a wrinkled piece of paper.

The skimpy bikini program took a commercial break. "Hey Ricky, I gotta tell you something."

Ricky didn't hear him, he was busy studying the way Suzy swirled the last letter of his name making the bottom of the, *y*, into a heart—just like the dot on the, *i*.

"Richard!"

THUD. The impact of the flying pillow caused the back of Ricky's head to hit the headboard.

"What!" Ricky sneered at Laury and rubbed the back of his head.

"Didn't mean to scare you, but I just remembered something you oughta know."

Ricky sighed. "Alright, what ought I to know."

Laury clicked off the television. "Competition bro—that's what."

Ricky cocked his head and frowned at Laury.

"You've got a little competition for Suzy-Q."

"Whaddya mean?" Ricky's voice was shaky.

"Well, there's this hot-shot punk kid on junior varsity. He's a pretty good puck handler and I think he was born with skates on his feet. Anyway, I got a feeling Coach imagines his daughter and hot-shot together someday—and of course, his daughter is your little Suzy-Q."

Ricky looked at the letter and then at Laury. "How would you know anything about it?"

"Some Saturdays Suzy would show up with her dad for practice. On those days, and only on those days when Suzy was with him, Coach would call Ryan off the ice and point to the bench—the bench where Suzy was sitting. I saw it happen three or four times before me and the guys put it together. Yep, I think you may have a little competition on your hands."

Ricky leaned his head back and stared at the ceiling. He let out a slow breath. "Competition."

"What—" Laury raised a brow—"you don't like a little competition?"

"No."

"Don't like competition?" Laury let out a short laugh. "My roomy's a computer geek."

It wasn't that he didn't like competition. He just didn't like beating others. He'd tried sports and was athletic enough but he always found himself rooting for the underdog—even if it was the other team. "I don't even own a computer."

Laury squinted and shook his head. "You don't like competition and you're not a geek—what do you do? What could Suzy-Q possibly see in you?"

Ricky ignored the remark. "Well, I don't have to worry about it 'til next week...maybe by then—" Ricky forced a smile—"there won't be any competition."

"Nice thought, too bad it ain't so. Haven't you heard?"

Ricky shook his head.

"Coach is gonna be here, and so is your competition."

Ricky's heart sank. "Why?"

"Coach is supposed to give us a closing pep-talk the last day. Then he's spending the week-end at some fancy resort on the lake with his family."

"What's that got to do with, hot-shot, what's his name?"

"Coach invited Ryan, that's what. I overheard him. 'It'll be good for your soul' Coach said, 'and you can do me a favor, keep an eye on my daughter.' "

Ricky started to sweat. "Suzy's dad invited Ryan to spend the week-end with them at—"

"No. He told Ryan to attend this rally. Coach and Suzy will leave from here and go to the resort...Coach told the whole team that."

"You liar. Ryan's not here—he wasn't on the bus."

"It's the truth. I think his folks gave him a ride. They were going skiing or something."

"How do you know?"

"The hot-shot talks too much—always bragging about some expensive thing his rich daddy bought him. He'll be here skating circles around your little Suzy-Q—like a shark...you can count on it."

"Great."

"Let me see that." Laury jumped up and reached for Ricky's letter. "I'll give you some pointers."

Ricky shook his head. "No way—"

Laury grabbed the letter.

Ricky pulled.

It ripped in two.

Ricky froze—except for his chin.

"Oh crap—sorry man." Laury held out the torn paper.

Ricky rolled off the opposite side of the bed and walked to the window.

"Come on man—it's just a stupid piece of paper."

Ricky spun around his face red hot, his blue eyes burned. "You're stupid! You have no idea—" Ricky held up the torn letter—"this is important." His chin took off chattering his teeth on the last word. His eyes blurred. Ricky wiped his sleeve across his eyes. "Relationships are important."

"Sorry dude...really, I am. Look, I've had a million of those from chicks. You will too. You'll just throw it away in a few days or a week anyway, right?"

"Has your dad ever called you a stupid, worthless, brat, while his stinky spit flew all over your face? Have you ever felt his fist in your face? Or watch him push your mom to the floor and jump on top of her...have you ever cried just to drown out the shouting?"

Laury put his hand on Ricky's shoulder and looked at the floor.

"Well, do that—then come back and tell me if a letter from someone who likes you is just a stupid piece of paper. To me, it's important—and no, I won't throw it away."

"Hey, I never knew. I thought your folks were cool. Should I have my dad call them?"

"No." Ricky grabbed the other half of the letter from Laury and pushed past him toward the door. "They're dead."

Ricky made his way to the lobby and dropped into a chair in front of the fireplace. The invisible aroma of burning wood filled the air.

And just as invisible, dribgnos floated near Ricky's ear. "You should show some respect. Her father wants her to date a hockey player."

She'll probably like him better anyway—a hockey player just like her dad. That's what her dad wants. I should respect that.

David wasn't at his usual spot by Ricky's side, so dribgnos hovered close. "She wants a man like her dad—not a boy like you."

Ricky felt his chin wanting to quiver. I'm such a stupid boy. What was I thinking?

drignos spoke straight into Ricky's soul. "Torn in two, just like you. You'll never have a relationship. Never."

Ricky looked at the wrinkled letter. That's how we'd end up anyway...torn in two.

The fire popped.

"Burn it" dribgnos hissed.

Ricky watched the flames dance. He stood up, took a step toward the fireplace, felt the heat, stretched out his hand with the wrinkled torn letter—heard the giggle.

dribgnos cursed.

David was beside Suzy.

"Ricky!" Suzy was wearing fuzzy slippers and pajamas with hearts all over them. "What are you doing down here?"

"I uh..." he stuffed the wrinkled letter in his back pocket.

"Oh the fire is so beautiful." She walked up and held her hands out to the fire. "Wish we could make S'mores."

Ricky stood next to her. She didn't see me almost burn the letter. Good.

"I was going to get some extra pillows." She giggled with that cute little dimple. "A bunch of girls are in my room, they were sitting all over the floor and I thought I should get them some pil—are you by yourself?"

"I um...I was just—" he pointed at the fire—"watching. Thinking and stuff."

She hooked her arm through his. "Whatcha thinkin' about...me?"

Ricky felt heat from the fire—or was it him, or her? He smiled.

They sat on the love seat near the fire and talked about nothing and giggled about everything, until one of Suzy's friends showed up.

"Hey girl we've been waiting for you." She looked at Ricky. "Oh...where's the pillows?"

Suzy squeezed Ricky's hand. "I'm sorry, I forgot. I was—"

"Never mind I'll get 'em." The girl walked to the front desk.

"Maybe you should go back with her" Ricky said.

Suzy looked at him with a small smile. "Yeah, maybe I should."

Ricky whispered, "See ya tomorrow."

"Okay...dream of me." She jumped up and caught up to her friend.

He watched Suzy get on the elevator and then walked to the front desk. "Can I borrow some tape?"

Ricky placed the wrinkled pieces of paper together. The rip had gone right through one of Suzy's hearts. He taped it together like he was putting together one of his models. Perfect.

I mend the broken hearted.

Ricky smiled.

dribgnos cursed.

David laughed.

23

Ricky and Suzy spent every available moment together and he was headed her way. But then he heard it, again.

For three days in a row, the words echoed inside.

Go for a walk.

It wasn't a bad idea—Lake Superior was only a short walk down the hill—except the timing was off. The mid-morning service was about to begin.

Besides, there she is...my girl.

Ricky shrugged off the feeling when he spotted the blond bobbing pony tail. She was seated near the front, saving a seat for, her guy.

He was, her guy, she said so that morning when she introduced him to her roommate at breakfast. He couldn't remember the girl's name, but the words—I want you to meet, my guy, Ricky—replayed in his mind like a favorite song.

Ricky floated up the aisle, his eyes glued to his girl.

She hadn't seen him, when he heard it again. It wasn't loud so everyone could hear, but inside, like an inner urging.

Go for a walk.

He stopped dead in his tracks. Go for a walk?

This time the voice was loud—out loud—too loud.

"Walk!"

Ricky spun around.

Charlie held a can of Coke in one hand, and a Bible balanced two donuts in the other. In one fluid motion, Charlie took a swig and waved the can. "Walk man—I almost spilled this."

Ricky side-stepped."What else is new, Charlie?"

In that instant, Ricky knew what he had to do.

He glanced toward Suzy. He didn't see her at first, his breath caught. The crowd shuffled a bit and there she was, shaking her head toward a young man in a hockey jersey. Probably telling him she was saving the seat for, her guy.

The kid was tall and dark haired and athletic looking. Suzy was blond and blue-eyed and beautiful. Oh no—it's hot-shot.

Sure is stuffy in here, and crowded. All eyes were on Ricky—or so it seemed. A thousand butterflies flittered across his stomach. I've got to get out of here.

He quick stepped through the hotel lobby, ducked behind a group of business men in suits and made it out the front door. The fresh air filled his lungs and he could breathe.

More than that, he felt like he was back on track. Like the world was right. He didn't understand, he just knew.

Okay Lord, I'm going for a walk...now what?

Obedience brings understanding.

Ricky smiled, the cold wind whipped against his teeth. He pulled the zipper up to his chin and cinched the draw strings tight on his hood.

As real, and as invisible as the crisp Duluth air, a smiling angel named David, walked beside Ricky, and said, "How could one word from Coca-cola Charlie, get you to go for a walk?" David pointed at dribgnos, who flittered around like an annoying fly. "Me and the mockingbird, have been telling you to go for a walk for three days."

dribgnos repeated the words of David just like lucifer instructed.

Ricky didn't notice.

David laughed and said the old familiar phrase angels use when puzzled and amazed by humans. "People have a tendency to be human."

The light grey sky turned dark, and a temperature drop turned spitting flurries into large floating flakes that caught on Ricky's lashes, and melted on his lips.

White streaks appeared in the sidewalk, as if stroked by an invisible brush. Down the hill he plopped. His cowboy boots slipped now and then. At the base of the hill, the sidewalk leveled and Ricky looked straight to the lake—Lake Superior.

Wow, it's as big as an ocean.

Right then Ricky was flat on his back.

His hands still stuffed deep in his coat pockets, he lay there, with his mouth open, catching modern day manna. If only Sally could see him—she warned him not to get another pair of those stupid cowboy boots.

All of a sudden he was a little boy, on his back in the snow, next to his birth mother, Jenny.

They lay head to head, making snow angels. And then, one of them made a soft giggle, then, the other made a little bigger giggle. Back and forth it grew into an outright fit of laughter. As they lay there catching their breath, Ricky had asked, "Mommy, how come I don't have a Grandma and Grandpa?"

The question she never answered, still hung in the air.

Something caught his eye, and when he rolled his head to the side, he saw an old man with his gloved hand on the handle of a red, wooden door. The man nodded hello, stomped the snow off his feet, and stepped inside.

Ricky let his gaze drift back toward the hoary sky. It looked like his letter. White spilled from every wrinkle and floated like love letters from heaven, rounding every sharp corner, and every jagged edge, mending the bright and shiny and the dark and grimy, together as one, under a blanket of white. He thought of how he mended his letter, and paid special attention to the rip through the heart.

I mend the broken hearted, and put the lonely in families

He caught one more flake on his tongue, and in that moment, he knew exactly, what he had to do.

~

"I don't get this." dribgnos stated the obvious to David.

"What else is new?" David said.

"You tell the kid to skip church? For three days in a row. That sounds like something I should be telling him." A crooked, wicked grin crossed dribgnos's face. "Whose side are you on?"

"I'm on the Right side—and you know it. You're confused, because you're too religious."

"You've got to be kidding—you, an angel, calling me, a demon—'too religious.'"

"You are. Religion reflects separation from God." David nodded at the demon. "And I'd say you're about as separated as you can get."

dribgnos looked down—toward hell.

"Religion was the stick used to crucify Jesus." David looked toward the red door. "You're too religious to understand what's happening here."

dribgnos tried to speak but no words would come.

"Religion divides. Relationship restores. Do you remember the curtain?" David asked.

"The one in the Temple that separated the people from the Holy of Holies—" dribgnos smiled—"the one that tore the day we killed God?"

"You mean, the day death died, that curtain tore from top to bottom—from God to man. God ripped that religious curtain wide open, allowing access straight to the Holy of Holies, to Life, to His presence—that's relationship. And no religious spirit saw that one coming."

"Nobody cares angel boy—" dribgnos yawned—"boring."

"Only the blind say such things. No real child of God claims boredom. They're too busy going about their Father's business, doing the next thing, like skipping church to raze hell."

dribgnos scratched his throat trying to find a word hidden somewhere.

"Remember dribgnos you repeated my words asking Ricky to skip church. As a matter of fact, you've agreed with everything I've said for a long time now...whose side are you on?"

dribgnos found his voice."Ah, dear David, I've repeated...yes. But, agreed? Not a chance angel boy."

"The sin of familiarity isn't unfamiliar. I've known all along what you were up to—angels aren't ignorant of the wiles of the devil. Keep trying though. After all, maybe your efforts helped get Ricky here today."

dribgnos growled. "What are you up to? The kid should stick with the group, not wander off alone. You must be slipping over to our side, angel boy."

dribgnos knew it wasn't true—or at least he thought he knew. But what if it were? What if the angel switched sides and joined him? Then lucifer would sing his praise. Then he'd be safe from the tormentors. Like all demons, dribgnos drifted in and out of confusion. With the-father-oflies as his leader he had trouble grasping truth but latched easily to a lie...especially if it stroked his ego.

David gave dribgnos a look that said, are you out of your mind. "First, the kid, has a name, it's Ricky. Second, you think he should have stayed up with the group, huh?"

"Absolutely." dribgnos remembered lucifer's words.

Keep them in a pack, like sheep to the slaughter. Keep them thinking acting and looking like their neighbor, blind leading the blind. Make sure they don't wander off seeking their own identity, calling and destiny. Tell them they're a grain of sand like every other, not unique in any way. Let them be comfortable, quiet and apathetic. lucifer had said, apathetic, like it was his favorite dessert.

dribgnos pointed up the hill. "The kid should have stayed with them."

"I remember a Boy about Ricky's age who didn't stay with the group. His parents couldn't find him until days later. The Boy simply said, 'Didn't you know, I must be about My Father's business?' Ricky's just going about His Father's business."

"His father's dead!" dribgnos knew David wasn't talking about any man but about Ricky's True Father—The Father to the fatherless.

David encouraged Ricky toward the red door, the one the old man had walked through. The door had The Tavern carved into the wood.

"Are you nuts!" dribgnos said. "First you tell the kid to leave church, and now you lead him into a saloon."

David stayed behind Ricky and, like always, kept himself between the young man and the demon. He urged Ricky through the door and threw the words over his shoulder, "The Lord works in mysterious ways." The door closed behind Ricky and David slipped through it like water through a sieve.

dribgnos tried to follow but hit some kind of barrier, and it wasn't brick and mortar that stopped him.

Confusion was one of dribgnos's specialties and right then he was surrounded by it, so he should have felt right at home—only problem was, he was the one confused.

The demonic host preferred people to remain predictable. Ricky had slipped through the noose of religion and predictability and dribgnos felt lucifer's noose tighten around his throat.

demons didn't mind if folks went to church—actually they liked it. "Religion is hell's amusement park." lucifer had said. "Religion keeps their bodies doing the right things so their hearts and minds don't have to. Make them act righteous, oh so righteous—more righteous than everyone."

dribgnos remembered how lucifer had pointed a jagged talon right at him when he said, "A holier-than-thou attitude is the garment of demons, lust over the being who wears it. But if they won't wear the garment—" lucifer had scowled—"strip them naked. Pour hot scathing words of shame and blister them with false humility."

dribgnos circled The Tavern as lucifer's words circled in his brain. "But, keep them from relationship. Relationship is a cancer to the sinner's soul—it will eat at sin until they become born-again. Prayer develops relationship. Keep them from prayer at all costs."

dribgnos should've been able to slide right through the walls of The Tavern like smoke through a screen because angels and demons are spirit beings created with microscopic cells that float unhindered through the larger celled items of planet earth. To be seen by the human eye, they simply expand their cells like a sponge in water.

dribgnos shot toward the side window like steam from a kettle, he hit and bounced and rifled back and ricocheted like a super-ball shot from a cannon in a racquetball court, back and forth he flew hitting every spot on every side including the roof and even under the floor—but it was no use, he couldn't get in. It's a stinking bar and i'm a demon—i've never had trouble getting into a bar.

he drifted toward the front window and tried to look inside, but a brilliant light blinded him and immediately he knew what he was up against.

He'd heard the angels call it, Shekinah Glory. The majestic presence of God. And of course, no demon or anything contrary to the perfect will of God could enter His presence, no more than darkness could penetrate light.

But...why here? At the top of the hill, sure, where hundreds of kids turned a hotel conference room into a church service. But here? God's presence in an old worn out tavern? No way. It made no sense. David's words haunted the demon—you're too religious.

As he backed away from the window, the brilliant light faded just enough for him to see inside. Angels everywhere shoulder to shoulder lined the perimeter forming an impenetrable barrier. It reminded him of the angels around the walls of Jericho as they stood ready to crush the walls down flat at the sound of the trumpet—now that was a miserable day, dribgnos thought.

he looked through the window as much as he was allowed until he saw Ricky. David, like a faithful Golden Retriever, was standing beside him. Ricky was shaking hands with someone. A flash shot through dribgnos like a hot sword. "How can this be?" dribgnos moved closer to the window and the white hot light blinded him again until he moved away.

From a safe distance dribgnos stared through the window at the boy and then fixed his eyes on the man holding the pipe. "Relationship" he spit the word like it was poison on his tongue.

All he could do was wait. And hope lucifer didn't find out. With that thought he spun around, and looked for any of his low lord's spies, or worse—tormentors.

That's when he noticed the other demons.

dribgnos settled in beside them, as if sitting in the waiting room of a doctor's office, they waited, with their eyes glued to the red door.

Ricky skipped church and went to a bar. dribgnos smiled. No matter how this turns out—that will please lucifer.

The biggest demon spoke first. "Best not mention this to lucifer." And then, as an afterthought and most likely to stop any backstabbing demon from running to lucifer and repeating what he'd just said, he added; "he has enough on his plate—i'll handle this."

Of course, he wouldn't handle anything. There was nothing to handle. All they could do was wait...wait and then attach themselves to their charge after they left this...this...Doctor's office disguised as a tavern—or whatever it was.

24

Ricky couldn't see. He went from blinding white to pitch black, with one step.

At least it was warm.

The smell of alcohol triggered a thousand painful memories. This was a mistake. I better get—

I AM with you—do not fear.

A blanket of calm wrapped around Ricky and a flicker of light caught his eye—he blinked and tried to focus as his eyes adjusted to the dark. A sweet aroma drifted on a cloud of blue.

The old man was seated with his back to Ricky. He drew a flame into his pipe with short puffs of smoke in between. His elbows rested on a dark colored bar that looked like it had at least a hundred coats of varnish. The match burned in his right hand, and Ricky could see in the mirror behind the bar, that the old man was staring at him through the flame. Just before the flame touched his fingers he dropped it in a glass ashtray and spun around on his stool to face Ricky.

When their eyes met the old man's jaw dropped and so did his pipe. He caught it in the palm of his hand just before it dumped soot and ashes in his lap. For a moment the old man's mouth hung open as if a word got stuck in his throat. But then, his shiny blue eyes blinked a couple times, and his chin bounced a few times under a beard the same color as the clouds, and the stuck word fell out..."Richey?"

"Richey? No."

"Shiver me timbers...what brings you in here, Son?"

Ricky stared at the pipe and then into blue eyes— familiar blue eyes—that sparkled against tanned leather skin, like beacons on a weathered sea. He wore a faded blue hat that read, Captain.

"What brings me here...um well, you do sir." Ricky stepped toward the man and stretched out his hand. "My name's Ricky."

The old man set his pipe in the ashtray, stood and shook Ricky's hand. "They call me Mac" he pointed to the stool next to him. "Have a seat."

Ricky did as he was told.

Mac fished his pipe from the ashtray and brought it back to life.

A big man walked out from the back room with a white towel over his shoulder and a case of long necks in his hands. He cocked his head and opened his mouth about to say something that looked like—what are you doing in here kid? But instead he looked at Mac, and pointed his chin at Ricky.

Mac held up a hand and nodded. "Pete, meet Ricky."

Pete nodded at Ricky and then looked at Mac and then back at Ricky and stared. "Boss?"

Mac raised his eyebrows and offered the slightest crooked grin.

Pete's eyes dropped to the pipe and he shook his head.

"Aye." Mac pressed a calloused thumb over the bowl of the pipe and set it back in the ashtray. "It's your fault, Pete."

"Nobody makes you do anything you don't want to and you know it." Pete slid back the silver lid on a chest cooler and started to unload the case of longnecks.

Mac looked down at Ricky and said, "Where were we? Oh yeah, you were going to tell me what brought you in here."

"Um, well, I saw you outside when I was..."

"When you were making snow angels." Mac's smile was warm and filled with humor—like he just thought of a funny joke.

"I slipped on the ice—" I was only thinking about snow angels— "and then, I saw you and heard...I mean, well, I, um...I knew right then and there that I needed to come in here."

Mac nodded and looked at Ricky's reflection in the mirror behind the bar. "Okay. Where were you headed before you slipped on the ice and saw me...home?"

Ricky cleared his throat, twice. "No. I was just going for a walk, I didn't really know where I was headed until I saw you...then I knew."

Mac lifted his hat and scratched his head. His grey eyebrows furrowed. "Going for a walk when a snow storm is fixin' to blow in? Why?"

"Well, I didn't know why. But, for three days I felt like I was supposed to."

"Huh?" Crows feet appeared next to Mac's narrowed eyes.

Ricky let out a nervous chuckle and then pulled in a deep breath. "Okay, see...I'm with my youth group up the hill, at that humongous hotel. We're having a big youth conference thing. I don't like crowds too much, but I just got a new girlfriend and so, it was okay, because I could sit with her and then being around all those people didn't bother me so much. But then Charlie, who always drinks Coke, told me to walk, and since I think God was already telling me to go for a walk, when Charlie said it real loud, I just knew I had to go...but still I didn't know why. I just knew I had to. And then, I fell down and for some reason, I remembered my mom and me making snow angels when I was little, and I asked her about how come I didn't have a grandpa, and then I saw you, and I think I heard—"

Ricky stopped, caught his breath and looked at Mac with big blue eyes and swallowed a lump and said—"I think I heard, The Voice."

He stopped again to check Mac's reaction. When Mac didn't flinch or laugh or gasp he continued. "I think I heard God say—"

The Lord is near the broken hearted and puts the lonely in families.

"And then, I knew why I was supposed to go for a walk—to tell you that."

Ricky shrugged his shoulders. "Sorry if it sounds dumb...maybe I—I don't know. Maybe you think it's just my imagination, and that's okay, because, maybe it is."

Mac's eyes looked wet when he said, "He spoke to you. I know that for sure and certain."

"You do?"

"Yep. Want to know how I know."

Ricky nodded.

"Because I always thought God told me I'd have a big noisy messy happy family, but things didn't go the way I planned, so I figured I just imagined it."

Ricky looked sad. "So, you don't have a family?"

Mac smiled. "Yes, I have a wonderful family. It's just..."

"Not a happy one?"

"Well, it's happy. It just didn't turn out the way I planned—or wanted. But, I reckon you could say it's even bigger and noisier and messier than I'd expected. Thanks to

you—God speaking through you—I can appreciate that now."
Mac patted Ricky on the back. "Thanks."

Ricky looked at Mac's reflection in the mirror and
said, "Wow...shiver me timbers."

Mac raised his voice and slapped the bar. "Pete, bring
my man here the good stuff."

Ricky lifted both hands palms up. "No, I—I don't
drink."

"Oh, you'll like this. My Mags used to make it for my
son when he was about your age."

In about two and a half minutes Pete emerged
through the swinging doors with a tray at shoulder level
holding three mugs of hot chocolate over flowing with
melting marshmallows and a candy cane for a stir stick.

"Where you from Richey...I mean Ricky?" Pete asked
and then sipped his hot chocolate.

Ricky wiped a chocolate mustache off his lip with his
sleeve and said, "Richey?"

"My son's name is Richey—you two could've been
twins." Mac said.

"Oh...that's why you keep calling me Richey. Is he my
age?"

Pete laughed. "He's old enough to be your dad."

Mac said, "But when he was your age—you two
could've been twins."

Ricky thought on that for a couple breaths. "Anyway,
we live in St. Peter. It's quite a ways from here."

"Do you have a big family?" Mac asked.

"Nah, just my mom, dad and sister—she's almost
fifteen and thinks she knows everything."

Mac let out a small laugh. "When you turn fifteen you'll know everything too. St. Peter huh? Lived there your whole life?"

Ricky hesitated, lifted his mug and held it to his lips for a while, and then finally after wiping his mouth, with a napkin this time, he said, "Pretty much."

Mac nodded and let out a slow breath.

Pete grabbed an empty beer case and walked through the swinging doors out of the room.

Mac picked up his pipe and gave Ricky a sideways glance. "It's aroma therapy—makes the place smell good." He lit the pipe just like before and then asked, "So, Ricky, is that your real name?"

Ricky licked the cocoa off his lip, "My name's Richard MacArthur Paulsen."

Mac looked back at the mirror and took a slow pull on his pipe. "That's a good name."

"Yes sir." Ricky noticed something familiar reflected in the mirror behind the bar and he spun his stool around.

The whole place was made out of wood. The ceiling, the floor, the bar, the stools, the tables and the hand carved intricate design bordering the mirror which stretched the entire length of the wall behind the bar, but what caught his attention were the shelves on the opposite wall.

From the ceiling to about four feet off the floor shelves were adorned with model sailboats—the wood kind—Ricky's favorite.

~

Mac watched Ricky float trance-like toward the sailboat wall and heard him whisper, "Well shiver me timbers," he said it just like a true sailor would.

"Did you do these, Mac?"

"Yeah, it's kind of a hobby,"

Ricky admired the boats and Mac studied the boy. "You like sailboats do ya?"

Ricky slid his finger along the side of one of the boats. "I have one just like this back home." Ricky spun around and asked, "So, are you like a real sailor or something?"

Captain Richard MacArthur Johnson had sailed the ocean more times than he could remember, he felt more at home on the water than on land, he and his son ran Maggie's Charter Service and he was a certified licensed sailing instructor—a real sailor? Mac just said, "I sorta like sailboats."

Pete made a laugh that sounded more like a grunt.

Ricky's eyes got big. "I love sailboats—I don't know why either. I've never even been on one. But, I've put together a bunch of models and someday, I'm going to have a real one of my own and sail around the world."

Mac thought he could be listening to Richey when he was that age...or himself.

The conversation sailed back and forth. Ricky told how he loved to save his allowance and buy a model sailboat just to give it away because, "it feels good."

Mac's blue eyes twinkled when he talked about how he and his wife and son had done the same with real sailboats, only most of the time they sold theirs.

Finally Mac gave Ricky a serious look. "Were you scared?"

Ricky wrinkled his nose. "Huh?"

Mac smiled. "Were you scared when you knew you had to come in here?"

"No." Ricky looked at his boots. "Well yes, but still, I had to do it."

"It takes a lot of courage for a man to face his fears."

Ricky smiled. A man. He stood a little straighter.

"To stand up for what he believes. That's something to be proud of, Son." Mac held out his hand. "It's a real honor meeting you sailor. I'm afraid you best be casting off, though. The temperature's dropping and the snow's still falling. Thanks for the message mate and..." He paused and looked deep into Ricky's eyes, right to his heart. "Keep listening to The Voice."

"Yes sir, I will." Ricky grabbed Mac's hand and pumped it twice—strong like a young man should. He turned walked to the door and turned around.

Mac hadn't moved and Pete was frozen behind the bar. All eyes were on Ricky.

"Um...It was sure nice meeting you guys." Ricky lifted his shoulders up and down once. "Maybe I'll see ya again sometime."

Mac cleared his throat and ran a quick backhand over his eyes. "That'd be great, Ricky."

Ricky pushed back and eased the door open.

"Hey Ricky," Mac's voice cracked a little.

Ricky's breath caught in his throat and his eye brows went up. "Yeah Mac?"

"You're gonna get your sailboat—and you'll make a fine captain when you do."

Ricky giggled. "Hope so." He shrugged his shoulders. "Someday."

Mac nodded and lifted a wave. "Someday."

Pete waved. "Nice meeting you."

"You too...bye." Ricky lifted a little smile and a small wave and slid out the door

By the time the big red door closed, two chins had taken off on a beat of their own.

~

Ricky looked like a snowman by the time he made it back to the hotel. His pant legs were white with a layer of snow and ice, the fur lined border of his parka hood was frosted white and his eye lashes were frozen.

He snuck up the stairwell—avoiding the lobby, so he didn't get busted for skipping mid-morning service—and found his room.

After changing into dry clothes, he ran warm water on his hands until the cold sting was gone and then glanced at the digital clock between the beds and hustled out the door.

He jumped three steps at a time down to the first floor, and fast stepped into the Lake Superior room, where the afternoon class had already started.

He couldn't find Suzy so he found a seat, sat down and acted like he'd been there all along. He scanned the audience, maybe she's not here yet. He sat his notebook and bible on the seat next to him and hoped Suzy would see him and sit next to him. After all, he was her guy.

Ricky's mind drifted back to the old man and the bar and the sailboats and his blue eyes—they looked so familiar.

A guy in a hockey jersey walked by and Ricky watched as he sauntered toward the front. That's who wanted to sit with Suzy in the first session. But she had waved him off obviously saving the seat for Ricky—except Ricky never showed up.

The jersey stopped about four rows from the front, the place was packed, where was he going to sit? But then, Ricky noticed an empty space about a half dozen seats from the aisle. The kid in the jersey pointed toward the empty spot and a girl, a beautiful girl with a pony tail pulled up with a pink scrunchy. The girl, Ricky's girl, tossed a nervous look over her shoulder, looking for someone, and then she lifted one shoulder up and down and nodded.

Jersey slid into place, like a puck into the goalies net.

Ricky felt sick, why didn't I see her? He couldn't hear a word the preacher said. He was too busy staring at the back of a blond pony tail...and thinking about an old man with deep blue eyes.

After that, Ricky slid into his default setting of being invisible, avoiding confrontation. He didn't want to fight for Suzy, if she wanted the hockey jock, Ricky wouldn't stand in her way.

He managed to avoid Suzy, telling himself it was best, until the last day of the youth rally. She chased him down the hall and fired, "Where've you been? What's wrong? Why are you avoiding me? Did I do something?"

About the time he started to answer, Ryan Taylor walked up wearing the same jersey. Didn't he ever change clothes? He puffed out his chest as he stood next to Suzy, crossed his arms and stared at Ricky.

"I guess I better, um—" Ricky pointed his thumb back over his shoulder "—you guys have fun." He turned and walked away, feeling like a loser. Only this time, he didn't want to lose.

Suzy huffed, "What do mean, you guys—Ricky!"

Ricky pushed through the door with the gold sign that read, Men, just as he heard Ryan's voice say, "Come on Suz, or we'll be late for Chapel."

Suzy didn't care. She followed Ricky into the men's bathroom and planted both hands on her hips. Her eyes narrowed and her mouth dropped open like she was ready to give Ricky a piece of her mind.

But Ryan stood holding the door halfway open and his voice echoed off the walls. "Come on Suz, your dad's saving us a seat."

Suzy blew a strand of wild hair off her lips and stormed out almost knocking Ryan to the floor in the process.

Ryan grinned at Ricky and disappeared.

~

Ricky finally slipped out the door with the gold sign that read, Men, dribgnos told him he was in the wrong room, he needed the one that read, Boys.

David was right there by Ricky's side, but said nothing.

Coach Smyth gave a pep talk that had the kids on their feet ready to, "check the devil to the boards and score a hat-trick for Jesus," and then whisked Suzy off for a weekend get-away with the family.

The bus ride home was sleepy for everyone but Ricky—he rode a roller coaster. What's wrong with you? Why do you want to be alone all the time? How come you get so nervous around a bunch of people? And Suzy—she's gorgeous you idiot—why'd you avoid her?...The Tavern was so cool, and that old guy, Mac and his sailboats, and Pete and his awesome hot-chocolate...wonder if I'll ever see them again.

25

Ever since Ricky walked into, The Tavern, Mac couldn't keep from sailing memory's ocean—in search of buried treasure.

He dunked another peanut butter cookie into his coffee mug and his wedding band clinked against the side of the cup. He chewed and swallowed with his eyes fixed on the little sailboat he'd dusted off and displayed in the center of the mirrored wall behind the bar. It was blue on the bottom and white on the deck with a small blue cross hand painted on the top of the main sail.

It was perfect, accept for one thing. It didn't have a name.

"That's it!"

Pete popped his head up from behind the bar. "What's it?"

"His name...it changed."

"Who? What?" Pete's forehead wrinkled. "Huh?"

"Ricky is mine."

Pete tilted his head.

"Ricky is Richey's..." Mac grew a smile and sat up straighter than he had in years. "He's my grandson...I think."

"You're losing me here Boss." Pete shook his head and raised his hands. "What's going on?"

Mac couldn't believe what he was starting to believe.

"Richey and his wife, Jenny, were together before Richey deployed."

Pete nodded and narrowed his eyes, "Yeah, that's pretty common Mac. But—"

"That was probably around thirteen years ago…how old do you figure Ricky is?"

"Now Mac, drop an anchor here for a second. I know you always wanted a family, but—" Pete pointed at the red door—"but, just because some blue eyed boy walks in here that happens to like sailboats and have the same color hair and eyes…and looks just like Richey, and has the same name and build and…Mac, you may be on to something."

Mac dropped his head. "It may be my fault."

"Go slow Mac, I'm still trying to catch up to the whole Richey's got a kid idea."

"I don't like to talk about this around Richey, but Mags and I saw Jenny with another man after we heard Richey was MIA. I tried to teach the scum-bag she was with some manners, and then told Jenny I never wanted to see her again. She must have left after that."

Pete rubbed the top of his head. "Whoa."

"She must have been pregnant with Richey's baby and didn't know it." Mac rubbed his eyes. "Or maybe she did, and was afraid to tell us…maybe, she wasn't sure who the baby belonged to."

"But the same name—she must've known." Pete said.

Mac nodded. "After he was born it wouldn't take a blood test to see he was Richey's."

Maybe Jenny straightened out her life and got married. But how? She and Richey never divorced? She just disappeared. Maybe Ricky has a wonderful life with loving parents and he doesn't know anything about Mac and Richey. Maybe it's better that way. Maybe Mac should just forget about the boy and leave well enough alone.

Mac closed his eyes and whispered a prayer inside his head. God, should we contact Ricky, should we tell him?

As soon as he opened his eyes, Pete was standing straight in front of him, both hands planted firm on the bar and resolve in his eyes. "Well Boss, I think ya oughta tell him."

Mac never thought he'd hear God's voice right out loud. And if he did, he never thought it'd sound just like Pete. Until just now...when it did.

~

The next morning Mac sat at his usual spot at the bar with a phone in one hand and a pen in the other.

Pete finished wiping the bar and flipped the white towel onto his shoulder in one fluid motion. "So, you're gonna call—good. What'd Richey say? I'll bet he lost his mind. I'll bet he thought you lost your mind."

Pete stared at Mac.

Mac stared back.

Pete's eyes grew. "You have told Richey...right? You know—your son—the boy's dad."

"Not yet...no sense hoisting sails if you're not goin' to sea. I'm just, doing the next thing. I haven't even got the number yet."

"Aye Capt'n" Pete gave Mac a crooked salute to match his crooked grin. "You'll never know, or sleep, 'til you make the call. And sometimes you best hoist a sail to test the wind—at least make the call."

Mac started to correct Pete. Tell him there's a multitude of ways to test the wind before hoisting a sail— landlubber. Instead he picked up the phone. "Aye," and punched three numbers.

"411 operator city and state please..." And just like that, within a minute Mac had a phone number scribbled on a bar napkin that could connect him to his future—his grandson.

How could it be? Only a little over a week ago a young man with deep blue eyes slipped into his bar, from out of nowhere to tell him, *God is near the broken hearted, and puts the lonely in families.* Mac covered the napkin with a trembling hand and rested his eyes on a little model sailboat with blue on the bottom and white on the deck and a hand painted blue cross on the sail.

Pete set a cup of fresh-brewed black coffee before his boss—his friend. Mac nodded thanks, but his thoughts were a million miles away. Back to when his son was young, full of dreams.

Now, how do I tell Richey?

~

Deep blue oceans stared at each other across the table. "What?" Richey set his fork and knife down and patted his full stomach, "I can tell you want to talk about something. Missing the Florida heat?"

"No, that's not it." Mac wiped a napkin across his weathered beard and pulled a slow deep breath and smiled, "You get that from your mother."

"What, my good looks?" Richey smiled a crooked one eyed smile.

"Yes...and more, the way you can read people. That's a gift."

"Okay—my gift tells me there's something you want to talk about—so spit it out."

Mac figured it was like going for a swim in cold water—you just had to plunge. Easing-in wasn't an option. "Alright, this is probably going to shock you, so I'm glad you've got a good heart." He sucked in a quick breath, "I think Jenny had a son...yours."

Richey's mouth dropped open and all oxygen fled from his lungs. He sat becalmed—not a breath.

Mac waited.

Jenny would have come back. She would have at least told him. "Impossible." Richey said. The word dropped like an anchor.

Mac looked deep, puzzled, cocked his head, "Impossible...you mean you and Jenny, never—"

"No. Not that—we did. But how on earth can you think after all this—"

"I saw him—that's how."

"Where? When?" Richey looked around as if he might be hiding in the room somewhere.

"Twice actually, I told you about the young boy at the Jiffy Lube years ago."

"Dad...I'm sorry I didn't give you any grandkids, but you can't go on thinking that some—"

"Richey, listen. That boy that handed me that sailboat out of the clear blue is the same young man that walked into The Tavern about a week ago and I know he's my grand—"

"You can't know this. Did you have a DNA test done?"

"His name is Richard MacArthur Paulsen."

Richey stopped breathing. "Paulsen? Jenny remarried? But, we never got divorced."

Two men, strong enough to cry, allowed high tide to spill. Deep blue stared at deep blue. Silent waves rolled between them for several minutes.

Finally Richey whispered one broken word. "Jenny?"

"I don't know Son. He was with a youth group at the Hyatt." Mac smiled. "He said he went for a walk because he felt like God told him to. And when he saw me walk in The Tavern he knew he had to tell me, *God is near the brokenhearted and puts the lonely in families.* Mac shook his head and whispered, "Amazing."

"I can't believe it." Richey said staring at a spot on the table between them.

"He almost drooled on the sailboat shelves." Mac's eyes glistened.

"What about the one?"

"His?" Mac smiled. "He didn't notice it. I didn't think about it."

"My oh my." Richey sat back, wove his fingers together behind his head, and stared at the ceiling. "Dear God...I have a son?"

Mac cleared his throat. "I have his number."

~

Richey's stomach did a flip and he felt blood rush from his head. He pushed his plate to the side, rested his head on folded arms on the table, and concentrated on breathing.

"Do you want...should I...what do you want to do?" Mac said.

Richey's breathing settled. I have a son...a son. He must be how old, twelve—thirteen? Wonder if he knows how to sail...swim...fish? He must already know how to ride a bike. Wonder who taught him?

Richey imagined pushing his son on a bike, "Pedal, pedal." He could hear his son saying "Daddy, don't let go, don't let me fall." Richey could hear his own voice laughing, "I won't let you fall..." And then he watched his son pedal away weaving a little but not falling.

Then his mind switched to the water, sailing, just him and his first mate—his son. And then, Jenny sat beside him. Her smile, her laugh, floated in the wind, but then, a strong gust hit their sails and heeled the boat onto its side, and as they started to roll over the boat wasn't a boat any more—but a car, flipping over and over until it stopped upside down, and the little boy's silent tears fell over a quivering lip.

Richey bolted upright. "That's it! My dream, the little boy in the dream is my son."

Mac slid a wrinkled napkin across the table. "Call him."

Richey plucked his cell phone off the clip on his hip and reached for the napkin and froze. He looked at his hand. Three and a half fingers started to shake. Richey felt beads of cold sweat on his forehead—his scarred forehead. He couldn't. "I can't."

"Why not? God opened this door."

"Maybe He did it for you—not me." Richey swallowed hard and wiped sweat and a one eyed tear.

This is what I get...my punishment for not listening to the warnings, for plunging ahead against my parent's wisdom and getting married to the first pretty face I found. And now it's too late. Even if he is my son, there's no way I want to destroy his life by letting him know that he has a monster for a father.

"Dad, I'd probably scare him to death, and then what?"

Richey broke and tears fell unhindered. The words came out, but they were chopped between sobs as he pushed the napkin away.

"You call—meet him—tell him I'm dead. You won't be lying. I died when Jenny left."

"Son, I can't—won't, do that." Mac slid his hand across the table and covered Richey's. "I love you. We can...we must do this. Your son needs you."

Richey made a laugh that held no humor "Needs me?"

"Yes, every child should know their father...their grandfather." Mac blinked and spilled a tear.

"He has a family—the Paulsen family. He probably doesn't know I exist and showing up would only screw up his world. When you saw him, did he look like an abused child? Didn't you say he was at a church thing? Didn't you say he talked about God? So, sounds like his life is just great. What gives me the right to step in and say 'Surprise! Guess what? I'm your one-eyed, three fingered one and a half eared freak of a dad—miss me?' "

Mac stood up fast. "Stop it Richard MacArthur Johnson, Junior! I will not allow you to talk about my son like that. I love you more than life and you are the most handsome man I know. Those scars are only ugly to you. To me and to anyone who knows you they are a badge of honor...of courage, of character and integrity and everything else that is lovely in this world—even a blind man, or woman can see that."

"It's not a blind man—or woman—I'm worried about. ...I'm sorry Dad. I need some time...please?" Richey stood and the two men embraced, and the angels in the room smiled, and the Father in heaven smiled and a little boy five hours away wondered about the grey haired man with the ocean blue eyes...and he smiled.

But...they didn't make the call...yet.

26

Ricky swept the tiny paint brush one more time and looked at the word, Suzy, on the back of the little sailboat. Hope she likes it. A robin landed on his window sill and whistled approval.

Ricky and Suzy had walked home from school together, every day for a week. Ryan, the hockey jock, didn't like it, and threatened to teach Ricky a lesson. But Ricky wasn't worried.

Steve Shostrum had put word out that anyone who messed with Ricky, would have to deal with him. Ever since that day in the hall—when Steve flipped to the floor and Ricky tripped over his own shoe string—Steve decided to be Ricky's bodyguard.

Ryan wouldn't admit it, but he was more afraid of Ricky, than the bully. Rumors had spread about Ricky being some sort of ninja warrior.

That's why he's such a loner. They'd say. That's why he backs down from fights—'cuz he's afraid he'll kill somebody. He almost accidentally killed Steve. You should've seen it. One minute he was walking along minding his own business, and then all of a sudden, Steve attacked him from behind. In a flash, like he had eyes in the back of his head, Ricky did some kind of ninja drop and roll thing and just like that, Steve was flat on his back. And then Ricky bowed his head and said some kind of prayer—like one of those kung-fu dudes—like Karate Kid. Better not mess with that prayer ninja.

As Ricky walked toward Suzy's house, the April sun warmed the smile stuck to his face. Hope her dad's not home. The smile dropped. He looked at the little model sailboat and felt stupid. What am I thinking? She'll think I'm some little kid bringing her a toy to play with. And her dad?

Oh boy, if only it were a hockey stick, then I'd be in like a puck in a net—like Ryan.

Ricky spun around and ran right smack dab into Suzy. SMACK. Full body impact. Since they were about the same height, their faces smacked like a hard un-puckered kiss. To keep balanced, their arms slapped clumsily around each other on impact.

They laughed until Suzy snorted, and that made them giggle all the more until they collapsed in slow motion onto the sidewalk, smiling and catching their breaths.

Suzy sat cross legged and leaned back on her hands. "I was trying to sneak up on you. Why'd you turn around?" She narrowed her eyes and pointed at him. "You really are a ninja."

What could he say? I turned around because I felt stupid for bringing you this sailboat...instead of a hockey stick. "Ninja—me? No way." He smiled, "Navy seal."

A remaining giggle fell from her lips, "Whatcha got there?" Suzy pointed her chin at the sailboat in Ricky's lap.

"Oh, um—" Ricky made a nervous laugh.

Suzy saw her name on the back and snatched it from his lap. "Ricky, pleeeaase tell me you made this for me. I love it! You are so good at this."

Ricky smiled and shrugged his shoulders. He felt his face grow warm and knew his face and ears had turned as red as Suzy's cute little sweater.

"We're going to ride one of these in real life this summer, Daddy booked the cruise yesterday. Some sunset cruise on a boat called Maggie. Wanna come? I'll ask, maybe you can come too."

"Yes! I'd love to." Then Ricky thought about Suzy's dad. "But...if I can't, that's okay, because one day I'm going to get me one of my own, and I'm gonna sail it across the whole ocean."

"Well, this boat isn't in the ocean, but way up north on that huge lake that's as big as the ocean. You know, where we went to the youth rally. Where...you ditched me and left me with that smelly Ryan Taylor." Suzy rolled her eyes and acted hurt.

Ricky's mouth dropped open to say something...anything but he just sucked air.

Suzy touched his shoulder and gave him a smile, "It's okay I forgive you."

When Suzy said, I forgive you, Ricky thought of something his mom had said: When people forgive, love happens...She loves me?

~

Ricky looked at the little boat. "I should teach you stuff...just in case."

Suzy made a small frown. "In case...what?"

"Oh nothing...but what if the boom knocks the captain out of the boat and you have to rescue him and sail back to land before a rogue wave capsizes the boat and leaves you a hundred miles from shore."

"What? Could that happen? What's a boom? What's a rogue wave? Are you trying to scare me? Maybe I better tell Daddy this is a bad idea."

"No! It's a great idea. I was just kidding—" Suzy's fist hit his shoulder—"but you should know what stuff is. What if the captain yells, 'Comin' about, watch the boom'?"

Suzy lifted her shoulders up and down.

"Okay, this is the sail." Ricky pointed at the little sailboat sail. "This flagpole looking thing the sail is attached to is the mast. And this pole on the bottom of the sail is the boom. When the boat turns, the wind swings the sail from one side to the other—over your head. Depending on how high the boom is you may have to duck when it swings. And, the boat will lean to the side the sail is on—so you'll sit on the opposite side."

"So how can that be fun if you always gotta worry about getting knocked out of the boat by that boom thingy?"

"Don't worry, it won't swing unless the captain is changing directions, that's called, coming about. So, if the captain yells, 'Coming about!' duck first and look for the boom later."

"You're so smart Ricky," Suzy batted her eyelashes, tilted her head and smiled.

Ricky sat a little straighter. "This is the rudder; it steers the boat. The captain will move the rudder from the helm—the steering wheel. And on the bottom, which is the hull—" he turned the little model over—"is the keel. It makes the boat go forward instead of the wind blowing it sideways, and it weighs a ton to keep the boat upright."

Ricky went on to explain that right on a boat is starboard and left is port and the front is bow and the back is aft and the ropes that pull in the sails are called sheets—

"Sheets? That's dumb." Suzy wrinkled her nose. "Why not call the sails, sheets? 'Cuz they look like sheets anyway— and just call the ropes, ropes?"

Ricky smiled. "That's a good question. Ask the captain when you go, okay? Anyway, this big sail is the main and the smaller one out front is the jib or foresail. The pulleys the ropes—I mean sheets—go through are called rigging and..."

Suzy wasn't listening. She was watching the way his blue eyes danced and the way his mouth formed the words. Wonder what it would be like to kiss him right now—right on the lips.

A barking order from a coach's voice shattered their perfect piece of paradise. "Suzy! Come home. Now."

"I gotta go." She leaned over and real quick like, kissed Ricky on the lips—right in front of her dad.

~

Ricky could hear her giggling as she trotted across the street toward the glaring father. Oh no, she's gonna get killed—I'll never see her again. That was my first...and last, kiss.

Ricky sat on the sidewalk and watched her glide, unafraid, all the way up the front steps and into the clenched jaw of her father. Only, when she got close, his jaw slacked and a smile appeared. Ricky's eyes got wide. Wow, didn't see that coming. Maybe coach is human after all. Ricky could hear Suzy's laughter as her father scooped her up into a twirling embrace, then he set her down and his eyes swung toward Ricky, still sitting—like an idiot—on the sidewalk.

Ricky jumped up and quick stepped toward home, and when he thought, or hoped, no one was looking, he jumped up as high as he could toward the heavens and clicked his heels off to the side.

~

Chet Smyth shook his head and Suzy's hand flew to her mouth and only slightly stifled a burst of laughter. "What am I gonna do with you Suzy-Q?"

They stood on their front porch facing the street. Suzy was in front of her father, leaning back, his hands rested on her shoulders and her hands cupped on top of his. They both watched Ricky continue his walk toward home.

Chet smiled, "How'd this happen?"

"What, Daddy?" Suzy said still watching Ricky.

"How'd you go from...eweee icky boy germs...to ohhh boy, I gotta get me one of them?"

Suzy made a dreamy sigh... "Not them...just Ricky."

Her dad groaned as he opened the door and they made their way into the house.

Suzy let out one more giggle as her eyes turned from Ricky rounding the sidewalk into his driveway. She lifted the sailboat, "Daddy, look what Ricky made me. He loves sailboats...I have a question."

~

Spring turned to summer and as much as Suzy begged, Ricky still couldn't go with them on the cruise.

"It's just for family Suzy, can't you see that?" Her father had told her "at least a hundred times."

She'd say, "But daddy, Ricky is family."

Her father would just shake his head.

"It's okay Suzy," Ricky had told her.

She said, "Someday when you have your own boat and daddy wants a ride—you tell him no way."

Ricky hustled up some lawn mowing jobs and a paper route to save money for the same thing he'd always saved money for—only bigger.

He'd seen some real cheap sailboats on the internet. He'd even found some that were free—they were the ones that needed work.

Someday.

Someday Ricky would have his own sailboat and Mr. Smyth would want a ride but Ricky would say, no way.

That's not true.

If Mr. Smyth asked for a ride Ricky would give him one, even if it was in the middle of a hurricane. He'd never turn Suzy's dad away because, someday, if Ricky had his way, Mr. Smyth would be Mr. Father-in-law-Smyth.

27

"Watch your step ma'am. Please have a seat right over there." Mac pointed to the starboard side of the cockpit. "And young lady sailor, you can sit right next to the pretty lady right there."

Suzy giggled as Mac pointed to where Suzy's mom, Sheila had just taken her seat.

Mac extended his hand to Chet, "Welcome aboard sir." Mac shook Chet's hand, appreciated the strong grip, and swept his left arm toward the young ladies.

"You folks must be fine sailors since you picked such a perfect day, seventy-five and sunny with a fourteen knot southerly wind."

Suzy raised her hand and her feet bounced up and down off the cockpit sole. Mac nodded toward her and smiled. "We've never been on a sailboat before, Sir Captain, Sir."

"Well I never had either until my first time. So, we're in the same boat, so to speak. You can call me Mac." Mac tipped his hat.

"Suzy...you can call me Suzy, Mr. Mac" She giggled.

"A few things before we launch." Mac's mouth shifted into auto-pilot as he discussed the trip, what they'd see, sailing terms, safety, refreshments, snacks, where the head was located—he explained what head meant to Suzy and finally... "Most importantly, enjoy the cruise and the beautiful sunset your Creator painted just for you this evening."

And then, without hesitating, he pulled off his hat, bowed his head and said, "Dear Heavenly Father, I humbly acknowledge that you are Captain of this vessel and Creator of the waters we sail upon. In all my years, whether stormy seas or becalmed waters, You've been ever faithful to bring me safely back to the harbor. Now, I thank you for the honor of hosting the Smyth family aboard *Maggie*. May they experience a joy-filled life lifting journey. Thank You. In Jesus name I pray, Amen."

Mac always prayed before a launch. He didn't ask anybody if they'd mind—he just did it. It's God's boat—who am I to not invite Him to ride along?

After that he asked Chet to help him cast off and they were underway.

Suzy and her mom's wide eyes and unending smile told Captain Mac what he wanted to know—they loved it.

It wasn't that way with everybody. Sometimes folks looked scared to death. Other times they'd have that I'm-gonna-be-sick look. When that happened he'd make sure they were seated furthest aft on the leeward side.

"Oh look Suzy—" Suzy's mother pointed—"there's a lighthouse. That's so ships can find their way to shore at night or in a storm—right Captain Mac?"

"Yes ma'am. Lighthouses are the streetlights of the sea. They help us find shore without running up on a rocky reef."

"Wow, look at that!" Suzy pointed at a barge as big as a football field, filled with iron ore. I bet he wouldn't wanna get stuck on no reefy rocks."

Mac and Sheila smiled at Suzy—reefy rocks?

Before anyone could comment, Suzy squealed, "Dolphin, dolphin!"

Sheila giggled, "No honey, there's no dolphins in fresh water—they live in the ocean. It was probably just a big fish."

"A humongous fish," Suzy stretched her arms.

"Could've been a big Sturgeon or Muskie" Chet offered.

Mac loved it when someone like Suzy was on board. She was a natural water lover. She couldn't absorb it fast enough.

Chet stood next to Mac at the helm. "Your eyes look familiar—have we ever met?"

"Not that I recall, Chet. Some years ago I was down near your neck of the woods for a funeral. Did you happen to know Scott Meyers?"

Chet didn't know Scott.

Mac thought Chet looked a little wobbly on his feet each time they'd hit a wave. "What do you do for a living Chet?"

Chet's chest grew a little. "I'm a hockey coach."

Just then the wake from a freighter rolled under from starboard and rocked them from side to side. Chet lost his balance and grabbed Mac's arm with both hands.

Mac smiled. "A hockey coach...on ice?"

Chet laughed and rolled his eyes. "Hard to believe, huh?"

Mac stepped back and asked Chet if he wanted to grab the wheel. After a few instructions about how to guide the boat, Mac told Chet he'd run down and grab some drinks and snacks.

When Mac walked away, Chet's smile looked like a boy with his first car.

Mac pulled in a deep breath and looked from the sky to the water—taking it all in. Thanks. The slapping of the waves, the cool mist breaking over the bow, the wind slipping through the sails, Mac was at rest, this is where he breathed the best. He missed the salt air, but to his surprise there were seagulls, so he could still hear their familiar call. God was good, even through all the heart wrenching, dream shattering pain. God was good.

Mac thought of a blue eyed boy named Ricky...and maybe He's not finished yet.

Mac handed Chet a bottled water. "Where do you coach?"

Chet was still at the helm and showed no signs of wanting to give it up. "I coach junior and senior high near where we live in St. Peter."

"St. Peter...that's close to Mankato, right?" Mac's stomach did a couple flips because he knew exactly where St. Peter was at. It was Ricky's town.

"Yep, ten miles north of Mankato."

What are the odds? God? "When I was in Mankato for that funeral, the strangest thing happened—I'll never forget it. I needed to get the oil changed in my old pick-up and I was sitting on the tailgate in the Jiffy-Lube parking lot, finishing a burger. All of sudden a young man walked out the door and straight up to me, he never said a word...just looked at me with those big blue eyes. And then, he handed me a little model sailboat...didn't know me from Adam, and he handed me a sailboat of all things. It was kind of like this one, too. I still have it." Mac shook his head, still awed by that day.

But, Mac didn't tell Chet about how Ricky had showed up at, The Tavern, or how he'd looked at him with those same blue eyes and said, *God is near the brokenhearted, and puts the lonely in families.* He definitely wasn't going to tell him that Ricky was his long lost grandson. If he said all that—they'd think he'd lost his mind. No, he'd said enough. Best leave well enough alone.

If God was involved, there'd be no need to force the wind. God would make it blow in His due time.

Chet glanced at his daughter, "Sounds like a boy we know"

Mac's eyes scanned the horizon as he put his hand on Chet's shoulder. "Alright crew, are you ready? We're going to turn this thing around."

"Come about!" Suzy raised her hand and shouted at the same time. She whispered to her mother, "Ricky taught me that. He knows everything about sailboats." Sheila laughed right out loud and hugged her daughter.

"Yes Miss Sailor Suzy—you're exactly right." Mac pointed toward the bottom edge of the sail. "Ladies, the boom is about to swing over our heads to the opposite side of the boat. When it does the boat will lean in that direction, so you'll want to switch seats." Mac pointed to the seats on the opposite side of the cockpit.

"Aye Aye Captain." Suzy saluted and giggled. "Don't let that boom thingy bonk you on the head and knock you in the water Captain Mac."

"Thanks mate, I'll be sure to watch out for it." I love that kid.

Suzy raised both hands in the air. "Okay everybody, when the captain yells, 'Coming about!' duck first and look for the boom later." She smiled real big and nodded at Mac and then said to her mom, "Ricky taught me that too."

Mac looked at Chet. "Alright master helmsman, come about!"

Chet just looked at Mac with a deer in the headlights look. "Me—do what?"

Mac laughed and pointed at the helm. "Spin the wheel mate, spin the wheel."

Mac motioned with his hands for Chet to spin the wheel starboard, into the wind.

Chet did the opposite.

"Other direction—into the wind, always into the wind."

Chet corrected.

As the bow crossed the southern breeze the sails swung about over their heads to starboard and heeled *Maggie*. The sensation was normal to Mac, and he adjusted his footing. Chet lost his balance, and if not for the wheel and Mac grabbing his shoulder, he'd have hit the deck.

Sheila and Suzy let out similar squeals as they switched seats. Suzy shouted to the wind and the waves, "I wish Ricky was here he'd just loooooove this!"

Mac's breath caught. Did she say Ricky? He smiled and tried to sound casual. "Who's Ricky?"

"He's my boyfriend," Suzy blurted out.

"He's a boy from across the street...and a friend. She's too young to have a boyfriend." Suzy's dad deadpanned.

"Oh, no, Daddy, he's my boyfriend and one day he's going to have a boat just like this and we're going to sail around the whole world. He taught me all about sailing. Like that—" she pointed at the big sail—"is the main sail. And that—" she pointed at the smaller sail over the bow—"is the jib. And those ropes aren't ropes they're sheets." She stopped, took a breath and looked at Mac. "Why is that? Why do they call ropes, sheets? Ricky didn't know, so he asked me, to ask you."

Mac wanted to jump up and do one of those flips, like the dolphins at Sea World. That's my grandson they're talking about—my grandson—and he's teaching about sailboats...awesome. "Ricky did a good job teaching you all those things. And the sheet question is a good question—"

"That's exactly what Ricky said," Suzy blurted out with a giggle.

"Most folks—even sailors don't know why the ropes that control the sails are called sheets. But...since my family has been old salts for generations I think I may know the answer to this very good question."

"I can't wait to tell Ricky," Suzy patted her hands together in little claps.

She must really like him—a lot. "The word sheet most likely comes from a shortened version of an Old English word, sceatline, meaning sheet line. The root word is sceata meaning, lower part of sail. So the sceatline, or sheet line is the line for the sceata, or sail. Did that make sense?"

"Wow, thanks, Captain Mac. You probably know as much about sailboats as Ricky—I wish you could meet him. You'd just love him."

I already do. Mac nodded, clenched his jaw to calm the quiver and blinked hard to hold the salt.

Chet pointed toward the sky "Look at that sunset. Isn't it just beautiful?" He stepped back gesturing for Mac to take the wheel. He did, and Chet quick stepped to the seat next to his wife and daughter.

The cruise ended with Sheila exclaiming how much she enjoyed it and that, "the sunset was by far the most breath-taking I've ever, ever, ever seen."

Chet promised to do it again and Suzy whispered to her mother, loud enough for everyone to hear, "Next time maybe we can bring Ricky."

28

Mac poured two glasses of milk. "What are the odds Richey?" A gallon ice cream bucket sat between them on the old butcher block table.

Richey raised his eyebrow and one shoulder up and down.

Mac slid one glass to Richey. "Of all the places they could have gone. Out of all the charter services they could have picked—they picked ours. What are the odds?"

Richey pulled the lid off the ice cream bucket and grabbed two peanut butter cookies. He gave one to Mac.

Mac pointed the cookie at Richey. "Your son's girlfriend—" Mac's smile filled the room—"maybe your future daughter-in-law, that will make you a grandpa, just took a cruise on our boat."

Richey shook his head as he dunked the cookie up and down in his milk.

Mac dunked the cookie in his milk one time and ate half of it. "All she could talk about was Ricky this and Ricky that, and how he would looooove to be with them—that's the way she said it—loooooove." Mac's excitement could be felt through the whole kitchen.

Richey lifted his hands and opened his mouth, but nothing came out. He let his hands drop back to the table and his gaze fell on his wounded hand. He clinched his jaw and squeezed back the tears.

The oak ship wheel clock made the only sound.

Mac rested his forearms on the table. "Do you remember the widow, Mrs. Turner back home, in Tavernier?"

Richey lifted his eyes but not his head, "Sure, why?"

Mac narrowed his eyes. "But do you remember the old ramshackle place she lived in?"

"Yeah, after her husband, Joe, died, she just couldn't keep the place up."

Mac crossed his arms. "What kind of woman was she?"

"Well, from what I knew of her she was a God fearing woman—good Christian woman." Richey's eyes questioned what this had to do with anything.

"Well what about John Hinches, remember him?"

"Yes dad, I remember him...why?"

"But—" Mac pointed a finger straight in the air—"did you ever see the old beater he drove?"

"As a matter of fact, I rode in it once when I ran out of gas. He was kind enough to pick me up. He's a good man. What are you getting at?"

"One more question. Do you remember the missionaries that visited church a few months ago?"

Richey nodded.

"What was your first impression?"

"Um...I don't know...thought they were weird. I mean, come on...grown men wearing skirts."

"They're called kilts. What was your final impression of them?"

"Well, once I got past the skirt, and heard what they had to say—and all they'd done—I thought they were brave warriors for Christ, really. They put it all on the line. I don't think I could do it. I know I couldn't wear no skirt. But you're trying to make a point...I think, so what is it?"

Mac rapid fired the questions at Ricky. "How could Mrs. Turner be a God fearin' woman if she lives in an old shack? How could John Hinches be a good man drivin' an old beat up truck like that? And how could those missionaries possibly be warriors for Christ dressed like that?"

Richey's mouth hung open as he shook his head from side to side. "What on earth are you talking about?"

"What am I talking about? Well, I'll tell you what I'm talking about—you."

Mac's voice was louder than he wanted it to be, but he couldn't help himself. He pointed a firm finger at his son.

"You, Mr. Richard MacArthur Johnson Junior...you are a spirit. You have a soul and you live in a body. Your body isn't who you are—it's where you live. Shack or palace it doesn't matter, it's just where you live.

"Your body is the vehicle that carries you from place to place in this world—Rolls Royce or old beat up pickup truck it doesn't matter—it's not you, it's just your vehicle.

"Your body is your earth suit while you visit this planet—faded blue jeans or kilt, it doesn't matter—it's not you, it's just what you wear.

"So what, if your house or your car or your clothes are a mess—you're not. You are beautiful and precious in His sight...and mine. Any anyone with eyes can see that. So quit rejecting the gift God keeps shoving in your face."

Mac snatched another cookie and leaned back. "There...that's what I had to say."

Ricky said the words real slow. "I am a spirit, I have a soul, and I live in a body. That's good. Did you think that up?"

"Of course." Mac looked serious, for about two, maybe three seconds, until his mouth wouldn't cooperate and lifted into a smile, followed by a single laugh. "I don't remember, I heard it from Billy Graham...or some preacher."

"Well, it sounds right. Thanks. What's his number?"

Mac produced the same old wrinkled napkin he'd scribbled the number on months earlier, he was holding it in his hand, because he knew his son...he knew he'd ask for it.

Ricky was riding his bike delivering papers when the phone rang. Rebecca and Sally had gone to the grocery store and Martin was at a doctor's appointment.

The answering machine picked up, "You've reached the Paulsens, Martin, Rebecca, Sally and Ricky, please leave a message." The recording was a team effort. At first it sounded like the whole family said, "You've reached the Paulsens." And then, one by one each person said their own name—ending with Ricky. In unison they all said, "Please leave a message." There was laughter in their voices the whole way through.

When the beep sounded alerting Richey that it was his turn to speak, his mouth went dry and his brain went numb. His mouth opened but no words would come. He looked at his dad.

Richey and Mac had faced enemy fire in their day and stood up to it with medal winning honor, but this—this wasn't something they'd been trained for.

Mac shrugged his shoulders, "Say something," he whispered. Richey held the phone out to his dad. Mac reached for it, and then pulled back shaking his head, "You've got to do it."

"Um...this is, ahhh, my name is...I'm Ri—" Richey ran his fingers through his hair trying to pull some brain cells awake. "My name is Richey, I mean Richard, or Richey, it doesn't matter, um and my number is..." Richey rattled off the number. "Oh, and my last name is Johnson. I'll try again...later maybe...or you can call me maybe, if you um...you want to, please. Thanks. Bye."

Richey pushed the red button to end the call. His head dropped to the table with a thud. "I sounded like an idiot, didn't I?"

Mac stood and went to Richey. "No son, not at...well, yes...yes you did—" Mac laughed right out loud as he hugged his son and kissed him on the top of the head. "I'm so proud of you."

"Proud of me? For making a fool of myself?"

"For facing the biggest fear of your life and headin' into the wind...when it'd be easier to cut and run." Mac rubbed his son's shoulders. "Relax man you're tighter than a sail in a gale."

Mac's hands rested on Richey's strong shoulders and he bowed his head. "Father, I reckon You know better than anyone, what it's like to long for a Son. Well, this here's my boy, and You know I love him more than anything else on this earth. He's just faced his biggest fear. He did it because he knew it was the right thing to do. He didn't think about it—he just did it, and I'm proud of him. He did it because he knew You'd want him to. So now, Lord, the seeds have been planted. We leave the next move up to You. Thanks for giving my precious, brave, handsome son all the courage and peace he needs to follow through with whatever you have in store. In Jesus...Your precious Son's name we pray, Amen."

When Mac lifted his hands off his son's shoulders Richey said it felt like a million pounds had been lifted. A calm assurance filled the room, and they knew whatever lay ahead—God would be there, and that was enough.

"Thanks dad. What will I say when they, if they, call back?"

"That's a good question, I've been praying about that." Mac looked toward the ceiling.

Richey smiled. "That's no surprise...what do you think?"

Mac smiled as he rubbed his bearded chin. "Well, you can't tell Ricky without explaining everything to his parents first."

"That's another question...the answering machine didn't say Jenny it said, Rebecca." Richey shook his head. "Maybe we're all messed up here...a coincidence fluffing our sails, with nothing behind it."

Mac said, "What're you saying?"

"What if we're wrong?" Richey asked. "Maybe we should wait until we see some evidence in black and white. Like adoption papers or, I don't know...something."

Mac sat across from Richey and looked out the window. A tree limb danced in the wind.

"For many years and thousands of miles I've ridden the wind. I've never seen it—not even once. But, I've felt its kindness, warm and gentle, and I've endured its fury, cold and hard. I don't have to see the wind to know it's real." Mac looked deep into Richey's soul. "I don't have to see evidence in black and white to know this blue eyed boy with a heart for the sea, is my grandson...your son."

"Aye," Richey lifted a crooked smile and a cookie. "My son."

Mac lifted a cookie too, "Your son."

"I just wish there was a way we could meet, without him knowing. To see if he could handle—" Richey pointed a three fingered hand at his face—"to make sure I didn't scare him." He let his hand drop back to the table, next to a stack of mail. It was mostly junk mail, but one color brochure pictured a thirty-two foot yacht and read, Win A Northern Lights Sunset Cruise.

Richey smiled.

29

Rebecca held groceries in one hand and fumbled with the house keys in the other. She managed to unlock the door and bump it open with her hip.

Her daughter, Sally, was right behind, carrying a bag filled with bread and chips. "Mom, can we have pizza and chips for supper?"

Rebecca pushed the blinking light on the answering machine as she walked by, "Sounds good to me, and we can eat out back on the picnic table—how's that?"

She set the plastic grocery bags on the kitchen table as some man named Richey or Richard or it doesn't matter rattled on.

"Oh, and my last name is Johnson. I'll try again...later maybe...or you can call me maybe, if you um...you want to, please."

Beck scrunched her pretty nose and made a silly face toward her daughter."What a strange message."

Inside her stomach tied itself into a knot. Johnson? Richey or Richard Johnson...wasn't Johnson Ricky's last name?

Rebecca hit the save button so she could listen to the message again, when the kids weren't around. And then she'd take the time to write the number down...and maybe even call it back—probably not. Maybe call the social worker, what was her name? Mary...no...I'll think of it later.

Ricky pushed through the back door, sweaty from running his paper route. He struggled with four plastic grocery bags dangling from one hand. "I like these plastic bags better than the paper ones—you can carry a lot more stuff."

Rebecca smiled at her son.

Ricky's other hand held a rolled up newspaper, inside a plastic sleeve. He flipped it to his mom. "Extra-extra read all about it!" He smiled and headed straight to the fridge, after plopping the bags down on the kitchen table. "I'm so thirsty I could drink the whole ocean."

Sally couldn't help saying, "Well, that would be dumb, because you'd still be thirsty."

Ricky took a swig straight out of the milk carton and put it back. A milk-moustache covered his lip. "Huh? How could I still be thirsty if I drank the whole ocean?"

Sally loved playing school, and she was always the teacher. "For one, you couldn't drink the entire ocean—it's too humongous. For two, the water is salty and salt makes you thirsty. So, for four, even if you could drink the whole ocean—it wouldn't do you any good."

Ricky just smiled with his blue eyes for a long moment, then closed the fridge and wiped his arm across his mouth real slow and said, "Sis, when are you going to learn how to count?"

Rebecca let out a single laugh. Sally shot her mother a look.

And then one at a time Ricky flipped out a finger, "For one, for two, for four—"

"And for five—" Rebecca tried to use a scolding voice but the smile in her green eyes softened the tone—"you're not suppose to drink out of the carton."

Ricky looked at both of them and tried not to smile. "You mean...for three."

Sally and her mother huffed at the exact same time, "Boys."

Rebecca set the paper Ricky had tossed her on the counter, "Thanks for helping with the groceries you're such a strong young man."

Ricky stood a little taller and his chest grew an inch or two. "Dad says a man helps when he can."

"And he's right. So, young man, help your sister unload the rest of the groceries while I run upstairs for a minute, I'll be right back to help."

Ricky started to object but then said, "Okay, if we can have pizza tonight."

Rebecca threw a knowing look at her daughter letting her know to keep quiet, and then looked at Ricky as if considering his request. "You drive a hard bargain...but alright, you win. Help Sis, I'll be right back."

Beck took two steps at a time and quick stepped to her bedroom closet where she pulled out a manila folder labeled, Ricky.

She leafed through the twenty or so loose papers. There it is...Marilyn Harper. That's her name. She pulled her cell phone out of the front pocket of her faded jeans and punched in the social worker's name and phone number and saved it to her contacts list. For a moment she let her mind go back to that day in Marilyn's office. She remembered the social worker shaking her head as if something was wrong, but then, said it was probably nothing. That always bothered Rebecca. I'll call her first thing in the morning—after the kids are outside.

~

"Pizza's ready, come and get it!" Rebecca set a large deluxe and a medium cheese pizza on the picnic table.

Martin, Ricky and Sally dropped their croquet mallets where they stood and trotted toward the fabulous healthy feast of pizza, corn tortilla chips and sweet tea.

Ricky grabbed two slices of deluxe and covered them with chips and smashed the chips into the pizza. His dad, Martin, did the same. Rebecca and Sally slid one slice of cheese pizza on their paper plate.

After everyone was seated around the table, without saying a word, they held hands and bowed their heads. They always took turns saying the prayer, this time it was Beck's turn.

"Lord, thanks for this time we have together and for making us a family—" her voice cracked a little—"that nothing can tear apart, amen."

Ricky had a mouth full of pizza as soon as his mom said amen. But Sally and Martin didn't move.

Martin cocked his head and raised an eyebrow.

Sally voiced what he was thinking. "Mom, you forgot to pray for the food."

"Oops sorry, Lord, thank you for this meal, we pray You'll perform a huge miracle and make it healthy. Amen." She lifted her piece of pizza. "Better?"

Ricky finished his first piece and started on his second when he blurted out while still chewing, "Sure wish we had some grandparents."

"Where'd that come from?" Martin asked.

Both sets of grandparents were gone. Martin's mother and father were missionaries and both had died in a plane crash when flying into Haiti while Martin was in college. Rebecca's father had passed away on Rebecca's twentieth birthday from a heart attack and her mother had lived with them until she passed away three years later— while Rebecca was pregnant with Sally. The doctor said it was pneumonia...Rebecca said it was a broken heart, from missing dad.

Ricky shrugged, took another bite of pizza and swallowed the rest of his glass of sweet tea. Then he looked over where they'd been playing croquet. "I don't know. Sitting out here reminds me of a show. They sat around the table like us and prayed like us and played croquet like us. Only they had a grey haired grandpa and grandma always there. And at night, when they were all in bed, they'd show the outside of the house and you could hear them taking turns saying goodnight to each other. Like this—" Ricky lifted his voice—"goodnight Sally, goodnight Mama and Daddy, goodnight John-Boy, goodnight grandma, goodnight grandpa...I liked it. I think it was called The Walnut Family."

"You mean Walton's. It was called Walton's not Walnuts...you nut." Sally had to correct.

"Oh yeah," Ricky nodded and raised his glass indicating he wanted some more ice tea, Martin was sitting next to the gallon jug and filled Ricky's glass. "Now that, was a family."

"So, what's wrong with our family?" Rebecca didn't mean to sound hurt, hoped she didn't.

"Nothing, this family is great." Ricky looked at his dad's plate. "Aren't you gonna eat that?"

Martin shook his head. "You can have it—I'm not too hungry."

Ricky, the bottomless pit, grabbed his dad's pizza and took a bite before saying, "I just thought some old folks would be fun to have, that's all."

"Maybe Sally should pray God will bring this family some grandparents." Martin said it with a smile, but after he said it, the words hung in the air. And one by one each person sitting around the Paulsen picnic table nodded their head.

Sally nodded real big and smiled at Ricky. "Yeah, I prayed for you."

That night after everyone had crawled into bed and all went silent, Rebecca replayed the day in her mind—like she always did. And just as she remembered the strange phone message, the silence broke.

"Goodnight Sally." Ricky's voice filled with humor rang out. One by one they took turns telling each other goodnight until finally Ricky said..."Goodnight Grandpa and Grandma."

After that the house fell still as everyone drifted to sleep with smiles on their faces and in their hearts.

~

The next morning before Rebecca had finished cleaning the dishes from breakfast the phone rang.

Martin had already left for work and Sally and Ricky had gone for a bike ride to the park.

"Hello Paulsen's."

"Hello Mrs. Paulsen, this is Richey Johnson."

Rebecca's knees felt weak, she dropped to the chair next to the phone. "Yes, I believe you left a message yesterday, but...you didn't explain the reason for your call. You sounded a bit...um—"

"I know, I'm sorry about that, I sounded like a bumbling idiot. But, hopefully I won't repeat that today. I hope I didn't alarm you."

Alarm me? Yes as a matter of fact you did. "No. Of course not. Are you new at this?"

"Yes ma'am you could say that...I'm bran spanking new at this. Um, anyway, I'm calling to let you know that you and your family have won a free all expense paid sunset cruise with, Maggie's Charter Service."

"Maggie's Charter Service?" Rebecca shook her head. "I've never heard of you. We're not interested in buying anything like a timeshare, or any of that kind of stuff. Thank you." She started to hang up, but added, "Where are you located?"

"We're in Duluth, Minnesota ma'am."

Duluth...Ricky was in Duluth at the youth rally. Ricky said Suzy and her family just got back from some kind of boating thing in Duluth. Maybe they signed us up for some drawing or something. "Well, um, I'm sorry what did you say your name was?"

"Richey, well actually, Richard MacArthur Johnson, ma'am. Oh, wait. You mean our company. It's called Maggie's Charter Service—named after my mother."

Richard MacArthur Johnson—coincidence? Rebecca swallowed. He sounded so polite, not at all like he was trying to sell anything. "So what's the catch? What are you trying to sell?"

"Nothing ma'am this is a free trip—we don't sell anything—no catch. The only expense would be fuel from your house to Duluth...but, we can help you with that too."

"Can you send some information my husband and I can review, and then get back to you?"

"Yes ma'am that's a great idea, I'll send you a packet today. Where should I mail it?"

Rebecca spilled the address, and then looked at the ceiling and shook her head. I can't believe it. I just gave our address to a perfect stranger.

"And, Mrs. Paulsen, ma'am, just to set your mind at ease, I can give you the name and number of someone near you, who recently sailed our sunset cruise. They gave us permission to give their name and phone number as a reference."

"Sailed? Did you say sailed—as in sailboat, with wind and sails? I was thinking big floating restaurant, motor, boat, ship, type thing."

"Yes ma'am, wind and sails—the only way to float." Richey's smile could be heard over the phone.

"Oh, I see..." Rebecca leaned back in the chair and felt her shoulders relax. "My son Ricky's a sailboat nut, and I have no idea why. As far as I know, he's never even been on one."

Richey said it soft, "As far as you know?"

"We adopted Ricky when he was around seven."

"Oh, that explains it." Ricky said.

Rebecca made a small laugh. "He even wears this necklace with a sailboat pendant. He's had it ever since we brought him home and he won't take it off. So maybe sailboats are in his past or something...we just don't know."

"Yep, sailing's in his blood that's for sure...or, I mean, at least that's what it sounds like to me. Don't you know anything about his parents?"

"All we were told was that his parents were killed in a car accident. He bounced from shelter to foster home, until we were blessed enough to meet him." Rebecca stood up. "I'm sorry, I'm sure you don't want to hear all this—"

"Yes I do" Richey's words came out fast, too fast. An awkward silence followed until he said, "I'm glad to hear Ricky's found a family that loves him, as much as you obviously do."

"Oh we love that little boy with all our hearts...I suppose I shouldn't say little anymore, he's growing like a weed and already has a girlfriend. I can't imagine him not being a part of our family. Do you have any children Mr. Johnson?"

The phone was silent for a moment. "Sailing's in my blood." Richey said. "As far back as I know my granddaddies were sailors. I can't imagine doing anything else."

Rebecca considered his comment for a moment and nodded into the phone. "I used to sail. When I was in high school we lived on Lake Washington and owned a little Sunfish—nothing big like you're talking about. But it was fun."

"The wind is no respecter of sails." Richey said.

"What's that mean?"

"That's what I asked the first time I heard my grandpa say it. The beauty of sailing isn't influenced by the size of the ship."

"Yeah, that's true. After all the big motor boats went in for the night, I'd go out in our little boat. I'd listen to the wind slipping through the sail, the water sliding past. I can still hear it, still feel the breeze on my skin, see the sunset over the water—I see how it could get in your blood."

"Sounds like you may have sailing in your blood, too."

Rebecca let out a small laugh, "Maybe you're right Mr. Johnson. Anyway, if you'll send us the information, I promise we'll look it over and get back to you, okay?"

"Yes ma'am—and you don't have to call me Mr. Johnson—Richey is fine."

"Well Richey, I'll do my best, if you stop calling me, ma'am—Rebecca will do just fine."

"Thank you, ma'am—Rebecca. I'll send our information right away, today."

"Sounds great—this must be your way of advertising, right? You give away a free cruise, and if it works out you gain a relationship for life...am I right?"

"I couldn't have said it better myself."

They said goodbye and Rebecca set the phone on its cradle and stared at it for a long moment.

Lots of people are named Richard and even more are named Johnson. Richard MacArthur Johnson is probably a common name, too. But the same name and same love for sailboats...Rebecca's eyes drifted toward the ceiling, "God what's going on?"

~

Richey flipped his phone closed and let his head drop slowly until his forehead rested on the kitchen table. Jenny died in a car accident...I have a son. Richey laced his fingers behind his head. I need help, God. Now what?

30

Sunday morning Mac and Richey sailed *Maggie* to the Bayside Church. It was the only church along the Duluth shore line that had boat access—not a good reason for picking a church.

The pastor wasn't a good preacher, either. He stuttered. But it was a good church because the pastor loved God and lived it, and most importantly, he was a man of prayer.

"I'd rather listen to a stuttering preacher that knew how to pray than an eloquent one that didn't." Mac had said. "He may not be a good preacher, but he's a great pastor."

When that man prayed, there was no stutter, and even God paid attention. And he read the Bible like he prayed—no stutter. Mac figured he should've been named Moses.

When the service consisted of singing, Bible reading and prayer it was beautiful...when the pastor tried to preach—it was painful.

The singing was over. Pastor Olson had made his way to the front and finished his opening prayer. "N-nice t-t-to see y-you th-th-this m-m-morning, p-please o-o-open..."

Mac and Richey sat near the back of the church. They had their Bibles opened to where Pastor was reading, but neither one of them were paying attention. They were thinking of all the time that had gone by since Richey had talked to Mrs. Paulsen.

Seventeen days.

Richey had talked to her on a Thursday and mailed the information packet, they made up special just for them, on Friday. If mail delivery takes three or four days—maybe not counting the weekend—they should have received it by Wednesday or Thursday the following week. By now they'd have had the information for about ten days. If they were interested at all, they should've called back by now.

Richey had prayed every morning that would be the day they'd call. And each night when the call didn't come in he'd pray they'd get a call the next day. Until last night, he was frustrated and said, "God, I've prayed. I've obeyed. Nothing's happening. Why don't You hear me?"

Pastor was continuing his reading of Psalm 68..."Father to the fatherless, defender of widows—this is God, whose dwelling is holy. God places the lonely in families; he sets the prisoners free and gives them joy..."

Mac and Richey popped their heads up at the same time and then back down to find the place where he'd just read something about, *Father to the fatherless and lonely in families.* Richey elbowed his dad and pointed to verse five and six. "Father to the fatherless..." and verse six "God places the lonely in families."

He had their attention.

After the Scripture reading Pastor Olsen would pray again and invite anyone who wanted prayer to make their way to the front. For those who couldn't or didn't want to go forward they could simply stay where they were seated and a prayer counselor would find them. They also opened up private prayer rooms for those who had personal prayer needs. It was a praying church. Not much preaching—but a whole lot of praying.

Mac and Richey made their way to the front of the church and waited. They both had their Bible by their side and each had a finger stuck in Psalm 68.

Pastor Olsen was kneeling next to little Joey Walter, he was saying something about his best friend George, being sick. "I'll be lonely if he gets dead, 'cuz he's my bestest friend—" he twisted the toe of his tennis shoe into the carpet—"my only friend." The little boy sniffed, wiped his nose with his sleeve and made a quick nervous look around the room. He cupped his hands and whispered toward the pastor's ear—loud enough for ten people to hear. "If he gets dead he won't go to heaven, 'cuz he was naughty."

Pastor Olsen gave a questioning look.

The little boys eyes got real big and he said in another loud whisper. "He jumped on the table and ate grandma's birthday cake. Nobody saw him 'cuz we were praying. We had our eyes squeezed shut like this." He squeezed his eyes closed. "That's why God made him bad sick...but he's really really sorry. I know 'cuz his face was sad, and he didn't wag his tail no more when mom made me tie him up in the back yard." Joey wiped wet cheeks with his palms, gave Pastor Olsen a quick hug and asked, "Can you tell God he'll be good, and to make George not sick no more? Please. I asked...but He must not have heard me 'cuz nothing happened."

Pastor hugged the little boy for a long moment and then started to pray. "Father, You know every sparrow that falls. You don't make them fall—but care enough to know when they do...how much more You must care for puppies...and best friends. Joey thinks You made George bad sick for being naughty. He prayed for him to be all better, but nothing happened, so now he thinks You don't hear him. Lord, Joey needs to know You...as his best friend."

The wise pastor opened his eyes and let them drift toward Mac and Richey.

"And that You always hear...even when nothing happens." Pastor Olsen leaned back and looked Joey in the eye. He placed a hand on each of the young man's shoulders and smiled. "And thank you Lord, for making George all better, amen."

Richey turned to leave. That's all I needed—God hears even if nothing happens. God's got this. But, before he took two steps Mac grabbed his arm, and when he turned around Pastor Olsen was standing in front of them.

They wanted him to pray that God would make the Paulsens call to set up a cruise—so they could see Ricky. Simple. They explained the phone call, the waiting, the anxiety...but they knew that wasn't what he wanted to hear.

Pastor Olsen always prayed that the Word being read during the sermon, would do the preaching for him—since he obviously wasn't gifted in that area. So, when someone wanted prayer, rather than spend time talking, and stuttering, about the details—he wanted to know what part of the scripture reading during the service, "j-j jumped out a-a-and t-t-tugged at y-your h-h heart"

"Verses five and six" Richey and Mac said it at the exact same time.

The pastor chuckled, and then read Psalm 68: 5-6.

A father of the fatherless, a defender of widows, Is God in His holy habitation. God sets the lonely in families...

Without looking he flipped to Psalm 34:18 and quoted.

The Lord is near the brokenhearted...

He closed his eyes and his Bible at the same time. He tucked his Bible under one arm and grabbed Richey's right hand and Mac's left. He didn't notice Richey's wounds—because love doesn't see, or feel, scars.

"Lord our God, thank You for Your Word that is forever settled in heaven. And Your Word tells us You are a Father to the fatherless, defender of widows, You dwell in holiness and yet see the lonely and place them in families. Mac and Richey have received Your Word and long for a dream—the one You've given. The dream and calling within all mankind to be fruitful and multiply—to be part of a family. Thank You for casting every demonic hindrance into the deepest depths of the ocean, and for angels to assist in the completion of Your high calling."

He went silent for a long moment. And then for a few seconds each, he placed his hands over Mac's ears and then over Richey's. "Thank You Lord for filling these ears with the sounds of babies. With thankful hearts, we rest in You. In Jesus precious name we pray, amen."

"O-okay g-gentlemen—" Pastor smiled—"m-m my w-wife a-and I w-will s-s start l-looking f-f for b-b baby c-clothes."

"Babies?" Richey raised his hands. "Whoa Pastor, I don't have a wife...I don't even have a girlfriend." He looked at his dad. "And he's not Abraham—he's too old."

Mac nodded. "We'd settle for a relationship with Richey's boy—" Mac smiled real big—"my grandson."

Pastor Olsen shook his head and without a stutter said, "No...I hear babies." He looked at Richey. "Calling you Daddy." He looked a Mac. "And calling you Papa." His eyes got real big when he noticed he didn't stutter and he looked straight up, through the church ceiling and into heaven. When he looked back down, he was smiling, his eyes were glistening and when he blinked happy tears spilled.

Richey dropped to the front pew. "W-w what do we do n-now?" Richey stuttered, he wasn't mocking the Pastor he just couldn't get the words out right.

Pastor Olsen clapped his hands one time and pointed at Richey. "N-now y-you know h-h how I f-f feel." And then he looked serious at Mac. "You must preprayer."

Mac repeated to be sure he heard right. "Preprayer?"

Richey said, "Prepare. How?"

"No. Pre-prayer. Y-y you c-c can't p-p prepare until y-you preprayer...pray gentlemen, pray."

Pastor Olsen hugged both men, gathered his notes off the pulpit, and was gone.

~

A few weeks later the scripture reading was out of Exodus 29. It had to do with a special gathering place called the Tabernacle. God made the place holy and met and spoke and dwelt with His people there. Eight times in that one chapter the word Tabernacle appeared. It jumped off the page and floated in front of Mac and Richey.

The next day, Richey stood in front of a red door with a chisel and a can of paint.

He placed the chisel against the door. "I feel like Moses, about to carve out the Ten Commandments."

Mac said, "I noticed you were picking up a stutter. Let me know if you need anything Moses, I'll go call the Pastor."

Five hours later Richey was done. Just in time, too, because Pastor Olsen was supposed to be there around 3:00.

Mac had asked the pastor and his wife to stop by the bar for an important prayer matter. And since Pastor would swim the lake of fire to be able to pray—they knew he'd show up.

At first the pastor wasn't in favor of Mac and Richey owning a tavern, but after praying about it, he felt at peace—which he didn't even pretend to understand. He just shrugged his shoulders and stuttered, "God's b-b bigger than m-m my r-religious b-box."

The atmosphere of the bar had changed without anyone really trying to make it happen. Little by little they'd gotten to know all the regulars and the place was more like a gathering for a family of lost and lonely rough necks.

Mac built a wooden box with a slit cut in the top like a mailbox. He burned the words, Preprayer Box, into the wood. He figured God would forgive him for stealing the Pastor's word since it was for a Good cause.

On each table and scattered on the bar were miniature versions of the Preprayer Box. Only the small boxes held paper and pens for folks to write out a prayer request and stick it in the big Preprayer Box on their way out.

Mac and Richey couldn't believe how many people used it. It became a full time job just praying for all the prayer requests.

That wasn't the only change, either. They built a small stage along one wall, and hooked it up with lights and a sound system. A couple nights a week some singers from church would play and sing. Occasionally, Richey would stand behind the microphone and read a scripture and share whatever was on his heart. The old-timers started calling him, Preacher.

At five minutes to three, Pastor Olsen and his wife, Rachel pulled up beside the curb, next to the door where Richey had been working.

"They're here" Richey hollered inside the door.

Mac walked out and stood next to Richey in front of the door.

"Hi Mac, Hi Richey," Rachel did most of the talking when she was with her husband. They walked arm in arm wearing identical smiles.

Mac and Richey stood shoulder to shoulder in front of the red door—wearing smiles of their own.

"S-so h-how c-c can w-w we p-pray f-for y-y you?" Pastor Olsen managed.

Mac shook his head, "Not us—" he pointed over his shoulder toward the building behind him—"this place."

Rachel looked down, her husband raised his eyebrows.

"I know you have a hard time with a Christian owning a bar, don't worry, we're not going to ask for you to pray for business to increase."

The Pastor and his wife smiled.

"But, remember when you read about the Tabernacle? And how they prayed and God's glory filled the place? Well we want to pray for that here. We think God wants to do something here, and He gave this place a new name."

They parted like the red sea and displayed what Richey had been working on all day. What once read, *The Tavern,* now read, *The Tavernacle.*

Pastor Olsen lifted his hands to the sky. "Oh Most Holy God, Creator of heaven and earth, we give you praise. Sanctify this Tavernacle of meeting to bring You glory." Pastor dropped his arms and looked from Mac to Richey and then pointed at the door. "From, The Tavernacle, sons and daughters will be sent to the world."

And at that moment the sun broke through a cloudy sky and shined so bright it made their eyes water...and scattered every demon within fourteen square miles.

31

In the place where demons and angels exist, there is no time. Calendars and clocks mean nothing. dribgnos wasn't worried. Sure, time had passed but Ricky hadn't moved toward any eternal breakthroughs. Yes, it was unfortunate that he met Mac and that ditzy girl named Suzy, but they're no threat. Mac spends all his time on a boat or in a bar—how much harm could he do? And Suzy's dad's a hot tempered hockey coach. So what if Suzy's mom prays, she's just a mom—what harm could she do?

Ricky's becoming just like everyone else on the planet, sheep walking toward the slaughter, following their stomach. Ricky wants a girlfriend—let him have her, that'll keep his mind off God, and on his cute little Suzy-Q.

Besides, the last order given by lucifer was "back off the kid—he's praying too much." lucifer would prance and bark "If trials drive them to their knees, then back off and give them ease."

Of course, what else could they do? Prayer does to a demon what light does to dark—makes it flee. But, dribgnos saw the report and smiled. Ricky's beloved daddy had a strain in his DNA that would send them all spiraling into the pit of depression. Then, the whole family would curse God and die. All is well, dribgnos told himself. All he had to do was wait and watch. And soon, at the opportune time, he'd have his victory.

~

"Come on, Mom, hurry! You've got to see her—she's beautiful!"

Rebecca pulled her hair into a pony tail and slid it through the back of the baseball cap. "Okay Ricky let's see what you've got." Ricky pulled her into a jog out the back door and to the back of the garage where Martin was unhooking an ugly trailer holding an uglier boat.

Beautiful? It's growing stuff. "Oh Ricky...how nice," Beck smiled.

"I know, right. I told you she was a beaut. Maybe I'll name her after you mom...or maybe Suzy. Don't feel bad, I'll get another one just as nice, and name her after you, okay?"

Beck raised her eyebrows and swallowed. "Yeah...okay. So um, what's next, is she ready to sail?" Does the thing even float?

"Well, not exactly. But that's why I got such a good deal. I mean two-hundred bucks for a boat like this, and the trailer—what a steal, huh? Only a month's earnings."

"What do you have to do?" I hope he doesn't ask me to get in that thing.

"Well for starters I'll read all I can about a Newport 16—that's what she is you know. The keel winch cable is broke, the hull may need some fiberglass work. There's a main sail and a jib—they both need a little patching. And I'll let everybody pitch in to help scrub her up to shipshape—it'll be a blast, right?"

"We can help? Thanks..." Rebecca's voice was small. She tried to catch Ricky's enthusiasm, but scrubbing mold off fiberglass just didn't do it for her. She turned around and noticed Martin sitting on a chunk of firewood.

"Are you alright honey?" Rebecca knelt down next to him and looked into his eyes.

He let out a little cough and shook his head. "Those antibiotics are gone and I don't think it's any better."

The doctor had said the cough and weariness was from pneumonia and he prescribed seven days worth of antibiotics.

"I'm calling the doctor, come on let's get you inside to rest." Rebecca helped Martin up and gave Ricky a sad look, "Later okay honey...promise."

"Sure mom—" Ricky hustled over—"let me help." Ricky walked on one side of his dad, and Rebecca was on the other. "Dad, how come you didn't tell me you were sick? We didn't have to go."

Martin's words were slow...paced between labored breaths. "I was feeling fine earlier son...I'm just a little tired. Besides—" he let out a little cough—"we couldn't let a great deal like that get away, now could we?"

~

The next day Martin was admitted, into the Blue Earth County Hospital. After a few days and numerous tests they found a growth on his lung.

Beck listened to the beeping heart monitor and watched seconds tick off the clock and thought about time. Where'd all the time go? It seemed like only yesterday she was in that very same hospital giving birth to her daughter, Sally—and now, Sally was almost old enough to drive a car. Ricky was a teenager. How could I be the mother of two teenagers? She looked at Martin, he was sleeping—that was good, it meant he was getting better, right? Life goes by so fast—too fast.

Martin opened his eyes, "Beck." He smiled with his eyes. "I had a dream. It was...different."

Beck rested her hand on her husband's arm, "Tell me about it."

Martin nodded and glanced toward the glass of water on the hospital tray perched over his bed.

Beck stood and helped him take a drink by propping the pillows behind his head and pouring fresh water and ice into the glass.

Martin eased back and stared at the ceiling. "I could see hands shaping a lump of clay. It was like I was looking through the eyes of the one shaping the clay—but the hands weren't mine. I knew the hands were His." Martin looked at Beck and pointed toward the ceiling.

Beck raised her eyes to the ceiling and back to her husband and nodded understanding.

"A giant puzzle lay in front of the hands—it stretched out as far as I could see. It was out of focus—except when I looked to the far end. I knew, somehow, the first two pieces placed were, Adam and Eve." He looked at his wife and smiled nodding his head as if to say: really, I know—crazy, huh?

Beck's mouth dropped open.

"The hands kept pulling pieces of clay from the lump and setting them in place in the puzzle. Each piece of clay fit perfectly into the puzzle and each time the puzzle became a little clearer. Pretty soon, I could make out the faces of a few people in the puzzle, like my dad and mom. They had a few Haitian's around them. And behind them were grandpa and grandma..."

Beck's eyes lit and she sat on the edge of her chair. "All the people who've passed away are pieces to the puzzle, right?"

Martin nodded once real slow...and then narrowed his lips and shook his head from side to side. "Not everyone. I didn't see Uncle Charley, but Aunt Beth was there."

"You mean..." Beck narrowed her eyes. "You mean, only the ones who knew the Lord? That's the only ones you recognized in the puzzle?"

"Right," Martin nodded. "Maybe it was a puzzle version of The Book of Life. But...not everyone was dead. The people who had passed away were black and white. But others I couldn't recognize were in color—living color. And after being set into place, some got up and walked away. When that happened, the hands would sweep down and tenderly pick them up, and put them back into the lump and start reshaping them again."

"Wow..." Beck whispered.

"All of a sudden, I knew stuff." Martin lifted his shoulders up and down. "Like...I knew the hands were God's and He was The Potter we were the clay. Just like he formed Adam out of the dirt, He was shaping all of mankind piece by piece—person by person and setting them right where they'd be a perfect fit. But, they had a choice to stay where God put them, or get up and walk away. And if they walked away, He didn't give up. He'd pick them up and keep trying to work them back in. But, once the puzzle was complete, whoever had chosen to walk away...not good."

Beck scooted her chair close to the bed and put both hands on Martin's arm.

~

Martin took a sip of water, and leaned back on the pillow. He closed his eyes and didn't move, or hardly breathe for a full minute.

He didn't want to continue. But he had to, or he'd never be able to tell Beck what needed to be said. He took a deep breath and replayed the last part of the dream, or vision, or whatever it was. The part where one of the black and white pieces came into focus—it was him. Give me strength Lord.

"Martin..." Beck's voice broke. "You—" she shook her head and sucked in a deep breath—"you weren't in the puzzle, right?"

Martin opened his eyes and rolled his head toward Beck.

Her green eyes glistened—about to spill.

Their eyes locked, he clenched his jaw and nodded.

Beck jumped to her feet, bumping the tray and spilling Martin's water. "It's just a dream. It doesn't mean you're going to die—at least not anytime soon...right?"

Martin pulled in a slow deep breath and waited for his wife to sit back down. He stretched out a hand toward her and she held it with both of hers. "Whether a day or a hundred years—life is short. I'm ready."

Beck started to get up again, but held her place on the edge of her seat. "You shouldn't talk like that. It's not your time. You're too young—we have kids...you have me. Don't give up, Martin—" she dropped her head—"please, I need you."

"I don't know anything for sure. But after seeing that...I've realized something."

Beck released his hand long enough to wipe her eyes.

"I've come to realize, we—all of the human race—are a part of each other. A piece of—"

Beck squeezed his hand. "A giant puzzle...I get it. But you said it yourself; you can get up if you don't like the spot where you're placed."

"I can...maybe. But it doesn't make it right. Do you remember hearing about the king who became ill, and he was told to get his house in order, because he was going to die?"

Rebecca brightened, "Yes, it was Hezekiah, it's from the Bible. He prayed and the Lord gave him fifteen more years. See, God wants to heal."

Martin's eyes drifted out the window, toward the cloudy sky. "Do you remember the rest of the story?"

Beck shook her head.

"Three years after Hezekiah was healed, his son Manasseh was born. He became one of the most wicked kings that ever reigned. He implemented human sacrifices and dealt openly with demons. He led the nation to be more vile than the heathen nations around them. If Hezekiah had died, Manasseh would have never been born."

~

Beck couldn't believe her ears. "You must be loopy on the drugs they're giving you. Are you saying God wants to kill you to prevent something worse from happening?"

"No, my precious Beck, I'm not saying that at all. I don't think there's any circumstance where I'd willingly give you or one of my children a deadly disease—and God is much more kind and more loving than I."

"So, what are you saying, then?" Beck's words were quiet, slow—but her heart was racing.

"I don't know. And that's the point. We can't see the big picture, God does. It's our job to trust Him. We may get our way—like Hezekiah—but is our way the best? Even Jesus prayed, 'Not My will, but Yours be done.' And, Beck, for some reason...I'm at peace."

"Well they haven't found anything but a growth on your lung. Surely they can cut that off or give you some stronger antibiotics or something. We'll get through this. And then you can take your peace and your vision on the road. Tell the whole world about it. But you're not going to die. Not now. Not until we're old and grey." Beck rested her head on his chest. "You can't give up—promise me Martin."

Martin ran his fingers through her hair. "I'll never give up on loving you, I promise."

On day five he was gone. The local doctors had no idea what happened. They sent his body to Rochester for an autopsy, and after several days they received a report that the growth on his lung was cancerous and had spread to the lining of his heart, which created too much fluid causing his heart to collapse.

Rebecca blamed herself. She remembered how, sometimes, an uneasy feeling would come over her, an impression that something was wrong. A few times she woke in the night, thinking Martin was gone. But, she'd reach over and he was always there. So, she just brushed it off. But now, she felt like she'd been prompted to pray—and blew it. So her husband was dead, and she was alone. Just. Like. That.

The kids didn't even get a chance to say good-bye to their father, because, until the doctors told them otherwise, they held onto the hope that he'd pull through, and be home after a few days, as good as new.

Ricky wavered between being numb, and feeling that he'd caused it—just like before. He'd say, "It's my fault. I killed him. He got sick after helping me get that stupid boat." The sailboat sat on the trailer, untouched since they'd brought it home.

Sally wouldn't leave her room, she just cried. And if anyone mentioned anything about God—she'd scream, "I hate God!"

Life inched forward one painful sad breath at a time. Seasons changed but nothing in them did. One day looked like the next. Breathe, eat, sleep, do it again. No purpose. Round and round, day after day, month after month, life was a numb, meaningless blur.

~

dribgnos danced. he'd won. "i've got him right where i want him—in an apathetic trance." Ricky was protected by that annoying angel, David. But Martin's unexpected demise made the job of thwarting God's plan for Ricky a cinch. "This is too easy. Ricky's sister hates God as much as i do. Ricky's listening to his old friend, guilt. And more importantly—he isn't listening to *The Voice*."

dribgnos remembered lucifer's words and didn't even try to trouble the Paulsens. "Once a soul turns from Him, it's on the slippery slope to hell. So don't get in the way—don't wake it." dribgnos hovered and gloated but didn't interfere. And that's why he didn't notice a change in the atmosphere around the Paulsens. he didn't see the area being saturated by something that would send all of hell into red alert.

~

Prayer in the hands of love is the most powerful force on earth

Across the street a mom and a little girl were building a fire. As if stick by stick on an altar, they laid their prayers, asking for a miracle for their friends across the street. Every morning and every night and at every meal they'd pray. Day after day, month after month—they prayed. Because love never gives up, never loses faith, is always hopeful, and love never fails.

One Saturday morning before Suzy got out of bed, she prayed—like she usually did. "Lord You are near the brokenhearted and in Your presence is fullness of joy. Thanks for being with the Paulsens." When she asked if there was anything else she could do, an old sailor popped into her head. "Captain Mac!" She jumped out of bed and ran into her mother's room. "Mom, we've got to call Captain Mac."

~

Five hours north, whenever first light splashed orange and yellow waves against Lake Superior's shore, an old man and his son bowed their heads to pray—just like they'd done every day for a year.

"Lord, one more day we give You praise. You are a Father to the fatherless, defender of widows, You dwell in holiness and set the lonely in families. Only You can restore the years. Though our eyes see nothing—we still believe. And though our ears are dull we still can hear—the laughter of children, the sound of babes and the chatter of a big, noisy, messy, happy, family, amen."

At first it was a forced prayer. Something they knew they had to do. And on the outside—as far as they could see—nothing changed. But inside, something was different. They had reached a place where they could honestly say, "Peace like a river or sorrow like sea billows...it is well, it is well, with my soul."

~

"Maggie's Charter Service," Richey answered.

"Hello, this is Sheila Smyth. My family and I chartered a sunset cruise over a year ago and..." she paused, not knowing exactly where to go next.

"Would you like to book another cruise?"

"No...that's not why I'm calling. Or wait. Yes, maybe it is. Can I book a cruise and gift it to someone else?"

"Yes ma'am you certainly can..."

After Sheila hung up she eyed her daughter, "Suzy, now we've really got some praying to do."

32

Mac lifted the dock box lid and held it open while Richey dropped in the rest of the cleaning supplies. With the lid closed Mac sat on the box.

Richey disappeared below deck and then returned with two bottles of water. He handed one to Mac and then sat down next to him—neither said a word for a full minute.

Finally, Mac whistled low and slow, "Maggie, you've never looked so good." Afternoon sun danced off the tanned and sweat soaked skin of father and son. They'd scrubbed and painted and polished *Maggie* until she shined.

"I think we're ready" Richey pulled fingers through wavy blond hair—he'd let it grow out from his customary navy cut. Now, he looked more beach-bum. His smile was bright, a little crooked. He wore a bandana around his neck and a patch over his left eye. If it weren't for the kindness that poured out of his deep blue eye, and the ever ready smile—he could look like a pretty scary pirate. But now he just looked tired—a good kind of tired.

"I'd almost given up hope. What's it been—over a year or so? I'm still having a hard time believing it. Sheila Smyth calls from out of the blue and asks if she can book a cruise for Ricky's family. And then, she asks us to pray they'll accept it. How strange. But—they're finally booked. I pray they show up."

Mac looked toward the top of the mast. "One more thing—she should be ready by now."

Richey stretched out the words, "That's right." He downed the rest of his water and laughed. "Oh...she's ready all right."

Mac narrowed his eyes as he looked at Richey, "What...you're crazy." He pushed Richey's shoulder and stood, looked at his watch, "I've got to go." He started to half walk, half jog up the pier, but then he spun around mumbling something under his breath about not having enough time to make it home so he'd use the marina shower. He hurried past Richey and below deck to find a clean shirt.

"You're talking to yourself...and I'm crazy?"

Mac paid no attention until he heard Richey's voice carry down the companionway steps. "You want to borrow my cologne?"

"No." Mac huffed, and then.... "Where is it?"

~

Beth Meyers had kept in contact with Mac over the years. She'd send e-greetings at holidays and once in a while send pictures of grandkids. Somewhere along the way she'd mentioned how she made quilts for all her grandkids.

Mac figured if she could do that, maybe she could help him with a project he'd been thinking about since just after attending her husband Scott's funeral—since the day he was given a little model sailboat, with a blue cross painted on the sail.

Mac had asked Beth if he could hire her to sew a blue cross on both sides of his main sail. He considered using paint like Ricky did on the model, but figured it would bleed and look awful.

Beth said she'd only do it if he'd allow her the honor of doing it for free. Mac negotiated that if she would come to Duluth he would pay her room and board and take her on the first cruise under the new banner. She agreed and had driven up on Wednesday with her sewing equipment.

Thursday Mac met her for breakfast and delivered the sail and material he wanted her to use for the cross. After explaining that he wanted it centered about seventeen inches down from the top corner, he said, "I have a sunset cruise scheduled for Saturday, but Friday is open, for you—can you have it ready by then?"

Mac felt guilty about the way he felt when he thought of taking Beth on a sunset cruise—just Beth. It was a feeling he hadn't felt since Maggie, he was disgusted with himself— felt like he was cheating.

Beth told Mac, "You run a tight ship, Captain, but by sunset Friday your *Maggie* will be full sails ahead."

~

Richey was in the same room when his dad made the phone call to Beth. He had watched his dad's face turn red and heard the stain in his voice when he said he'd take her on the first cruise under the new banner.

At first he was angry—how could he cheat on mom like that? But then, he figured mom would want him to move on—it'd been long enough. And then...later, he felt jealous.

How come dad gets to move on and find someone, but I never will. The only girl I ever loved is gone...and she never loved me anyway. And now, I'm too—

He couldn't finish the thought. He knew where it was headed...it'd be impossible for anyone to fall in love with him because of his scars. But after his dad talked to him about who he really was—a spirit who had a soul and lived in a body—he decided he'd never feel sorry for himself again because of his physical scars. He still had plenty of other faults he could berate himself over.

Like, why didn't he listen to his folks when they told him to take his time with Jenny, and why did he volunteer for that fatal mission? He thought about the cross...the one that would soon fly at the top of their sail.

Sailing through life alone—it's my cross to bear.

~

Mac hustled through a shower and broke the speed limit driving to the motel where Beth was staying.

As he drove around the motel to the rooms with the lakeside view, he envisioned what was about to happen. He'd knock on the door and Beth's bright eyes and big smile would greet him. She'd have the sail rolled perfectly, with the blue cross on top. She'd be wearing blue cut off shorts and a white tank top. Her hair would be pulled back and a suntanned smile would ask if he wanted a Coke. Mac shook his head hard, and the vision of Maggie standing on the pier the first day they met, vanished.

He stood in the doorway and looked at Beth perched up on the bed, her legs tucked under her. She had a colorful, scarf like thing wrapped around her head in an attempt to keep her hair pulled back. He'd seen Maggie wear something like that. She was all faded denim, from her button down shirt that had the sleeves cut out, to her cut off shorts—he had that part right.

The sail was draped across the bed and her thighs. She blew a wisp of hair from her face with a tight lip that held a few stickpins.

Mac stood just outside the door, "Hi, why's the door open?"

She wiped a forearm across her eyes and forehead and spoke through the pins perched in her lips, "AC's broke."

"Oh no, did you call the front desk?"

"Yep. They said it'd be fixed shortly." She shrugged her shoulders.

"Beth, why didn't you call, you could've done this at my place."

"It's okay."

Mac stepped into the room. "Well, how goes it?"

"I'm sorry Mac." She made a sad face. "I wanted to double hem the inside perimeter of the crosses using my electric sewing machine but the needle broke—that needle never breaks. I don't have a spare, so I went to a few shops in town—got lost once—and nobody had a replacement. I hand stitched them and it's taking longer than I thought. I'll have it done by your cruise though, don't worry, okay?"

Mac only heard about a third of what she said. He was fascinated by the way her mouth moved as she held the pins, how that one strand of stray hair bounced across her face when she talked, how little drops of perspiration sat on her neck and nose, how her arms and legs looked strong and shiny. Mac looked at the sail draped across her thighs. It looked like it was over halfway finished. "Can I help?"

She puffed the bouncy stray hair off her face and the pins fell out of her mouth.

Mac reached down to retrieve them and their hands met. For a moment no one took a breath, the clock stopped ticking and their hearts stopped beating. And then everything blurred into fast motion and they each pulled their hands away leaving the pins where they lay.

"Um..." Beth pulled in a deep breath. "What did you say?"

"I...ah...help...can I help?"

"Other than almost poking myself—" she smiled and picked up the stray pins— "I think I've got everything under control."

"How much longer? Have you eaten?" Mac noticed a bottle of water sitting on the night stand and handed it to her.

"Thanks." She took the water and a long slow drink, "Probably two, maybe three hours."

Mac figured it would be too dark by then to take *Maggie* out. "Well then, are you up for some company tomorrow, on our first sunset cruise under this exceptional looking new banner?"

Beth shook her head. "Mac, I can't do that. Remember when Scott and I took our cruise? I wouldn't have wanted some stranger onboard. But, if you offer rain checks..." She looked up and smiled.

She was right—especially for the first meeting with Ricky and family—but a man's word is his bond. "Beth, I said you could have the first cruise under the new banner."

"I know Mac, thanks. But I can wait, really I don't mind. Just glad I could help. Well...that is if I quit jabberin' and get to work."

"Okay then...you still didn't answer my question about eating—did you?"

"I'll get something when I'm finished."

"How 'bout I order something...pizza?"

"Sure."

Mac ordered pizza and Cokes.

The only problem was Beth wouldn't stop sewing long enough to eat. So, Mac held a piece for her to take a bite of every now and then, careful to hold a napkin under it, so the sauce wouldn't drop on the sail.

They laughed and talked until the last stitch was pulled through and tied. And as they said goodnight a teenage awkwardness took over.

"I really like this view." Beth leaned against the door frame looking toward the water.

"Me too," Mac had his back to the water, looking nowhere but in Beth's eyes. "Maybe you ought to move up here."

"I suppose I could get used to it—" Beth lifted one shoulder and let it drop—"but how would I spoil the grandkids?"

"Well, maybe I could give you a hand in that department."

~

Mac brought the sail in the house to show Richey. "What do you think?"

"I love it. It's perfect, a cross for a Southern Cross. Why didn't we think of this a long time ago?"

"I reckon maybe I just hadn't met the right sail mender." Mac's smile was bigger than usual.

"Kids." Richey shook his head. "I know you didn't rig up and then take her back down, just to show me. What happened?"

"Complications. She didn't get it done until just a little while ago." Mac smiled. "We ordered pizza."

"I can tell—" Richey pointed at Mac chest—"sauce there on your shirt."

Mac remembered feeding Beth, making sure none dropped on the sail. Beth probably thinks I'm a slob. "Big day tomorrow, are you ready?"

Richey sat up straight. "I'm scared to death, dad."

Mac nodded.

"What if I scare Ric—?"

Mac lifted his hand and shook his head signaling—don't go there.

"I know. I've tried everything to keep from thinking like that. I feel like I'm about to step out of the boat, in the middle of the ocean, and try to walk on water." He pointed at the TV and the book on his lap. "I've tried watching the tube, reading...I even polished your oak ship wheel clock, for crying out loud." He lifted a crooked smile, "It looks good though."

Mac stood in front of Richey and said one word, "Preprayer?"

With that Mac knelt next to the couch, next to his son, and they did the only thing that can bring peace and courage before walking on water. Pray. It was the only thing that allowed either of them to get any sleep that night.

~

The sun came up, and like a couple kids, waiting for Christmas, Mac and Richey were already sitting on the deck of *Maggie*.

The mainsail with the blue cross was draped over Mac's lap, waiting for enough light to rig and set sail for a short test run...and just because they couldn't wait to see how the cross would look.

Richey didn't want to feel the way he did, but he was more concerned about how he looked, than about how the boat looked—he couldn't help it. After looking in the head mirror for the hundredth time he finally remembered to follow his dad's advice, pray. He did. It helped.

He didn't look any better, the scars were still there, but his vision improved.

He could see there was more to him than flesh and bone. He prayed the people about to board—especially one young man—would be able to see past his scars and into his heart. Give them your eyes, God.

~

After the longest day in history five-thirty came and Mac and Richey were seated in the cockpit staring up the pier toward shore. Mac looked at his watch. "What time are they supposed to be here?"

Richey gave his dad a look, "Same as always this time of year, around seven."

Six o'clock came and they were standing at attention near the gangway staring up the pier toward shore. Richey fidgeted, "I better check the fuel level."

"Tank's full. I topped it off this morning." Mac stood firm, eyes fixed on the shore.

"I better check anyway." Richey walked away and returned in about a minute. "Tank's full."

"That's good." Mac wiped his brow. "I better check the fridge."

Richey smiled. "I got supplies yesterday, even some ice cream bars."

"I better make sure it's cold." Mac disappeared below deck only to return about a minute later. "Want some water—it's cold."

"Thanks—" Richey reached for a bottle and then shook his head—"no, better not or I'll have to use the head right when they show up. Don't wanna make a bad first impression."

Six-thirty came and they were pacing up and down the finger pier.

Richey looked at the sun. "What time are they supposed to be here?"

Mac gave his son a look, "Same as always this time of year—around seven."

As if on cue they both turned and looked toward the open water and pulled hankies out of their back pockets and wiped sweat from their necks and brows.

The view of the waves, the call of a gull and the refreshing breeze allowed them to take a full breath and settle their hearts to a regular beat for the first time all day.

And then, from somewhere deep inside, Mac started to laugh. It started with a soft chuckle and a slap on Richey's back, but before they were through they were both sitting on the pier staring out at the water and laughing.

They laughed so hard, the tension over the meeting that was about to take place spilled out onto the water, the fears of whether they would be able to develop a relationship with Ricky drifted away, regret and doubt and shame rolled off the pier and sank to the bottom of Lake Superior.

They hadn't laughed like that in a long long time, since before Maggie got sick, before Richey met Jenny, before the Titanic sunk their lives.

They laughed so hard they must've looked like drunken sailors, to the mother and two children standing on the shore.

33

Ricky whispered to his mom as they walked down the pier toward *Maggie,* and the drunken sailors, "It's just part of the act—you know, putting on a show—just roll with it."

They stopped about three feet from the laughing sailors. Rebecca spoke. "Excuse me."

Mac and Richey were seated on the pier, their legs dangled toward the water. Their heads spun toward the sound of the voice, and six knees stared at them. As they lifted their eyes—still stifling the last bits of laughter bubbling to the surface—they met the Paulsens.

Ricky saw Mac and his mouth dropped open, and his eyes got as big as a mooring ball.

Richey made it to his feet and helped his dad by grabbing an arm.

As Mac struggled to his feet he winked at Ricky and pressed a finger to his lips.

Ricky held his breath.

"We're not drunk as you suppose." Mac straightened his six foot frame and made a single laugh. "I apologize, we just..." He pointed over his shoulder toward the water, then looked toward heaven, and then toward Richey. And in that moment, as they stood in the afterglow of an impromptu celebration, they noticed it. Something that had been missing for a long time, had returned.

Years ago it was a part of their lives. It could be seen in their eyes, and in the way they held their mouth, on the verge of a smile. But, it had died, a long time ago, with their dreams. But now, just now—it returned. As it filled their hearts and gave them strength Mac remembered hearing the preacher say, "The j-j-joy of the Lord is your strength." Right then and there he knew...joy had been restored.

Mac stood beside his son and wrapped an arm over his shoulders. His professional, Captain of the ship, demeanor must have gotten lost somewhere in the laughter. He patted his son's shoulder.

Richey may have wondered if perhaps his dad really was drunk, after all.

"You must be the Paulsens, let me explain our merriment, if I can..." Mac rubbed his hand across his beard. "I've got it. We are sailors—have been all our lives—we've traveled the ocean far and wide, through every kind of weather, even a hurricane or two. And, like any good sailor we've been in search of treasure. Buried treasure—our treasure—we lost it years ago. And by golly, we just found it again."

"Treasure—no way, really?" Sally's eyes were wide and her mouth hung open.

"Yes way—" Mac smiled—"and we're going to tell you all about it. But first...proper introductions." Mac hadn't planned what happened next, but somehow he knew what he had to do.

Mac's arm was still around Richey's shoulders. "Rebecca, Sally, Ricky—" Mac's eyes were dancing—"this pirate looking character is first mate, Richey Johnson and I'm very proud to say...he's my son." Mac's voice broke.

Richey squirmed and his eyes fell to his feet. Mac held him tight.

"He's a decorated war hero. He's earned the Medal of Honor, which you probably know, is the United States highest military honor."

Mac knew Richey was embarrassed enough to dive straight into the water, so he didn't let go.

"But, of all the honors he's been given, it's the badge of honor he wears on his body that distinguishes him above and beyond any other person I could ever hope to meet."

Mac stepped back and lightly pushed Richey forward toward the Paulsens.

~

Richey stood in stunned silence. What was dad thinking? Why would he do this to me? I'm gonna kill him...after I pass out.

A blue eyed boy stepped forward and stretched out his hand. "Sir, my name's Ricky, it's an honor to meet you."

Richey felt dizzy as he stretched out his hand toward Ricky...his son. When their hands met, Richey's chin started to move in quick little jerks, his bottom lip tightened and he couldn't speak.

Ricky didn't even seem to notice the scars or the one eyed patch as he shook the man's hand, but his eyes started to swim in a pool of blue.

~

Rebecca's stomach did a flip flop as her eyes bounced from Ricky to Mac to Richey and back again, she was seeing three generations of Ricky—the resemblance couldn't be denied. The queasy feeling returned—the one from Richey's first voice message.

~

Mac led them aboard *Maggie,* "for a sunset cruise you'll never forget." The light chatter and quick smiles told Mac that his spur-of-the-moment first impression speech actually worked. And rather than Richey's scars being a white elephant to tip toe around, they inspired awe toward this brave man of valor—even in Rebecca.

When everyone was seated onboard, Mac stood before them and made another surprise announcement. He didn't want to, and tried to talk himself out of it, but couldn't find a good enough reason. It scared him to the core. But that didn't matter because he'd learned a long time ago never to back down simply due to fear. He was never any good at being transparent, except with Mags...and even then, it was hard. But sometimes, many times, doing what's right, means doing what's hard. And he didn't understand. But, that was no reason to back down either, because obedience brings understanding. So, after he'd lost every argument within himself about backing down, he opened his mouth and let the wind in his soul have its way. "Before we cast off I have one more bit of personal information to share with you."

Richey shot his dad a look that said, now what?

Mac smiled with his eyes and nodded. Don't worry.

"Contrary to what you may think, due to the initial merriment you witnessed...my son and I have experienced the deepest pain a human soul can endure. It almost took us under." Mac looked at his watch, his eyes pooled. "Fourteen years, three months, four days, seven hours and fifteen minutes ago, I lost my Maggie...my wife...my best friend, my first mate...Richey's mother."

Mac lifted a slightly shaking hand toward his son. "Richey not only lost his mother...but around the same time, he also lost a wife. The only two women he'd ever loved." Mac's eyes traveled to the end of the pier. "But, just a few minutes ago we found our buried treasure. And you are witnesses—joy returns."

Mac wiped the back of his hand across his eyes and looked at each person one by one, with an intensity that could be felt. "If you don't quit—you win."

Rebecca nodded as her lips lifted into a smile.

Mac pulled off his hat and as he'd always done at the start of every cruise he invited The Captain of Captains to man the ship, only this time when he thanked God for the honor of sailing His waters, he meant it more than any other time in his life.

After they were underway the Paulsens did what all passengers do—gawk at the sights. The immensity of the Great Lake, the speed the wind carried the vessel, the lighthouses, the gulls, the swirling waves, the majestic shoreline in all of it captivating glory.

~

Ricky watched close as the main sail was raised and then stepped to the sheet for raising the jib.

Richey smiled and nodded.

Ricky pulled the sheet and watched the sail rise. It fluttered and popped and filled with invisible fuel.

The boat heeled to port and Mac shouted, "Full sails ahead."

Ricky tried, but the ear to ear smile wouldn't go away. He hadn't smiled in such a long time, it made his cheek muscles ache. But it was a good ache—much better than the one he'd carried in his heart for so long.

When Ricky noticed the cross flying on the top of the sail he pointed at it, looked at Mac and pointed at it again. He was speechless.

Mac laughed right out loud. "A fine young sailor gave me that idea."

~

Mac and Richey did their best to include everyone in their conversations, but every few seconds, they found their eyes latched on to Ricky.

Mac's tour guide voice kicked into auto-pilot and he carried on about facts and figures of Lake Superior...but the only fact that really mattered was that Ricky was his grandson but he just couldn't figure out how to say it.

"As we head east out of Duluth Harbor you'll notice the South Breakwater, Inner and Outer Light Houses. We'll continue our course east to southeast about eight to ten nautical miles depending on wind speed. Somewhere in there we'll cross the Wisconsin border."

Sally raised her hand. "You mean we're going to drive all the way to another state? Won't that take a long time and how do you know where the border is? Do they have a big sign floating out in the middle of the lake—Welcome to Wisconsin?"

"We're going to sail across the Wisconsin border, but the state is real close. The border isn't marked with any signs, it's invisible, but it's there just the same. We should be out about three hours."

Sally smiled.

"When we come about—"

"That means turn around." Ricky told his sister and mom.

"That's right Ricky—you're quite the sailor. When we come about, we'll head west into a most amazing sunset painted just for you, by the hand of your Creator. And as we approach the shore line, you'll see the Superior Entry Lighthouse, in Superior Wisconsin, and then the Point Zero Lighthouse south of Duluth. I'll point them out when we get there."

Rebecca was looking out across the water. "It's so huge."

Mac smiled. "Lake Superior's surface area is 31,700 miles, that's about the size of Maine. She holds around three-quadrillion gallons of water...enough to cover North and South America in a foot of water. Her average depth is four hundred eighty three feet, and drops to one thousand three hundred thirty two feet at her deepest. She's three hundred and fifty miles long and a hundred and sixty miles wide. And if you wanted to take a cruise around her shoreline, you'd go one thousand eight hundred and twenty six miles—that's like driving from here to Miami."

Rebecca smiled, "Like I said—it's huge."

A big fish jumped near the bow and Ricky and Sally pointed at the same time and laughed.

"We had a young lady sailor you may know, her name was Suzy."

Ricky smiled. Rebecca and Sally nodded.

"She thought she saw a dolphin, or a shark...I forget which. We see them in the ocean, but not here. A fish big enough to be mistaken for a dolphin or a shark is most likely a sturgeon. The largest lake sturgeon ever caught in Lake Superior was seven feet, eleven inches long and weighed 310 pounds. Muskies are the second biggest and they can get to be around six feet long and up to a hundred pounds. Both have teeth you wouldn't want to mess with—but not nearly as big as a shark's."

Ricky and Sally had taken turns at the helm with Mac at their side offering gentle instruction to stay on course. "Port a little...okay back starboard, starboard...there, steady as she goes."

Mac thought about how his honeymoon trip with Maggie crossed the line from life to death. Everything before that line was good and right, and everything after the line was filled with hurt and sorrow. A rogue wave had rolled over the calm sea of their lives and capsized everything that was good and right.

But...this trip, Mac prayed, would bring them back to life. Roll them back upright and restore the years. Lord, here we are—now what?

Don't worry—I've got this.

~

When not at the helm, Ricky stayed close to Richey and asked at least a thousand questions about the boat and about how far he'd sailed in the ocean and how old he was the first time he sailed alone and if he'd ever fallen overboard or gotten lost or sea sick...

Richey answered every question and wondered if his words sounded funny because it was hard to talk with such a big smile plastered to his face. He could only hope his answers didn't sound stupid, since his mind was spinning and his heart was praying. Lord, here we are—now what?

Don't worry—I've got this.

And when they had come about, everyone gasped at the multicolored sunset splashed across the sky spilling through the water and right into their boat—everyone but Ricky. He was busy helping reset the sails.

Richey leaned over to coil some loose line and a little sailboat pendant slipped out from under his shirt and dangled as bright as the star of Bethlehem.

Ricky's eyes grew wide as he stared at the pendant— the pendant that was just like his own. His mouth dropped and the words fell straight out of his heart..."Are you my dad?"

The waves stood still. The sails dropped silent and not a sound could be heard but the beating of five hearts.

Thump thump...thump thump...thump thump.

Richey raised his hand and started to set it on his son's shoulder, but stopped. He looked at his wounded hand and let it drop back to his side. He slid his good hand across his scarred face and clenched his jaw to stop the quiver in his chin.

For an eternity they just looked at each other without taking a breath.

Finally, Richey's lips parted and he whispered, "If, you'll have me."

Ricky didn't even flinch when he rested his palms on his father's cheeks and wiped away fresh tears.

When he did that—wiped away the tears—Richey felt loved, more loved than he ever imagined possible.

Rebecca looked at her son—and the man in front of him. The smile on her face showed she didn't see scars...just the father of her son.

And every sunset, on every wave, on every shore, in all its splendid glory, could not compare, to Ricky's smile—and the sound of his voice, when he said...

"Dad."

34

Ricky opened the journal and smiled.

The inside cover read:

To Ricky...my guy

Love, Suzy

The letters were fancy with a heart over the, *i* instead of a dot. And the bottom of the, *y* was curled into a heart.

Suzy always wrote his name like that—ever since the first note she tossed him on the bus.

His eyes drifted to the first page. It looked, like his mind felt...blank. He looked up at the little model sailboat on his desk, it was blue on the bottom and white on the deck. A small blue cross was hand painted on the top of the main sail and *Maggie* was painted across the back.

He let his memory float across the past two years— since he first sailed on *Maggie*...and then, he centered his pen on the top of the page.

Dear Journal

Yesterday Suzy—my girl—gave me this journal. I told her I was a sailor—not a writer. She said, "Richard MacArthur it will hurt my feelings if you don't use the gift I bought you." When she uses my name like that, I know she's serious.

So, here I go...

Time sure flies. It's been two years since I found out Richey and Mac were my real live dad and papa.

Dad says I have three real dads. One is him—of course. The other is Martin, who adopted me. Dad says, "One of the first things I'm going to do when I get to heaven is find Martin, shake his hand, and tell him thanks, for being the dad he didn't have to be." And then, my most important dad, is my Heavenly Father. He pieced our broken lonely hearts together like a giant jigsaw puzzle.

I fixed up that old 16' Newport. I named it, Martin. It sits in the back yard and I don't think I'd sell it for a million dollars. That'd be about a dollar an hour for all the time I've put into it.

Dad and Papa have given me sailing lessons and say I've become quite the sailor. We're planning a trip from Superior, all the way out to the Atlantic and down the east coast to Tavernier—where Dad and Papa grew up. I can't wait.

I spend every weekend with Suzy. Her dad bought a cabin near the lake and a 22' Hunter. I've been teaching him to sail. He's not too good on his feet though—can't imagine him on ice. Chet and I have gotten to be pretty good friends, sometimes, I think it makes Suzy jealous.

Mom has become a great sailor and Papa says Beth has become a right fine, first mate. Sally...she's an okay sailor. Of course, she thinks she's ready to run a sailing school.

The wedding last year was...weird. I loved it but, I mean, how often does a kid get to be best man, in a double wedding, for his dad and mom and grandpa and grandma, with a stuttering preacher to boot?

Oh, and remember that prayer? The one Pastor Olsen prayed about hearing babies?

Well, if you go anywhere near our house these days, you don't have to listen real hard, because when the windows are open, a baby's cry can carry a full city block. And if they both start crying, I think the whole neighborhood can hear.

At three months old little Josiah and Kayla can sure make a lot of noise.

But that's nothing compared to Christmas at Papa Mac and Grandma Beth's. When Beth's four kids and twelve grandkids show up along with me and dad and mom and Sally and the twins—it's one big noisy messy happy family...just like the Walnut Family on TV.

Papa sits on the porch and listens to all the noise. He rocks back and smiles at the sky saying something about how, God is near the broken hearted and puts the lonely in families.

Just the other day, after a big meal, I sat next to Papa out on the porch. Our rocking chairs creaked in tune to the family chatter floating through the walls like a song. But then, Papa stopped and looked at me with those eyes that held the sea. "Thanks for making our house smile."

When I asked what he meant, he started rocking again and stared out at the fading sky for a long time before saying, "Our ship had a personality of her own. When we were underway, to a special assignment, she didn't smile. She got real quiet and serious. Sounds didn't echo, but fell flat, with a thud. But, right before we'd engage in combat, or whatever our mission involved, we'd say, 'Make her smile boys.' And sure enough, after it was over, the ship's personality would change."

And right then, as if on cue, Dad's laughter burst through the walls from inside the kitchen and bounced around on the porch like a rubber ball.

Papa let out a soft chuckle and nodded toward the laughter. "Like that. After we completed our mission—she smiled. Her walls echoed with laughter. We'd gather, like a family, in the mess...wounded, banged up and weary—but we all wore smiles."

I smiled at his memory, and could see the connection to the laughter echoing through the walls. "But what's that got to do with me? I haven't done anything special."

He stopped rocking and pointed at me. "Oh, but you have." His set his hand on mine. His blue eyes spilled. "You were given a special assignment, and obeyed."

"Huh? I was? I did?"

"Small seeds grow big trees," he said.

I lifted an eyebrow and wondered why he always talked in riddles.

Papa's smile lit up the night. "You gave an old man a boat...and skipped church to go to a tavern."

I have to think on that for awhile...

Oh, and one more thing. I'm still listening to, The Voice. I think He has something real important for me to do, because when I get real still...I hear Him say, ***"This is just the beginning."***

~

Somewhere far away, deep in the Western Pacific Ocean is a place called the Mariana Trench—wherein is the deepest point of the earth's oceans. It plunges almost seven miles deep. And in this trench is a demon named dribgnos—he's hiding from those he calls, the tormentors.

When a rogue wave rolls all alone, or a gust of wind kicks up from out of nowhere—beware.

It may be the fury of tormentors, flying by in their endless quest for something...or someone to vent their rage.

Or perhaps, it's the flutter of angels on assignment.

Either way—it's time to preprayer.

~

Dear Reader,

Thanks for setting sail with me, as we rode the waves with a little boy, an old sailor and a wounded warrior. I pray the story touched your heart. But more, I pray you felt His touch and heard His Voice.

If angels and demons bicker back and forth like David and dribgnos—I do not know. But one thing's for sure and certain—a battle rages just outside our natural senses. It's a battle for your soul, and mine. I've asked the Lord to illuminate through this simple story, that battle, and the power of prayer.

In the making of this book, long before one drop of ink was spilled—tears were shed and prayers were said. You see, I've lived much of the pain within these pages.

Maybe you've felt the silencing grip of fear like Ricky? Or the lonesome agony of a lost loved one like Mac. Or, perhaps you've known Richey's rejection, or have carried scars that bar others from seeing your heart.

Maybe...you still do.

That's why I write. That's why I pray...for you.

We are partners, you and I. You're the other half of this writing ministry. Without you, without your prayers, I wouldn't be able to walk in this calling.

Prayer in the hands of Love is the most powerful force on earth.

If you'd like to contact me, use the email address below. It is an honor to hear from you, I read every word.

Oh, one more thing.

Can I ask a favor?

If you think this story can be a blessing to someone would you help spread the word?

I rely on you to share this ministry. Frankly, I'm not good at marketing, but I figure if you tell two people and if they tell two...it won't be long until we've reached the world.

It starts with you.

Also, if you want to write a review where books are sold online, that would be awesome, too.

Thank you my friend,

Doug

DougSpurling@aol.com

See more from Doug at *Spurling Silver* or *amazon.com/author/dougspurling*

94271898R00178

Made in the USA
Columbia, SC
24 April 2018